Return this item by the last date shown.
Items may be renewed by telephone or at
www.ercultureandleisure.org/libraries

east renfrewshire
CULTURE
and LEISURE

Barrhead:	0141 577 3518	Mearns:	0141 577 4979
Busby:	0141 577 4971	Neilston:	0141 577 4981
Clarkston:	0141 577 4972	Netherlee:	0141 637 5102
Eaglesham:	0141 577 3932	Thornliebank:	0141 577 4983
Giffnock:	0141 577 4976	Uplawmoor:	01505 850564

The Turncoat

The Turncoat

Alan Murray

FREIGHT BOOKS

First published 2016

Freight Books
49–53 Virginia Street
Glasgow, G1 1TS
www.freightbooks.co.uk

A CIP catalogue reference for this book is available from the British
Library.

ISBN 978-1-911332-02-2
eISBN 978-1-911332-03-9

Typeset by Freight in Plantin
Printed and bound by Bell and Bain, Glasgow

the publisher acknowledges investment from
Creative Scotland toward the publication of this book

Alan Murray is an historian and novelist, originally from Edinburgh but who has lived and worked in Australia, New Zealand and Japan in recent years. He has published eight non-fiction books and several radio short stories. He is a recognised expert on Australian coal miners and their communities. His debut novel, *Luigi's Freedom Ride*, was published internationally in 2014 and was widely praised. He lives in New South Wales, Australia.

To Jacqui and Dugald

What you are about to read is based on true events.

Prologue: Two nights of terror

The cool, unwavering courage of the people of Clydebank is evident, and when the full story of their heroism in the face of the Luftwaffe is told, they will take their place alongside the citizens of Coventry and London—
The Glasgow Herald, 18 March, 1941.

The full story was a long time coming. Winston Churchill's War Cabinet in Whitehall decided that revealing the truth of the horror of German raids on Clydebank, Glasgow's industrial powerhouse, on the nights of 13 and 14 March, 1941, could shatter civilian morale.

The official Whitehall line was that although Clydebank had been heavily bombed and its citizens had received a punishing blow, the fighting spirit of the people was undiminished.

No official mention was made of the 10,000 houses that were flattened or damaged beyond repair and that an estimated 35,000 people were left homeless.

Whitehall said 528 people perished.

Those who lived through the two nights of bombing knew they had been lied to. They believed the toll was at least ten times that number. They knew, too, that thousands more were blinded, crippled, burned, even driven mad by the terror of it all: the ground-shaking explosions that flattened whole streets in the blink of an eye and drowned out the screams and the cries for help, the blasts that ruptured gas pipes, water mains, lungs and eardrums, the flames that turned Clydebank into a crematorium.

The dead, the injured, the mad, they had been in the wrong place at the wrong time.

Clydebank was a target ripe for the razing. It was an industrial and maritime hub. Ships and workers came and went around the clock. Nobody really knew how many people were there when the bombs brought carnage. Of the 440 German bombers that flew over Clydebank, only two were brought down by Royal Air Force fighters. Anti-aircraft guns failed to score a hit on any of the marauders.

There was talk that some terrified gun crews, in action for the first time, deserted their posts as the bombs whistled down from the gaping bellies of German bombers. This was not Clydebank's finest hour.

The first night of bombing smashed, in addition to thousands of homes, shipyards, dry docks, a munitions factory and heavy engineering workshops. The second night saw the bombers return and destroy, with pinpoint accuracy, targets that had survived that first night.

The truth, along with the bodies, was buried under the rubble of the Clydebank Blitz.

Chapter one: The deceased

I grew up in Partick. It was a slice of Glasgow that had everything... drunks, criminals, tarts, rats, rickets, polio, diphtheria and hard men. In the Great Depression, Partick wasn't even working class. Hardly anybody had a job except for the standover merchants. Then there was the war and just about everybody had a job. If the German bombs didn't kill you, the war was a big improvement. That's the truth of it—

Jimmy Macrae, Glasgow Evening Bulletin, 1992.

The door was open. The men from Room 21A, Major George Maclean and Sergeant Danny Inglis, stepped into a room that smelled of mould and rising damp. Death in Partick had a scent of its own: Eau de Subsistence.

There was a male corpse on the bare wooden floor. The man's trousers were wet and dark with urine. His neck had been broken. Considerable force had been used to despatch him. The deceased was Billy Dalgleish. Major George Maclean and Sergeant Danny Inglis recognised him.

The two men showed their identity cards, first to the police sergeant and his constable and then to the duty police surgeon.

The duty police surgeon squinted through his horn-rimmed glasses and raised his bushy eyebrows.

'Military Intelligence. Quite a cut above the rest. And here's me thinking this would be a job for Uniform... just another shabby Partick murder. No scented days of wine and roses in this corner of Empire,' he said.

Sergeant Danny Inglis took an instant dislike to the duty police surgeon. Shabby? What would this sod know about shabby? Pompous tweed-suited bastard. Bow tie, mustard waistcoat, shiny brown brogues. Hankie in his top pocket. Plummy Kelvinside voice. That's what really grated. The plummy voice.

Glasgow, by and large, was a place where accents spoke louder than words. Clothes might make the man elsewhere. But in Glasgow it was the accent that determined if the man was worth talking to.

The duty police surgeon nodded towards Billy's body.

'Must be something important to catch your attention on a Saturday morning,' he said. 'Don't your type usually deal in the hush-hush, cloak-and-dagger stuff? The trench coat and trilby brigade?'

Major George Maclean, keeping his eye on the corpse, said, 'Walls have ears, you know. So maybe you should stick to doctoring, there's a good chap.'

The doctor craned his neck towards George and sniffed.

'My "doctoring" tells me some strong drink might have been imbibed last night. It seeps out through the pores, especially if you haven't had a bath this morning,' he said. 'Nicotine breath, too. The eyes look a bit sensitive to light. A late night, and a few too many drinks and cigarettes, bit of a hangover... that's what I'd say. And the accent... Edinburgh, no question.'

George nodded. 'A sleuth as well as a surgeon,' he said. 'Sherlock Holmes and Doctor Watson rolled into one. You're wasted on dead bodies... or is that all they'll let you near?'

Danny stared at the corpse. 'The man's head is just about twisted off,' he said.

The police surgeon agreed. 'Extraordinary force. Wouldn't like to cross swords with the brute responsible. I'll leave you to catch him while I get my skates on. Postmortem this afternoon. Report in the system by the end of the day,' he said. Putting a finger to his lips, he added: 'Shh... mum's the word.'

Then he was gone, without even a backward glance at the body.

'*Mum's the word...* smug, slimy bastard,' Danny said.

'That he most certainly is,' George said. Turning to the police sergeant he asked: 'So, what's the story here?'

'We came down here, me and the constable, to collect whoever this was and get him up to police headquarters. No names. No pack drill. Didn't know why and didn't ask. There was no answer when I knocked so I gave the door a wee push and it opened just like that. Whoever did for the bugger on the floor must have forced the door – a good shove was all it needed – did the deed and closed the door when he left. I doubt it was robbery. Nothing to steal. Poor wee sod. I called it in and now you're here.'

'Right enough,' Danny said, 'we're here, and he was a poor wee sod. You should be a detective with powers of observation like that.'

'None of the neighbours heard or saw anything,' the police sergeant said, ignoring Danny's sarcasm. 'Mind you, around here there's a disinclination to help the police with their inquiries. They mind their own business. What happens here gets sorted here. Anyhow, now you're here, I'm away for my tea break. The constable here will get the body moved.'

He might just as well have said the constable would take out the empties, the detritus of the night before.

George Maclean looked around the room. A few hours earlier Billy had been the best lead they'd had for months.

Now he was dead.

Danny shook his head. How, in the name of God, could a life come down to this? A body lying in its own urine. Dead eyes wide open, staring into eternity. Danny had seen any number of corpses in his years on the Job. And always he wondered how, in the name of God, could it come to this? If life had a purpose for the likes of Billy, it was a well-kept secret.

'The bugger just couldn't take a trick,' Danny said. 'Bombed out in the Clydebank Blitz. Wife and bairn evacuated to Ayr. Probably laid off or on short-time right through The

Depression. A struggle from start to finish; that would have been the life of Billy Dalgleish. Pay packet, pie and chips and five bob in the gas meter every Friday. A few pints every Saturday night. Skint by Wednesday.'

The only break Billy ever got was his neck.

For several minutes George said nothing. His thoughts drifted and whirled from past to present and present to past. His eyes panned around the room. He shook his head at the wretchedness of it all. What a barren, greasy shambles. Dirty dishes in the sink. Two overflowing ashtrays. An Orange Lodge banner pinned to a wall. King Billy, in all his triumphal feathered glory, astride a jet black war horse above the embroidered words '*United we stand – Loyal and True.*' It was the only reading matter in the room. To be fair, though, Partick people weren't widely recognised as big readers, save, possibly, for a glance at the form guide for the Ayr and Musselburgh races or the hatches, matches and despatches columns of the local evening paper.

Unlike Billy and his neighbours for a mile, probably more, in every direction, George was a big reader. The living room of his lodgings in Glasgow's comfortable West End, the University quarter of the city, had the feel of a good, tightly-packed second-hand bookshop with a pleasant aroma of coffee and tobacco. It was a safe haven, an Anderson Shelter, well away from the war and Partick and police surgeons with plummy accents and their easy contempt for the likes of Billy.

There were two bookcases in the living room and two more in the bedroom. George was a big reader. Mind you, he hadn't always lived in book-filled rooms in the better part of Glasgow.

He had been raised in the sooty, cabbage-smelling tenements that leered over the steep and sunless narrow lanes that ran, like intestinal threadworms, off Edinburgh's medieval Cowgate. Nobody along the length of the Cowgate had books save, perhaps, for rent books.

'You stick in at school,' his mother told him. 'That's how you can get away from this. Education is like a big red Corporation tram that can take you anywhere.'

She was right.

Education – Moray House Demonstration School in the Canongate, a full scholarship to Edinburgh University and an MA Honours First that left him fluent in German and well-versed in European history – was his escape from the tenements.

Proud as Punch and wiping away the tears that ran down her colourless cheeks, George's mother had attended her son's graduation.

'I don't care what the doctor tells me about having a good rest,' she said. 'I wouldn't miss this for the world, seeing you get letters after your name.'

So, weak and in pain, she left her sickbed for the first time in a week. She pressed a half-crown coin into her son's palm. 'We'll get a taxi. Give ourselves a treat. We won't see a day like this again,' she said.

George turned away, hiding the dampness in his eyes. He tightened his grip on The Widow's Mite.

Two days after the graduation, George's mother died, bleeding from her paper-thin lungs. Consumption was common, almost inevitable, for anybody who lived in the tenements for long enough.

George sometimes wondered if his mother willed herself to stay alive until she was sure her son had secured his ticket on a big red Corporation tram.

Graduation opened the door to a reporting job at The Glasgow Herald. Then the war came along in September, 1939, and George enlisted. After basic infantry training at Redford Barracks in Edinburgh he was earmarked, as a University man fluent in German and well-versed in European history, for a commission as a second lieutenant in Military Intelligence.

The posting to Military Intelligence surprised George.

His basic training left him with the impression that the army tended to count bodies rather than heads and that nobody 'up the line' was remotely interested in what was written on enlistment papers.

The view was reinforced by a drill sergeant who told his raw recruits on their first day in uniform: 'First things first, you didn't exist before you came here. I don't give a bugger if you were the Duke of Buccleuch… here and now you belong to me and the King. Me first and Him second.'

George took less than eighteen months to attain the rank of major. After Dunkirk there was no shortage of gaps in the ranks – commissioned and otherwise. Dead men's boots had to be filled.

Now, in a dreary room in a Partick tenement, George was staring at Billy's boots. They were scuffed, worn down at the heel. There was a hole in the sole of one boot. The broken laces had been knotted together.

George nodded towards Danny. There was nothing left to see or do in Billy's digs.

It was time for the men from Room 21A to talk with the Boss, Brigadier Ewan Stuart, MC, DCM, officer commanding, Military Intelligence, Glasgow/Clyde Sector.

'We better get out to Lochard House, Danny,' George said. 'You drive. But don't toot the horn. There's a bloody Clydesdale stamping about behind my right eye.' Then, to the Uniform man at the door, he added: 'Nobody in or out for now.'

Outside, Danny depressed the clutch, pulled the choke and keyed the engine into life. He tooted the horn twice. George swore. Danny shrugged and offered a mock apology. George, unimpressed, said: 'For Jesus' sakes, Danny, grow up.'

Then the two were off, silent.

At Lochard House, a Second Lieutenant with bloodshot, old and angry eyes in a young face escorted George and Danny towards Brigadier Ewan Stuart's ground floor lair.

The second Lieutenant walked with a limp and the aid of a stick. The small bronze oak leaf pinned on the left breast of his tunic indicated he'd been mentioned in despatches. His shoulder patches marked him as a 51st Highland Division man. Danny recognised the patches and the bronze oak leaf. He pointed to the walking stick.

'Dunkirk?' he asked.

The Second Lieutenant managed a quick, sharp nod. That's where he lost a leg, he said. But he was one of the lucky ones. Most of the 51st had been captured or killed.

'Brave lads,' Danny said.

'More like lions led by donkeys. Just like the last war, so they say,' the Second Lieutenant said, an obvious bitterness in his lowered voice as he ushered George and Danny into the Brigadier's big, comfortable office with its padded leather chairs, dark red Baluchi carpets and a carved teak desk that might easily be converted into a billiards table.

The place looked like a gentleman's den. Only the maps on the walls and the bulging files and folders stacked in emptied bookshelves suggested this was a place of work. Partick and the scent of mould and rising damp were a cosmos away.

'So,' the Brigadier said, 'Major Maclean and Sergeant Inglis, a surprise Saturday morning visit... I would've thought Major Maclean would have been busy crosswording in a dimly lit public house, frequented by soft-handed Bohemian prattlers or reading one of those turgid German books he seems to enjoy. All *sturm und drang*. Cover-to-cover angst. Half of them are nudists. You know, these Germans; leaping about in the buff whacking each other with bunches of twigs. And that damned Hitler... only eats vegetables, they say. Neither wonder he's barking mad. Cracked.' He shook his head, appearing bewildered by the fact that a vegetarian had plunged Europe into war. Then, he looked back at the other men in the room. 'Now, down to tin tacks, I assume you're here to deliver some news of import... some progress of sorts with your hitherto disappointing inquiries?'

The Brigadier could be a pompous sod when the fancy took him. And the fancy took him fairly often.

George said there had been progress, 'of sorts.'

The Brigadier told the Second Lieutenant with the limp and the old, angry eyes: 'Some tea would be most welcome… and ask Lt. Col. Rutter to join us. Tell him Major Maclean and Sergeant Inglis have some news, of sorts, and we await his presence… *sans* delay.'

The Second Lieutenant left the room.

'Broody young fellow,' the Brigadier said. 'Second Lieutenant Randal McCann. Some of the lads here call him Genghis. You know, Genghis McCann. Not sure he's all that amused. Lost his sense of humour as well as a leg *en route* to us. Hardly surprising. Forward Signals unit. Banged about at Dunkirk. Well, the entire 51st was banged about. Bloody shambles. As usual, the French just ran away. That's the standard French order of battle, you know… about-turn and run like buggery. They're not worth feeding. Normally, young Genghis would have been invalided out. But these days every man counts. And you don't need two legs for wireless intercepts and odds-and-sods jobs around this place. Passable French and reasonable German so he's handy. Not without flaws, though. My various and numerous sets of eyes and ears tell me he drinks a bit much for his own good… seems he's a bit of a regular Friday-and-Saturday-nighter in those hostelries near the University… your neck of the woods, Maclean, as I recall. Still, who wouldn't seek solace in his cups coming from the 51st to a desk billet like this? I don't think he subscribes to the proposition that he also serves who only stands and waits.'

Until then, George hadn't picked the Boss as a man familiar with Milton. You just never knew with some people.

Rising from behind his desk, the Brigadier stared into the gardens beyond the bay windows of Lochard House. He touched the jagged, disfiguring scar that ran from the corner of his left eye to his chin. In 1918 he'd spent two months in a place just like this, in Lewarde in northern France. It was the country house where, decades earlier, Emile Zola had completed *Germinal*, his masterpiece that chronicled the lives and hard times of Flanders coal miners.

In 1918, the house in Lewarde was a British military convalescent home where officers like Ewan Stuart were sent to recover from their wounds. He'd been lucky. Save for the visible scarring of his face and the angry pock-marking across his chest, the white-hot German shrapnel inflicted no lasting injuries. Others left Lewarde insane or crippled or blind or deaf. They joined the legions of the living dead. For Ewan Stuart, Lewarde meant eight weeks of clean sheets, good rations, pretty French nurses who smelled of formaldehyde, coal tar soap and books he'd never otherwise have read.

The Brigadier, turning away from the bay windows, said: 'Wouldn't think there was a war on. Marvellous place, Lochard House, five acres. I've rather settled in. All the home comforts in trying times.'

The comforts were courtesy of Lord Dunolly of Drymen. Lochard House had been his Glasgow pied-à-terre. 'Generous chap,' the Brigadier said. 'In the know, too. A sharp eye for the approaching storm clouds. A few months before this latest stink started, Dunolly advised Whitehall we could have the run of the place for the duration of any hostilities. This and his Altskeith Estate up in Perthshire. Very private, out of the way.

'Of course, you'd be aware that Dunolly's in London most of the time now. One of the very top dogs in Churchill's War Supplies Directorate. Very sound. Gets things done. Ruffles feathers.'

George Maclean knew all about Dunolly. He didn't share the Brigadier's favourable opinion of the Ayrshire coal magnate who'd earned his life peerage for gutting wages and slashing thousands of pit jobs after the failed 1926 miners' strike.

Nor did George have any regard for Lt. Col. Elphinstone Rutter. He'd been Dunolly's peacetime right-hand man. Now, in wartime, he was the Brigadier's administrative factotum: his penny-pinching pen-pusher. Physically, Rutter reminded George of a picture he'd seen in a biography of Cosimo de Medici: the long, sharp nose, death-mask face, narrow shoulders and fingers like talons.

'I suppose you could say I inherited Rutter with Lochard House and the Altskeith Estate,' the Brigadier said. 'He needed a bit of rank if he was to do the job as my little helper. Hence the King's Commission. Between you and me, I also think Dunolly wanted Rutter here to make sure somebody didn't pinch the silver, use the best crystal, lick the plates or urinate without lifting the seat.'

And while Rutter wasn't what the Brigadier described as 'the sharpest knife in the drawer,' he was, most assuredly, 'very adept at the nuts and bolts work, attention to detail seems to be his forte. Doesn't miss a trick or a try-on.'

George couldn't disagree with that. He'd even had it in writing a day earlier.

Chapter two: Lines of inquiry

Reference: Expenses. Please adjust your claim (April, 1941) to exclude 'Office refreshments – Gordon's Gin, two bottles, 26 oz.' These items are not allowable and no reimbursement will be given (refer to previous of March, 1941). As you are aware, earlier similar claims have been disallowed—

Elphinstone Rutter (Lt. Col.), Officer in Charge (Administration, Records and Allowances) Military Intelligence, Glasgow/Clyde Sector.

Twenty-four hours before the corpse of Billy Dalgleish was found, George received a curt missive that attested to Rutter's attention to detail. It reminded George that expenses claims for Gordon's Gin would not be reimbursed.

George crumpled the typewritten page and threw it in the general direction of a five-gallon drum that served as a wastepaper bin in Room 21A on the second floor of Glasgow City Police Headquarters. Room 21A was the Military Intelligence and Police Liaison Office, Glasgow/Clyde Sector. 'Bloody Scrooge!'

Across the room, Danny turned from the window overlooking the grand sandstone buildings that edged and defined Glasgow's George Square. He turned away from a view that bespoke the wealth and influence and self-assurance of a Glasgow merchant class that had prospered from, and gorged itself on, the money to be made from the slave trade, the tobacco trade, the cotton trade, the tea trade and, later, coal, and the age of steam that had shaped the River Clyde as the world's slipway. That merchant class had fashioned Glasgow as the Second City of Empire.

'And which particular bloody Scrooge are we talking

about this grey, Glasgow morning? Might it be the ever-vigilant Elphinstone Rutter?'

George nodded. 'Right first time, Danny. Elphinstone Rutter, lantern-jawed Keeper of the Purse.'

Danny raised an eyebrow. There was a hint of a smile, too. He said, with all due respect, that Room 21A probably had better things to do than fight a paper war with Rutter. It would be a good idea to stick to following the orders that had come two months earlier from the Boss, Brigadier Ewan Stuart.

Those orders were uncomplicated. For two nights – March 13 and March 14, 1941 – German bombers had battered Clydebank, Glasgow's industrial engine room. On the first infernal night, civilian casualties were high. The homeless could be counted in the tens of thousands. Factories and shipyards were pulverised.

On the second infernal night, the accuracy of the German bombing left no room for doubt that Hermann Goering's Luftwaffe had inside information on what had survived the first night of bombing. That information could only have come from German agents or sympathisers in Clydebank. Maclean and Inglis were to find those agents and sympathisers.

'The useful ones we'll turn and we'll hang those we don't want and I, for one, will whistle while they swing,' the Brigadier had said at the start of the investigation. 'Results. Results. Results. Get them any way you can. Feel some collars. Pull people in. Round up the usual suspects. Pimps, tarts, black-market wide boys, anybody. People who hear things. Slap them or tickle them, just get results.'

Two months passed and George and Danny were still no further forward. A few slaps and even a few tickles had yielded nothing.

George lit another Senior Service cigarette and flicked the spent match towards the five-gallon wastepaper drum and the crumpled note from Rutter. 'Anything from that wee chancer, Robbie Kirkness?' he asked.

Danny shook his head. 'Not a peep,' he said.

Maybe, George mused, prayer should be considered.

'Worth a try,' Danny said. 'Nothing else is working.'

He had a point.

Another Friday. Another week of drawing blanks. It was singularly unusual that even their best informant – black marketeer and all-round Glasgow spiv Robbie Kirkness – hadn't heard a whisper in his regular rounds of the pubs, where he traded in stolen cigarettes, and the brothels, where he sold, not always for cash, nylons and lipsticks.

There hadn't been a worthwhile whisper, either, from the red-headed reporter, Finola Fraser. She and George had worked together during his Glasgow Herald years. It was a widely held belief among the Herald staff that if a tree fell in the forest, Finola would be the first to report the event. She might even get advance notice. Finola had contacts everywhere. People in the newsroom wouldn't have been surprised if God was on her contact list. Anything was possible. Finola was a daughter of the manse.

Exhaling the blue-grey smoke from another Senior Service, George said: 'Maybe we should give Finola a call? We could arrange a get-together. It can't hurt, and—'

His words were cut short by the ring of the telephone. He raised the heavy Bakelite handset to his ear. He listened, nodding, and replaced the handset.

'That was Uniform,' he told Danny. 'They pulled in a drunk and disorderly resisting arrest last night. Shipyard worker plastered to the eyeballs. One scruff ran away when Uniform appeared and they lifted this one that's in the cells. He's ranting and gibbering about the second bombing and some Catholic that works in the yards. Uniform said we might want a talk with him.'

Danny shrugged. 'A Mick in the shipyards,' he said. 'That's one for the books. It's a Protestant closed shop down there.'

Three minutes later, George and Danny introduced

themselves – by name but not by rank – to the prisoner in an interview room near the cells in the basement of the Glasgow City Police Headquarters. The room reeked of sour sweat, tobacco and reheated mutton stew. A slightly built, wiry man sat opposite them. The arrest sheet said his name was Billy Dalgleish. He was a welded at John Brown's Shipyard, Clydebank. He'd been at John Brown's for 25 years, ever since he left school the day, and the minute, he was fourteen.

He had two previous convictions for drunk and incapable and two for petty theft. By Glasgow standards he was close to a cleanskin, barely blemished, almost a model citizen.

His face was bruised. His upper lip was swollen.

'So you're in for attempted suicide?' Danny said.

'Me… attempted suicide? Away you go. Are you sure you're talking with the right man?' Billy asked.

'The desk sergeant said you had a go at the police who arrested you,' Danny continued. 'I'd call that attempted suicide.'

Billy looked sheepish. 'Aye, well, that was all a bit daft,' he said, 'me raising a hand to the polis… but it was self-defence. They gave me a right smack or two, though. Near battered me to death.' He brushed his face with his fingers. 'Mind you this wasn't all the polis. There was a stoush with some Mick just before your boys lifted me… don't suppose there's any chance of a cup of tea and a fag.'

'Fag now. Tea later,' George said, pushing his Senior Service packet and Swan Vesta safety matches towards the prisoner. George nodded to Danny.

'This Mick,' Danny said, turning his attention back to Billy. 'When you got lifted you said something about the Clydebank bombing… does this mystery Mick have something to do with the bombing… maybe it's the Pope that bombed Clydebank, is that it?'

'Wait a minute, wait a minute,' Billy protested. 'One thing at a time.'

Billy said he wasn't close to any Micks. He was an Orange

Lodge man; a Loyal Order man, like everybody in his street. His memories about last night weren't perfect. But he remembered a fight and the police putting him into the Black Maria.

'Picked me up and threw me in like a sack of coal,' Billy said. 'No call for that... two big polis and me a defenceless, wee working man half their size. A good family man that wouldn't harm a fly. A King and Country man. Loyal and True. That's Billy Dalgleish.'

As for the Pope bombing Clydebank, Billy said nothing would surprise him. 'The Pope's a Cafflick and between you and me and these four walls, you couldn't put anything past the left-footers.

'Anyhow, last night I had a few and got lifted. Look, there's a lot worse goes on than me getting on the drink. Look, I had good pals killed in the bombing. Everybody in Clydebank had good pals killed in the bombing. A wee drink settles the nerves. Nothing wrong with a wee drink in the circumstances.'

Now, a cup of tea and another fag would be perfect and then maybe he could be on his way. Surely the polis had better things to bother with than Billy Dalgleish? How about it? He was starting the late shift that night. Some parts of the yards were back to full production after the bombing. It would be nice to get a sleep before his shift.

Danny leaned forward into Billy's space. 'You'll go when we're good and ready for you to go and not a minute before,' Danny said. 'Understand... or do you need a clip round the ear to help you get the picture?'

Billy leaned back from the table, anticipating a back-hander from the strongly built detective.

'Oh, Billy, Billy, Billy. You've upset Danny here,' George said. 'He's an awful man when he's upset. The things he's done, Billy. The things I could tell you would curl your hair. He put his deaf spinster sister in a wheelchair when she spilled his tea. Terrible temper on him.'

What George didn't say was that while Danny had a

spinster sister, Effie, it was not true that she was in a wheelchair or that Danny had raised his hand to her. The truth was that Danny had lived with Effie since the death, in childbirth four years earlier, of his wife, his childhood sweetheart, Chrissie Macdonald. It was Effie who nursed her brother through the bleakness of depression and self-destructive heavy drinking in the two years after his loss.

Billy bowed his head, eyes fixed on the table. 'I'm sorry,' he said. 'Didn't mean to upset anyone.' He swallowed hard and looked up again, hesitantly. 'Look, you have to understand, I'm feeling like death warmed up.'

George smiled. 'Perfectly understandable,' he said. 'Now, you have another fag and I'll hurry up the tea. You just have a good think. We'll start from the start. Nice and slow and steady. Take your time. What pub were you in?'

Billy said he'd finished the early shift the day before. There was always a one-day break between finishing the early shift and starting the night shift. Since the bombing destroyed his rented room and kitchen in Second Street, Clydebank, he'd been in digs at Partick Cross. The wife and bairn were evacuated to Ayr and he went down there when he could have two days off in a row.

'I had a wash and a wee snooze at the digs,' Billy said. 'Then I got the tram to Glasgow Cross. It would have been around six, six at night. With the wife and the bairn being away and me here on my own I thought I would have a quiet wee drink. There was a nip and a pint here and a nip and a pint there. I got started in the pub up near Barrowlands – the Sarry Heid.'

He nodded when George asked: 'You mean the Saracen's Head?'

'That's right,' Billy said. 'So there was a wee drink there. Then it was along to the Scotia in Stockwell Street. That's right, the Scotia. It's coming back. Then, from there, it was the Hole in the Wall and the Highlander. Then the Star and that's the place I got talking with this character.'

'What about a description?' Danny said.

'A good mop of black hair, big shoulders, clean-shaven. Smelled of Bay Rum hair tonic,' Billy said. 'Big hands, big, strong hands. Worked the yards, so he says. And there's me works in the yards as well – John Brown's, I told him... told him my name as well. He never said what yard he was at but he mentioned his name... wait a minute... it'll come back... Tommy, that's the one. He was buying the drink like I was his best pal.

'He wasn't a Glasgow man, though. He was Belfast, through and through. One word, and you can tell straight away. They all sound the same, with that funny way they talk. The Orange Lodge over here is full of Belfast men. Hard men. No question of that. Batter you senseless for a nip and a pint. Maybe just a pint if they were in a good mood.

'He was right nosey. Asking questions about what John Brown's was building, what bits of the yard was back at work since the bombs, what we had on the slips. Nosey, that's what he was. I told him that me and the wife and the bairn were bombed out in Clydebank. I said the wife and the bairn were evacuated to Ayr and I was in digs at Partick Cross. Never told him exactly where, though. There was something about him that wasn't right. He'd look right at you and then, just for a wee second, he'd have a quick look around. Like he was on the lookout or somebody was after him. I didn't say anything, though... he was buying the drinks.'

George slid his packet of Senior Service across the table again. The tea would be there soon. But for now, what else did Billy remember about the nosey Belfast man... what was the something that wasn't quite right.

'Well, he was a Cafflick. That's what wasn't right,' Billy said. 'There's no Cafflicks I know in the yards. And he didn't know anybody in the Orange Lodge. I mentioned some names and he never knew them. Well, that's a dead giveaway around the yards. You're either in the Loyal Order or you know people in the Loyal Order or you're a Cafflick.'

The tea arrived. Three cups and a pot on a metal tray delivered by one of the Uniform boys. Another Senior Service was offered. Billy gulped the tea and inhaled deeply on the cigarette. He was feeling better, so he was. The tea and the fags were doing the trick.

George said Billy was doing just fine. Just grand. The memories must be flooding back, clear as crystal.

'I had a fair few drinks with this character,' Billy said. 'Then I says to him I wanted to go back to the Sarry Heid. He decides he'll go as well. So we're walking along and he's still hammering away with the questions. By this time, because I've worked out he's a Cafflick, and I'm fed up with the questions, I get on my high horse – that's what happens when I've had a skinful. Billy the Lip, that's me.

'So I said something about the Cafflicks and the Pope and Hitler and that maybe this Belfast fella's on the payroll, him being nosey, you know. Then I said maybe we should come right up here, to the polis, and maybe the polis would be interested. It was the drink talking. Me and my big bloody mouth. The trouble it gets me into.'

'So,' George said, 'you mentioned the polis. What happened then?'

'Well, he just walloped me a terrible belt. Right here, right in the ribs. God Almighty, he could fairly hit.'

'And?' Danny said.

'So I'm shouting and carrying on then there's a polis whistle and he's off like a greyhound and I'm left getting another walloping from your lads before it's head first into the Black Maria. Thank you very much.'

George wondered if Billy might recognise his attacker. Billy wasn't that sure. Maybe. Maybe not. See, he'd been on the drink. Still, maybe a photograph would jog his memory.

George nodded to Danny, and the two stood to leave the interview room. Before he left, George pushed three cigarettes towards Billy. 'They'll keep you going. Just you settle down here for a bit longer, Billy,' he said. 'We're away. But not for that long. Here's some matches as well.'

'Don't burn the place down,' Danny said. 'I doubt there's anybody here would rescue you.'

Billy said maybe George and Danny could bring a fresh pot of tea and a bacon and egg sandwich, on crusty bread, when they returned. A full packet of Senior Service wouldn't go astray, either. And some hot water in a basin would be nice. And soap and a towel as well. A wash would be the go, so it would.

By the way, while they were at it, could they leave the door open? It would let the air circulate a bit. It wasn't as if he was a criminal mastermind under lock and key. In fact, he was helping the polis with their inquiries. That might even be worth a couple of quid.

'I'm scratching your back, how about you give mine a wee tickle, too?'

Danny frowned.

'Nothing wrong with asking,' Billy said.

★★★

Back in Room 21A, George lit a cigarette, pursed his lips, blew perfect smoke rings and asked Danny what he made of Billy's story of the 'mystery Mick from Belfast.'

There would be a few hundred, maybe more, Belfast men in the shipyards, Danny said. 'Before the war they came over the water in their droves. That was when the order books at the Harland and Wolff shipyard at Queen's Island on Belfast's Lagan River were close to blank in The Depression years. Workers were laid off in their thousands. The Clyde yards had most of the Royal Navy contracts. That's where the jobs were. That's why the Belfast boys came over here.' Then, with a dryness that came close to sarcasm, he said all he and George had to do was find a big-handed, dark-haired Mick passing himself off as a Protestant and smelling of Bay Rum hair tonic. Easy. No bother at all. It shouldn't take long. Bloodhounds might be just the job for this one. A wee sniff here and a wee sniff there. Sergeant Inglis awaited his orders.

George said Glaswegians should leave sarcasm well alone. Irony was their strong suit.

As for orders, well… a telephone call to Lt. Col. Elphinstone Rutter would be a good starting point.

As Officer-in-Charge, Administration, Records and Allowances, Rutter had access to the Clydebank employment registers. The registers contained photographs and details of every worker – name, place of birth, date of birth, trade tickets. Place of employment.

Danny dialled Rutter's number at Lochard House. Rutter answered. A written request for access to the registers would be required. Then the documents could be sent to Room 21A within 72 hours. Danny said the request for the registers was a matter of some urgency. If Lt. Col. Rutter couldn't assist *pronto*, the Brigadier might be the man to hurry things along. Perhaps Major Maclean might have a quick word with the man.

Rutter's tone changed instantly. 'Oh, a rush job,' he said. 'And why, exactly, might that be?'

'Well,' Danny said, 'it's exactly to do with our Clydebank inquiries. We've a man in custody who might be able to point us in the right direction… you know, Clydebank, the place that was flattened? Maybe you hadn't heard?'

Rutter ignored Danny's sarcasm.

'Leave it to me,' he said. 'You'll have the registers delivered within 24 hours. Of course, I'll have to advise the Brigadier of your verbal request and the address and the identity of the man in custody, what he's doing in custody, those sorts of things. I'll take these details now… how does that sound…?'

Danny said it sounded just the ticket.

'Excellent,' Rutter said. 'Always pleased to assist. We're all part of the same team. No question about that. I'll put two clerks on the job... straight away. No point in being the organ grinder if one can't put the monkeys to work. Cheerio.'

Danny replaced the telephone handset in its cradle. 'Right. Cheerio yourself,' he said.

Seconds later, the telephone rang again. George answered. The custody sergeant wanted to know if Dalgleish should go back to the cells. They needed the interview room.

'Keep him where he is,' George said. 'We'll be back down in a wee bit. Tell him we'll bring the sandwich and the tea and the fags. He wants to have a wash, so show him where there's soap and a sink down there. And can you organise a car to take Dalgleish back to Partick when we're all finished with him?'

Fifteen minutes later, George and Danny were sitting opposite Billy. He smelled of carbolic soap. He looked replete and relaxed.

'That's what I call service,' Billy said. 'A scrub, a clean towel... Fresh packet of fags, nice strong tea and a nice thick streaky bacon sandwich. You two could open a fancy bed-and-breakfast.'

Danny looked around, reflecting that, over the years, he must have spent thousands of hours in that room, and others just like it, with a passing parade of drunks and thieves and wasters and razor men and standover merchants who extracted, in blood and broken bones, payments for loan sharks and bookies and slum landlords and pimps.

None had ever spoken well of the service.

Danny had seen many a hard man brought into interview rooms. Invariably, after what Danny described as a good talking-to, they'd leave subdued, silent, bruised and painfully aware of their place in the Glasgow scheme of things. That place was two steps down from the sewer.

Regularly, Danny told them as they were returned to their cells or released on police bail: 'Today we did it the hard way. Next time, we'll do it the really hard way... is that clear enough for you? Or do you need a demonstration?'

The responses were always in the affirmative. Sergeant Danny Inglis had made himself very clear. A demonstration was not required.

Leaning towards Billy, George said: 'We've managed to persuade the higher-ups there shouldn't be any charges. It took some doing, Billy. Now, we've done something for you... so you need to do something for us.'

Billy nodded. 'That seems fair enough. No problem there, you just say what's to be done and mum's the word and Bob's your uncle.'

George spelled it out.

Billy would be having a few days away from work, just to be on the safe side. It wouldn't do to run into his best pal from the night before. Well, not until George and Danny were sure just who this best pal was. As far as the shipyard was concerned Billy would be laid up with a bad chest. It might turn into pleurisy.

Danny would organise a medical certificate for the shipyard. He'd give the yard a call first. Everything would be fine. Billy would be paid for his time off. Danny would take care of that, too. It would be like a wee holiday. A treat. You never knew, maybe Danny would arrange for Billy to have two or three days in Ayr with the wife and bairn.

'That would be lovely,' Billy said. 'And maybe Sergeant Inglis could find his way to paying for the bus fare down to Ayr and back. And maybe a wee bit extra for, you know, fish and chips and ice cream? That's what you do on a holiday. Fish and chips and ice cream.'

George said first things first. Bus fares and fish and chips and ice cream? Well, they would have to wait and see.

A car would take Billy back to his digs in Partick. Then, in the morning... the morning... Billy seemed confused. 'Wait. Wait. Wait. What morning are you talking about?'

'This is Friday,' George said. 'Last night when you got on the drink was Thursday. Tomorrow is Saturday.'

'Oh, right,' Billy said. 'Ah must've lost a day. Sometimes happens when I've had a drink. It's like I've been in a trance, hypnotised by the alcohol.'

'Billy,' George said, 'that's by-the-by. Right now you need to concentrate. Alright… on Saturday morning, a car will pick you up and bring you back here. Then you, me and Danny will look at some photographs. Don't you set foot outside your digs until you're picked up in the morning.'

Billy looked unsettled. 'Aye, right… but, well, easier said than done. The cludgie is out the back. It's a shared one.'

George and Danny exchanged glances. 'You can pee in the sink,' Danny said. 'Anything else, you just bide your time. Either that or stick your bum out the window.'

Billy said he'd probably bide his time.

George said fine, Billy could be off. 'Turn left at the door. Then right along the corridor. Then up the stairs and along to the front desk. The car is organised. Not a foot outside the digs until Uniform comes for you. You understand all that? And myself and Danny here will see you in the morning.'

'You've told me the same thing about three times,' Billy said. 'I might not be feeling the best, but my hearing hasn't gone. I heard you the first time. Cheerio. I'll see you in the morning.'

But Billy would see nobody in the morning. Billy would be dead. Today was Friday, and Billy was about to run out of Saturdays. Sooner or later, everybody runs out of Saturdays. It's the same in Glasgow as it is everywhere else.

***

If Danny had known Billy wasn't long for this earth he could have saved himself the bother of a telephone call – and telling a pack of lies – to John Brown's shipyard.

'Doctor Farquhar Kinnell here,' Danny told the male voice at the yard's Personnel Coordination Office. The voice identified itself as Hughie Strachan, senior shift roster clerk. How could he be of assistance to Doctor Kinnell?

'I'm telephoning about one of my patients, William Dalgleish. He's one of your boilermakers,' Danny said. 'Lives in lodgings in Partick since the Clydebank business.'

Danny covered the mouthpiece of the telephone handset and winked at George. 'William won't be reporting for the nightshift this evening,' Danny said. 'I've packed him off to bed with pleurisy. I'll look in on him tomorrow but I'd say he won't be out and about for several days. We'll give him a week off just to be on the safe side. Full pay, of course.'

'I'm not that surprised to hear that William is laid low,' Strachan said. 'Somebody just the other day told me there was a bit of pleurisy about.'

Danny said Hughie – 'you don't mind if I call you Hughie, do you' – was absolutely correct. Pleurisy was popping up all over the place.

'A medical certificate won't be necessary,' Hughie said. 'A call from yourself is more than enough. More than adequate considering how busy you must be. Well, everybody is busy these days.' Hughie would make sure William's night-shift foreman and leading hand were informed. 'Let's hope we see William back in a week. Every pair of hands has a job to do. There's a war that needs winning, Doctor Kinnell.'

Danny said no truer word was ever spoken. Again he winked at George who looked at Danny and shook his head. He mouthed the word 'chancer.'

'By the way,' Hughie said, 'I've been a bit under the weather all week. Perhaps, since you're on the telephone, you could spare me a minute or two. I've had this rasping cough for a few days now and there's phlegm that won't budge. A bit of a temperature, as well.'

There was silence from Danny. His eyes widened. His jaw dropped.

He scribbled a note and passed it to George. The note

said: *He wants medical advice!*

A scribbled reply from a smiling George said: *Don't ask me... you're the doctor.*

Danny cleared his throat.

Hughie asked: 'Doctor Kinnell, are you still there.'

Another clearing of the throat. Playing for time.

Danny said yes, he was still there. It was difficult to make a diagnosis over the telephone, but he'd make some suggestions. 'Aspirin should help with the temperature,' he said, 'and whisky, warm water and syrup of figs might loosen the phlegm. Not too much syrup of figs. It loosens the bowels as well as the phlegm. We don't want problems at both ends. If you're still under the weather in 24 hours you should see your own doctor. In the meantime, I better get my skates on. The waiting room is as packed as Murrayfield when we're playing England.'

Replacing the receiver, Danny looked at George and shrugged. 'Don't you give me that holier-than-thou Edinburgh look,' he said. 'If I didn't have to actually see patients in the flesh I'd probably make quite a good doctor. An over-the-phone doctor, if there is such a thing. Doctor Daniel Inglis, MB ChB. It has a certain ring to it.'

'Well,' George said, 'you fooled that fellow, and no mistake.'

'It's in the voice,' Danny said. 'You need that self-confident note. It's not that different to being a policeman. You just need to sound like you're in charge. It always works a treat.'

George said that right there and then he was hearing a voice that told him it was Friday afternoon. Until the files arrived from Rutter, and Billy had a look at the photographs, there wasn't anything worthwhile that he and Danny could do.

An early mark might be just the thing. Possibly a thirst-quencher at the Clachan in Byres Road, a stab at the cryptic crossword in The Glasgow Herald – there was always a copy in the lounge bar at the back – pie and chips from Tony's just opposite, then home, just round the corner, for a good book and a kip.

Danny said an early mark would get his vote. No contest. He could have a tub and a scrub before the big darts tournament – Plain clothes versus Uniform – at the Police Social Club in Albion Street, just along a bit from Tom's Bar and the Scottish Daily Express building. It might be a good night at the Club, so it might. Plain clothes were overdue for a win.

Chapter three: Enemies within

Three men have been arrested in relation to the alleged sale and use of counterfeit as well as illegally-obtained petrol and food ration coupons contrary to various provisions of Emergency Regulations. Quantities of alcohol and tobacco were also seized from the three. Police say those convicted of such activities represent the enemy within and face serious penalties that, in some cases, are punishable by death.   Contact Glasgow City Police for further information—
Police press statement 05/41.

The overnight transition from a sharp, grey Friday afternoon to the sharp, grey Saturday morning that brought the unwelcome news of the demise of Billy had been seamless. There was a constancy about Glasgow weather. Spring was something that happened elsewhere. Exotic places – like 'The Continent' – had spring. Glasgow just had a long winter that, in a good year, gave way to a short summer.

George arrived at his desk at 8.15. He lit a cigarette, inhaled deeply, and coughed. He might stop smoking tomorrow when he didn't have a thumper of a hangover and he hadn't slept in his suit.

Some of the cryptic crossword clues had been a shade too cryptic. More drink than intended was consumed as George wrestled with, and was defeated by, 5 Down: *A Matronly rebuke for Plato* and 7 Across: *Unseemly haste at Balaclava.* 8 Across was a stinker, too: *A rather light approximation of Napoleon's Horse.*

George left The Clachan at closing time. When he stirred on Saturday morning, he had no recollection of lurching home, bypassing Tony's chip shop, before passing out, fully-clothed, on the sofa in his living room.

★★★

It was 9.15 when Danny arrived in Room 21A. It was unusual for Danny to arrive after George.

'What a night,' Danny said. 'A night-and-a-half. We hammered the Uniform boys. God alone knows the last time that happened. Still, losers bought the drinks. That's the rule... and we weren't in a hurry to leave. We've been keeping them in free drink for long enough.'

There was a sharp single knock and the door opened. A Uniform sergeant wheeled in five plywood boxes, each the size of a tea chest.

'The docket says they're from some Rutter character. They're marked for the attention of yourself,' the sergeant said, nodding towards Danny. A signature on an official request form for the boxes was required.

'You Plain Clothes boys were lucky last night.'

Danny smiled and shrugged a winner's nonchalant shrug and signed the request form. The Uniform sergeant left.

Danny began to unpack the boxes. It could be a lengthy Saturday of looking at photographs if Billy's memory hadn't improved.

'I'll get a car sent round to Partick,' he told George. 'They can bring Billy straight up. Won't take long to get him here. Half an hour, tops.'

The half hour passed. Then another. Finally, the telephone rang. George answered then listened. He replaced the handset, raised his head and looked at Danny. 'We'd better get over to Partick,' he said. 'And then out to see the Boss at Lochard House. Our Wee Billy is now the Late Wee Billy.'

★★★

Brigadier Ewan Stuart and Lt. Col. Elphinstone Rutter listened intently as George told of Billy Dalgleish, his initial arrest, his interview at Glasgow Police Headquarters, and his overnight demise in his Partick digs.

Friday's promising lead had become Saturday's dead end.

'No pun intended,' George said.

The Brigadier was sanguine. It wasn't all bad news, he said. In fact, the demise of Billy might even be construed as good news, '*bonne chance*,' maybe even a bit of a breakthrough. It suggested that Billy, in his cups, might have stumbled on something and had been murdered for that stumble. An unlikely casualty of war whose death might not be in vain.

It was, so to speak, an ill wind, the Boss suggested. Billy's departure might have been his unwitting gift to the war effort. Not a completely wasted and drudge-filled life, after all. The trick, now, was to discover what, exactly, Billy had stumbled on.

George wondered aloud if the sterling war service of Billy would see him buried with full military honours, perhaps there might even be a pension for Billy's widow. A piper by the graveside, too, and the eye-watering sadness of a lament... *Going Home* or maybe *The Flowers of the Forest*.

The Brigadier, patronising, smiled. He was pleased to see the Major's Edinburgh drollery had not been blunted by the unseemly sights he'd encountered in Partick.

It seemed obvious, he said, that Billy might have been sent to meet his Maker because he'd threatened to take his suspicions to the police, suspicions that his drinking companion wasn't the man he said he was, suspicions that the drinking companion and Billy might not be on the same side. The mystery man had been having a whack at Billy, quite possibly with the intention of killing him, just before the Uniform men arrived. He was interrupted. He made his getaway leaving the job unfinished but well aware of the pressing need to finish that job.

George cut in: 'Fine. Fine. All well and good, Brigadier, but how did he know where to go to finish the job. He wouldn't have known where Billy was taken when Uniform lifted him… he wouldn't have known when Billy was taken back to his digs… he wouldn't even have known where Billy's digs were.'

Danny Inglis nodded and said: 'Not unless somebody on the inside…'

The Brigadier advised that such suspicions were best kept '*entre nous*' for the time being. He'd make a few inquiries of his own. He wasn't short of eyes and ears. Leave it to him. 'And a good idea to keep the newspapers away from the exact details of this.' This was something Rutter might attend to, '*tout de suite*'.

When the fancy took him, the Brigadier peppered his conversations with pidgin French phrases, a legacy of his service and convalescence during what he called '*La Not-So-Grande-Guerre*'.

The Brigadier, turning to Rutter, said: 'A quiet suggestion to the Chief Constable, Rutter, that any newspaper reporters ferreting around are told Billy Dalgleish hanged himself. Suicide. They never report suicide in detail. Usually they'll just mention a death and say there was nothing suspicious about it – one of the few shreds of decency the newspapers ever display. Police can just suggest, if they're pushed, that the poor fellow was feeling a bit low after all the bombing, that sort of thing.'

Rutter said the Brigadier's approach was sound. Keeping a lid on things made perfect sense. He agreed wholeheartedly. Then again, when it came to agreeing with all who outranked him, Rutter seemed a most agreeable man.

The Brigadier pointed to the door. Rutter might want to make that call to the Chief Constable.

Once Rutter had left the room, the Boss looked at the Major and the Sergeant. 'He's a handy gun dog… good for fetching things,' he said. 'Now, what's the plan of action?'

George and Danny exchanged glances. There was a brief

silence. Then Danny spoke. 'We could do a lot worse than have a word with Robbie Kirkness, for a start. He's my snout in Clydebank. We have a blether every so often. He hadn't heard a whisper the last time I ran into him. It's worth another try. We both served in the Highland Light Infantry in France in the last war, but I never knew him then. Different battalions. He did nine months in the Glasshouse at Colchester for thieving medical supplies. A hard place, Colchester, but he's a hard wee man, is Robbie. I put him away for six months... four or five years ago it must have been... receiving and selling stolen goods.

'He should have got more but we came to an arrangement. He'd give me the names of a couple of shysters doing break-ins in Kelvingrove and I'd have a quiet word with the Fiscal's Office about the sentence. We've stayed in contact since then. These days, Robbie keeps me in the picture and I keep him out of Barlinnie jail. He keeps himself nice and I see to it that the local polis leave himself to himself.'

Danny said Robbie had done quite well from the war so far. He wouldn't be hard to find. He'd be doing business in either a pub or a brothel.

Danny added: 'If any fresh whispers are doing the rounds right now, Robbie Kirkness would have heard them.'

Half an hour later, George and Danny were in Clydebank.

***

The place had the appearance and the feel of a necropolis. Shells of buildings stood like tombstones over untended graves.

Here and there, red markers warned of the unexploded bombs that had been unearthed and sandbagged as rubble was cleared. Most of these were high explosive 500-pounders. All it would take was a shaky hand, a sneeze, too much pressure when a detonator was being removed and half a street and a two-man team of sappers would be blown to kingdom come.

In some places there were mounds of stone and glass and roof slate and clay chimney pots and splintered timber and rags that had been clothes.

Here and there were pram wheels, chair legs, door frames, scraps of sodden paper, a headless, armless doll, an eviscerated knitted golliwog, the shreds of an Orange Lodge banner, a child's tin drum. Clydebank was a crime scene. The crime was murder on an industrial scale. The murderers had come and gone in the night.

George and Danny found Robbie in a corner of the near-empty, drab Slipway bar at the end of Springfield Street where it met Lorne Place. It was a pub favoured by the merchant seamen who crewed on the North Atlantic convoys. It was a short walk from the docks to the Slipway, and a short lurch from the Slipway back to the docks.

It was nearly empty that Saturday, Robbie said, because there were no North Atlantic ships in. The Slipway and the tarts were busy when the ships were in and it was quiet for the rest of the time. While it was always a delight, he said, to see Danny and Mister Maclean, a big dram would make it more so.

There was no immediate response from George or Danny.

'Isn't this whole place in an awful state?' Robbie said. 'German buggers. You know, if I was ten years younger I'd be right back in uniform. Highland Light Infantry. Rifle at the ready, bayonet fixed. I'd show them a thing or two. I did it the last time and I'd do it again.'

Danny said he didn't doubt this for a minute. Still, he was sure Robbie was aiding the good fight by keeping his eyes and ears wide open in the service of the Realm.

'Anything you might want to share with us, Robbie,' Danny said. 'Anything at all.'

Robbie, pensive, pursed his lips.

'There's always some rumours,' Robbie said. 'Nothing worth troubling the polis about, though. A few words here and a few words there. Just stories around the yards. No names, no pack drill, as we used to say in the HLI. Now, just a thought while we're here… would Mister Maclean be interested in some fags and maybe a few bottles of whatever takes his fancy?'

George indicated a preference for Senior Service and Beefeater gin. At the right price, of course.

'Easier said than done,' Robbie said. 'Seniors and Beefeater have been hard to come by – hen's teeth – since the polis raided a warehouse at Govan. They lifted my best supplier. Makes it difficult for honest tea leafs like myself. Still, I'll make a few inquiries, Mister Maclean. Rest assured of that. Senior Service and Beefeater. I'll see what I can do. If you're interested right now, I can do a very nice price on whisky… Johnnie Walker Red. But it would have to be by the half dozen. The fags… well, the Yank ones are easier to come by than the likes of Seniors and Capstan. Look, buy a dozen Johnnie Walker and I'll throw in, for free mind you, two cartons of Lucky Strike.'

'Johnnie Walker Red,' Danny said, 'is hardly what you'd call top-shelf, Robbie. It might be good for rubbing on horses but I'd draw the line on pouring it down my throat. Now, a nice malt, that's another matter. If you can get Talisker, you can count me in for half a dozen.'

George said thanks but no thanks. He'd pass on the American cigarettes. Whisky, well? Like Danny, he enjoyed a nice malt now and then. But he wasn't really a whisky man.

'Well, I can't say the same for me,' Robbie said. 'A Dewars, on the large side, wouldn't go astray if you're putting your hand in your pocket. It's always the right time for a nippy sweetie.'

Danny ordered a double dram. Robbie downed it in a single gulp.

'Now that we've oiled your tongue,' Danny said, 'how about you elaborate on these rumours you mentioned.'

'Look, this bombing business, there's more to it than meets the eye,' Robbie said. 'The first night wasn't a surprise. You could expect Clydebank to get a pasting because of the yards and the factories. But the second night… the Germans came back to finish off what they missed on the first night… and the only way they'd know what to come back for… work it out for yourself… somebody here in Clydebank told them what to come back for.

'Right here and right now, I'll tell you and anybody else who wants to listen that hanging is too good, far too good, for anybody that was helping the Germans.'

'So, what's the local word on who the Germans are getting their information from?' Danny asked.

'Well, there's rumours that there's Irish over here working for the Germans,' Robbie said. 'Mind you, there's always rumours about the Irish… there's rumours about everything. Just the other day there was a rumour that three German submarines had been seen sailing up the Clyde near Greenock. It seems, so the story goes, they took one look at the Greenock tarts and turned right back out to sea.'

George, mock-serious, said the submarines story sounded a bit far-fetched. Personally, he'd never heard a bad word about the Greenock tarts. But the Irish story might not be that far off the mark.

It was no secret, he said, that even before the outbreak of war, Irish Republican units had been active in England – setting off explosions in London, Manchester and Birmingham. There had been civilian deaths, serious injuries and property damage.

'Bloody Cafflicks and IRA men. German sympathisers, that's the Irish. The Black an' Tans should have finished them off when they had the whip hand,' Robbie said, pushing his empty glass towards George.

The proposition that the Black and Tans should have taken a harder line against Republican active service units and their sympathisers in their fight for a united and independent Ireland did not sit comfortably with George. He'd long since formed the view that the Black and Tans, their Whitehall paymasters and the landed Anglo-Irish had done more than the Republicans could ever do to exacerbate mayhem and bloodshed.

And wasn't it a fact that Irishmen – in their scores of thousands – had drained their veins, under the Union Jack, in Flanders? If the Irish wanted to run their own affairs there was nothing wrong with that. They were owed that much.

George said nothing. There wasn't much of a point in saying anything. While Robbie might have been, from time to time, Danny's useful snitch, he wasn't going to be Brain of Britain, or even Brain of Clydebank, any time soon. With people like Robbie you just kept quiet and looked like you didn't disagree. People like Robbie wouldn't change their ideas or their ways in a million years. They were like the Glasgow weather. They had that constancy about them.

George slid Robbie's empty glass towards Danny. 'Claim it as a meal allowance,' he said. 'Liquid lunch.'

When Danny returned with the refilled glass, Robbie continued: 'You just think about this. Just you think. There was hundreds and hundreds that just vanished in the raids. Never seen since. Neither hide nor hair. Very handy for some, very handy. There's more than a few in Clydebank that thinks not everybody that's vanished is dead and under the rubble or melted in the fires. There would be them that would have been up to no good and very happy to disappear. That's what I'm saying. Husbands that wanted to get away from wives. Toerags on the run from the polis. Gamblers who owed a bit of money to the hard men. Seamen who didn't want to do any more convoy duty.'

The second double dram glass was drained. Again, it was refilled by Danny. Robbie was warming to his story.

'I'll tell you something about vanishing. I'll tell you for a fact now that I think of it. There was two – not Glasgow men – that used to come in here, they might have been at Henry Robb's or the Scotstoun Yard or Brown's Yard. Two Irish.

Belfast men that haven't been seen – not by me – lately,' Robbie said. 'Never short of a pound, those two. Friendly enough, so they were. We'd have a yap about this and that. Never had to put my hand in my pocket with these two. It was all small talk… were the tarts busy with the sailors from the convoys… was there much overtime on the docks. They were always up for a wee bit extra work, they said. We just blethered about this and that. Just gossip… a natter, small talk. That sort of thing.'

George wanted to know more. Did Robbie recall the names of the two vanished Irishmen, the address of their digs, maybe?

Another double dram appeared. Then another. Robbie had a right thirst on him.

'Couldn't say they mentioned their digs,' Robbie said, 'but there was one went by the name of Tommy Duthie, dark hair, big man, strong build. Right strong. His pal was dark-haired as well, same strong build. Tommy MacSherry that was his name. Duthie and MacSherry, a hundred per cent certain that's the two names. Smelled of Bay Rum, the stuff the barber rubs on after a haircut. Makes you smell like you've had a bath that week.'

Danny looked at George. Robbie was fading fast. A few double drams and he was slipping away, a silly smile on his face.

George and Danny stood to leave. George slid a ten shilling note towards Robbie. The money would keep the whistle wet.

With a flourish, Robbie placed a finger to his lips: 'Shh… all quiet on the Clydebank front. Not a word to a soul. I'll keep you posted. No bother at all. Did you know me and Danny here was in the Highland Light Infantry in France. We put the fear of God into Kaiser Bill's boys when we got stuck in. Comrades-in-arms, the likes of me and the Danny here.'

Half-smiling, Danny said: 'Comrades my behind. I was killing Germans for two bob a day and you were doing time for thieving. And you're still a terrible wee tea leaf, Robbie. It's only me that stands between you and the Big House.'

Robbie was indignant. 'I'm a tea leaf right enough,' he said. 'But I'm hard-working. When Robbie Kirkness shakes on a deal, the deal is sealed. I've got my pride and my standards, and that's no lie. And anyhow, there's worse than me, much worse, in the Glasgow polis. Present company excepted, of course. Sergeant Inglis, in my humble opinion, is the finest man that ever pulled on a pair of size nine black boots. A polis and a gentleman, he is.'

'That's as may be,' said George said. 'But right now, myself and Danny have some boxes of papers that need seeing to back at the office so we'll be away.'

He said Robbie's help was much appreciated. Robbie, his words now slurred, said: 'A pleasure, gentlemen. And may I say you're truly generous to a fault. And there's not many polis I'd say that about.'

'Praise indeed, coming from the likes of you,' Danny said. 'If ever I need a character reference, you'll be the man I turn to.'

Back in Room 21A, it took the rest of Saturday and most of the hours of darkness for George and Danny to conclude that none of Rutter's boxes contained records of either Tommy Duthie or Tommy MacSherry.

'Doesn't mean they don't exist,' Danny said. 'Some of the Belfast men over here in the yards might work under different names. All sorts of reasons for that. They've run off from the wife, or they're in a bit of bother with the Royal Ulster Constabulary or the IRA hardmen, or they owe money. Or just maybe the files have been lost, misplaced. Maybe somebody else is looking at them. Maybe there's files the likes of us don't get to see. We just don't know.'

George said that what he did know was that they wouldn't come up with answers sitting there, dog-tired and red-eyed, in Room 21A. Did Danny have any ideas?

'Well,' Danny said, 'I'll just think aloud… let's suppose our mystery Belfast men can help us with our inquiries. They don't know if anybody is onto them, but they can't be sure. So they might be lying low, picking their time to make a run for it... like rabbits heading back to the burrow. If they do make a run for it they'll head for the Stranraer to Belfast ferry.

'A couple of hours will get them from Clydebank all the way south to Stranraer and then over the water. We need eyes on the ferry.'

'Right,' George said, 'you call Uniform and get those eyes organised.'

Danny spoke with the sergeant who'd delivered Rutter's boxes. He'd be obliged if the sergeant could telephone the Stranraer boys and ask them to collar any passengers with the names Tommy Duthie or Tommy MacSherry.

'Tell Stranraer that myself and Major Maclean will take over if they pull anybody in,' he said. 'And while they're at it, they might have a look at passenger lists for the last few weeks just to see if a Tommy Duthie or a Tommy MacSherry have crossed in either direction.'

George swung his feet from his desk. 'Right,' he said. 'Nothing else we can do here.'

***

It was approaching first light when George and Danny left Room 21A.

A kip and a bit of a freshen-up, they agreed, would do the trick. Five or six hours and they'd be fit as fiddles. That was the theory, anyway. Danny could drive George to Hillhead and pick him up later. Then, another run out to Lochard House would be on the cards.

First, though, that kip.

Chapter four: A quiet word

An official report is being compiled following the apparent sudden death of a man in his Partick lodgings this weekend. Police officers from the Glasgow West Division say the deceased is believed to have been in his late thirties or, possibly, early forties. Officers say while there is no evidence of death by natural causes, there are no suspicious circumstances. The man's name will not be released until relatives have been informed—
Glasgow Sunday Record, City Edition.

The ring of the bedside telephone wakened George. Blinking, he looked at his watch, the Swiss-made Helvetia he'd bought, dirt cheap, from a Berlin pawn shop during a student summer in Germany. The watch told George he'd been out for six hours. He didn't feel as fit as a fiddle. It would take more than six hours of sleep to do the trick.

He reached for the handset. The voice he heard belonged to Finola Fraser. She said: 'Another late night…'

George, still half-asleep, gave no immediate response. He could hear the tapping of typewriters. Finola Fraser was at work on the second floor of the grand Rennie Mackintosh-designed Glasgow Herald building in Mitchell Street.

'Hello… George… are you there… another late night?'

'And a good morning to you, too,' George said. 'Since you ask, yes, it was another late night. But all business and no boozing. More's the pity.'

'That business… it wouldn't have anything to do with a sudden death in Partick yesterday, would it?' Finola asked. 'The official line is that some man killed himself. I don't believe a word of it.'

George, well-used to Finola's directness, asked why that might be.

'I read the Sunday Record report of the Partick death,' she said. 'So, nosey me, with nothing better to do, went down there. Well, it's Sunday so it was either sit in the office, go to Partick or put a shilling in the plate at the Kirk. Partick seemed a bit less dreary. Cheaper, too.

'I had a natter with the Uniform man on the door of the dead man's digs. He said the dead man went by the name of Billy Dalgleish. A shipyard worker. He said a Major Maclean and a Sergeant Inglis had visited just after the body was discovered. "Sorry, Miss, nobody in or out until the Cloak and Dagger boys give the all-clear.' His exact words.'

Finola said maybe herself and George and Danny could meet up later. If there was a wee story somewhere she wouldn't mind getting it before the other newspapers. What about a nice Sunday afternoon tea and a chinwag at the Royal Stuart Hotel near the Glasgow Herald office. About half past four. How did that suit?

It suited just fine, George said. No promises about a story, though. Still, the Royal Stuart would make a nice civilised change from Partick. For a start, it was unlikely there would be a body on the floor. Anyhow, it never hurt to catch up.

'We'll talk later,' George said. 'Danny's at the door, and we need to be somewhere else. Cheerio for now.'

***

At Lochard House, the Brigadier leaned back in his chair and listened, eyes raised towards the ornately plastered ceiling, as George told of the Clydebank pub conversation with Robbie Kirkness and the fruitless search of Rutter's manpower records for any mention of two Belfast men, Tommy Duthie and Tommy MacSherry, named by Robbie.

George said it wouldn't be drawing too long a bow to

consider the possibility that either Tommy Duthie or Tommy MacSherry had been responsible for befriending and then attacking Billy. If that was the case, one or both of the Tommies might well have had a hand in Billy's murder.

'By the way, the police statement about the possibility of suicide being the cause of the Partick death hasn't taken in everyone. Finola Fraser from The Herald had a nosey around after she read the Sunday Record report on the death. She told me a Uniform on the door of the digs said Military Intelligence paid a visit a day earlier. She put two and two together and came up with myself and Danny. We'll be seeing Finola at the Royal Stuart later today. It won't hurt to tell her that there might be more to the death than meets the eye but that it's best left unsaid right now. She'll play the game, no question on that score. I've known her for years. I'll vouch for her. Absolutely. One hundred per cent.'

The Brigadier seemed pleased George could vouch for Finola, although he said that wouldn't be necessary. Lochard House – well, Military Intelligence, really – had a file on every newspaper reporter in Scotland. Some of the files went back quite a few years, to the thirties and the grim years of The Great Depression with its mass unemployment and hunger marches and strikes. That was a time when, the Brigadier said, dark forces were afoot. 'More than a few in the Fourth Estate flirted with them,' he said. 'You had the Communists cheering for Stalin on one side and a band of mad-eyed fellows – a few hereditary lunatics in the Lords, too – cheering for Hitler and Mussolini and Franco on the other side. Then you had the anarchists who just generally disliked everybody. It made sense to keep tabs on who was saying and writing and thinking what. Hence the files. I've read them all, cover to cover.'

He said the pre-war file on George made impressive reading – exemplary Edinburgh University academic record, fluency in German, summer months in Berlin, foreign literature buff, smoked, liked a glass of gin. Cryptic crosswords, too. No known or obvious perversions. Wasn't known to associate with deviants.

Some very peculiar types scribbled for a living, the Brigadier said. There was the odd obvious madman, a few degenerates, a sprinkling of sundry misfits and more than a few borderline alcoholics, compulsive gamblers and buyers of picture books that were sold under the counter and were wrapped in brown paper bags.

However, Finola Fraser's file indicated she was a very sound sort of young lady. Good eyes and ears. Never missed a trick. Well worth vouching for. Didn't betray confidences.

'She's very solid. Middle-of-the-road. A daughter of the Manse, you know,' the Brigadier said. 'She's the right type.'

Not that Miss Fraser hadn't flirted with the Bohemian aspect of life during her undergraduate years at St Andrews. She'd had a fling or two, and occasionally enjoyed the odd glass too many with some in her cohort. Liked Muscat, although she would settle for Port. But all that was behind her. She'd made a seamless transition from student to respectability and a position on the staff of the Glasgow Herald.

The Brigadier added: 'While we're on the subject of seamless transitions, I'll see to it that the Uniform fellow down in Partick will soon make his own seamless transition. He'll be off to the bloody Shetland Islands before he can blink. See how he likes spending the duration with the seagulls and those foul-tempered little ponies and those half-Viking fiddle-playing Shetlanders for company. I went up there last year to have a peek at... well, I won't elaborate. Three days was more than enough for me. It's a foreign land, you know. Flat as a pancake, wind howling every day of the year. Never gets light in winter and never gets dark in summer. The locals play the fiddle rather well but they barely speak English. We should give the place back to Norway. They fobbed us off with it God alone knows how many centuries ago. The whole kit and caboodle won't ever be worth more than five bob.'

As for the business of Duthie and MacSherry, the Brigadier said, he agreed with George's proposition that one of the Two Tommies might well have been the drinking partner of the late Billy Dalgleish.

One could speculate, the Brigadier said, that one of the Two Tommies, sensing that his newly acquired drinking partner might unburden himself of his suspicions to the Glasgow City Police, could certainly have felt moved to silence Billy Dalgleish.

But, of course, of course, that led back to the question of how one or both of the Two Tommies would have known where to find Billy Dalgleish after his release from custody. That really was a worry. As he'd said a day earlier, it allowed for the suspicion that there was a snake in the grass.

Major Maclean and Sergeant Inglis should bend their minds and their efforts to tracking down the Two Tommies while the Brigadier would attend to any mischief makers.

There was a knock on the door. Elphinstone Rutter entered. He didn't want to barge in, but he'd seen Major Maclean and Sergeant Inglis arrive. Had there been any progress? Was there anything he could do to assist?

Indeed, there was. 'There's a talkative bugger in Uniform. Seems to have been chatting with Finola Fraser,' the Brigadier said. 'Get on the blower and speak with the Chief Constable. Explain the situation. Even Partick walls have ears, that sort of thing. The Uniform man we're after was on the door of the lodgings of the late and until now unremarkable Billy Dalgleish. Tell the Chief Constable I'd regard it as his personal service to the war effort if this particular loose-lipped bugger is on his way to Shetland on the next boat. We can post his shaving kit next week.'

The Brigadier nodded to George and Danny. 'I suppose you'd better be off to your afternoon tea – black with one sugar in the case of the Major, according to his file – with the inquisitive Miss Fraser,' he said.

Leaving Lochard House, Danny said to George: 'Ten bob says he's got your inside leg measurement as well.'

George declined the wager.

'On the surface, he's a right Hooray Henry, the Brigadier,' Danny said. 'All pip-pip and chin-chin. But there's something in him that bothers me. Can't put my finger on it. You look at his eyes... he hardly blinks when he looks at you. You see the same in crooks when they're lying.'

'What? So you want to arrest him for not blinking often enough?' George asked.

'I've arrested people for less,' Danny said, smiling. 'Look, all I'm saying is that my copper's second sense tells me that what you see isn't always what you get from him.'

'And my second sense tells me,' George said, 'that we better get a move on into the city.'

***

Despite the constraints imposed by wartime rationing, the Royal Stuart Hotel still served a good afternoon spread. It was taken in a corner of the deserted reading room just off the grand lobby. Finola was there when George and Danny arrived. They were directed to the reading room by a desk clerk who recognised George from previous visits.

'Major Maclean,' the desk clerk said, 'always a pleasure to see you. Miss Fraser is here. Refreshments are being attended to.'

Finola handed George and Danny a copy of The Sunday Record, folded on page three just above the single paragraph that told of the death in Partick. It was the official line – no suspicious circumstances, next-of-kin were being advised.

'So, what doesn't the story say?' she asked.

George raised his eyebrows and shrugged: 'You tell me.'

George and Danny knew full well that what the story didn't disclose, Finola said, was that the dead man was Billy Dalgleish and that Military Intelligence, according to her Uniform informant, had attended the scene of the death. And there was one other thing.

'Not half an hour ago, before I came across here,' she said, 'I heard that a certain Uniform man was packing his bags for Shetland. A clip round the ear from the powers that be would have done the job. And don't you ask who told me about this Shetland business. I'm not about to get a second poor soul sent up there.'

George said that what might or might not be happening to a certain nameless Uniform man now apparently bound for Shetland had been none of his doing. Certainly, he'd told his Boss about the nameless Uniform and his words with Finola. 'There wasn't much in the way of an option. It was either I tell my Boss or he finds out for himself,' George said. 'And when – not if – he finds out for himself that I kept mum, I'm the next sod sent up to Shetland. There's not too many secrets in the secrets business.'

'And that Boss would be Ewan Stuart at Lochard House?' Finola said.

Danny said Finola was, as ever, well-informed.

It was, Finola said, her job to be well-informed. Her tone was brusque, irritated. Danny responded by saying that getting 'undergarments in knots' wasn't the best way forward.

Seeing the rising redness on Finola's neck, George sensed the need to avert a looming spat between Finola and Danny. Neither would take a backwards step when verbal push became verbal shove. They'd be like two dogs at opposite ends of the same bone. 'Come on, come on,' he said. 'All pals here.'

Point taken, Finola said. 'Now, just between pals, what about Billy Dalgleish and the manner of his departure?'

George, lowering his voice even though he and Danny and Finola were the only people in the reading room, said there was no doubt about the manner of Billy's departure. It was a broken neck and it hadn't been a do-it-yourself job. Not unless Billy was a contortionist.

'But who did the breaking?' Finola probed, 'and why did

you two get called in. Murder isn't exactly a sign of the Second Coming of Christ in Partick. There must be a murder every weekend down there… mind you, if I lived in Partick I'd want to kill somebody every weekend.'

Danny said wonders never ceased. He and Finola might be in agreement that the prospect of a life in Partick was one without any obvious attractions.

'You two can cosy up later and talk all you want about your new-found common ground,' George said. 'But right now some cards need laid on the table. And, just to be clear, whatever is said around the table, stays around the table. So you won't be writing anything and even if you do, the censor will make sure it isn't printed.'

'No complete surprises there,' Finola said. 'The Ministry of Information is no shrinking violet when it comes to wielding the red pencil.'

George outlined the arrest of Billy, the story of his suspicions during his boozy encounter with the mystery man from Belfast and his return to his lodgings. The mystery man from Belfast seemed like the prime suspect, and their most obvious lead.

Then again, Danny said, there was a suggestion – 'from a snout of mine' – that the mystery man wasn't operating alone. 'There could be two Belfast lads at work here,' he added.

'Outside you and Danny,' Finola said, 'who would have known that? There's the Uniform men who took Billy back to his digs… that would be about it, wouldn't it. Of course, it could be somebody out at Lochard House.'

George and Danny said nothing.

'Oh dearie me,' Finola said, reading their silence. 'That's put the cat among the pigeons.'

The desk clerk appeared. There was a telephone call for Major Maclean at reception. This way, please.

Five minutes passed, then ten. George returned. 'It was the Boss,' he said.

Finola leaned forwards. 'And…?' she asked.

'And,' George said, 'Me and Danny here have to be somewhere else.'

He was about to field Finola's inevitable 'where and why' question when the desk clerk appeared again. This time the telephone call was for Miss Fraser. It was, the desk clerk said, a call from Miss Fraser's office.

Five minutes later, Finola returned to the table.

'That somewhere else you mentioned wouldn't be Stranraer, would it,' she said.

George said nothing. Danny shot a dark glance at Finola.

'Whose undergarments are in a knot now?' Finola asked. She was smiling. George and Danny remained silent.

'The call was from Andy Auld, Chief Reporter back at The Herald,' Finola said. 'He got a tip-off. Seems to have been a bit of bother at the Stranraer ferry. There's been one man shot, a Belfast man by Andy's account. Another made a run for it. Andy wants me to get down there in the editorial car, find out a bit more. I'd say your Belfast lads might have made an appearance.'

George wondered aloud where the tip-off might have come from.

'Any one of a few dozen people who saw the whole thing,' Finola said. 'People are always phoning us with a tip-off or two and we send them a five-bob postal order for their trouble. Seems the police at the gangway in Stranraer tried to collar two passengers, both men. Andy says there's talk of some IRA tie-up.'

George asked if there was anything else. Finola shook her head.

Danny said in that case, Finola knew as much, probably more, than he and George did.

'In fact,' Danny said, 'probably half of Stranraer knows more than we do right now... small towns, big mouths. What a shambles.'

Shambles or no shambles, George said, he and Danny were bound for Stranraer. Two hours would do it. Easy. The first stop would be the police station. Then, the local hospital. The wounded Belfast man was there under guard. There was no immediate word on his condition.

'What about the second man,' Danny asked, 'the one on the run. Any word on him?'

'Not so much as a whisper,' George said. 'First things first, though. You and me Danny, off we go to the seaside. Drop in at your place and then mine. Might as well take a change and a shaving kit. I can't see us being back tonight.'

'I could bring my bucket and spade,' Danny said.

Finola looked at the two as they stood to leave. 'Don't suppose you could squeeze in one more,' she said. 'I won't get in the way. You never know, I might pick up a whisper or two. Come on... I'll phone Andy and tell him I'm saving petrol ration coupons and getting a lift to Stranraer with a couple of contacts... no names... he'll give it the nod ... come on... the Three Glasgow Musketeers. All for one. One for all. You know the story. How about it? Anyhow, if you can't fit me in... I'll just drive down myself regardless.'

Danny smiled. He had a certain grudging respect for her doggedness. He'd told George, more than once, that Finola had missed her calling, that she'd be a bloody good detective if there was such a thing, God forbid, as women detectives in the Glasgow City Police.

Looking at George, Danny said: 'Why not? She'll just cause bother if she goes down there on her own. She's like a Westie with a bone.'

'And you aren't?' Finola shot back.

George said fine, there was room for one more. 'Your place, Finola's place, my place and then the seaside,' he told Danny. 'One condition, though. Finola pays for the tea and the sandwiches.'

The deal was sealed for nine shillings.

Chapter five: Cautious men

Patient – MacSherry, Thomas: Two gunshot wounds upper left thigh. Extensive and permanent muscle and bone damage present. Significant blood loss. Severe pain. Morphine administered. Half-hourly vital signs monitoring. Condition after initial surgical treatment on admission: Fair to moderate—
Roderick Campbell, MB ChB, FRCS (Edin.), Surgeon, Stranraer Infirmary, patient admission notes.

The light of the day had all but gone when they arrived in Stranraer. It had been a pleasant drive. Windows down, fresh air that smelled clean and a bracing breeze that tightened the skin like an astringent. The war was somewhere else.

Glasgow, for all its compact central city Georgian grandness, sometimes looked best in the rear-view mirror when the road ahead was slicing through the green of the open, rolling Ayrshire farmlands that overlay the rich Ayrshire coalfields. This was one of those times.

From central Glasgow they motored by Paisley and on to Kilmarnock, the birthplace of Johnnie Walker whisky and the birthplace of the first printed edition of the collected poems and songs of Robert Burns in 1786. From Kilmarnock it was a short drive to Ayr, a town that the bard Burns once lauded, tongue firmly in cheek said some scholars, for its 'honest men and bonnie lasses.'

From Ayr the road held fast to the coast all the way to their destination at the head of Loch Ryan.

Just short of Stranraer they were stopped at a police roadblock. An Irishman was on the run and another Irishman had been shot. The man on the run was a dangerous character. A potential killer, by all accounts. Probably armed. And certainly not to be approached by civilians. The constable's description of the fugitive was halted when Danny showed his Military Intelligence identity papers. The constable saluted and waved the three through the roadblock.

'Hope you nail the so-and-so,' he said.

Three rooms were taken at the White Cockade Hotel. It came with Danny's recommendation. He'd stayed there before, he said. That was during his days with the Glasgow City Police Special Branch. He'd gone to Stranraer, with two other Special Branch men, to take custody of a prisoner.

'An IRA man,' Danny said. 'Shot and killed a teller in a bank robbery in Paisley and made a run to Stranraer. I watched him hang in Barlinnie Prison. Not the quick and easy death it's cracked up to be. Not the hanging I saw, anyway. A bullet in the back of the head, that's the way to do it. Bang. Cheerio. Quick. Easier to watch than somebody wetting himself on the end of a rope.'

George said Danny was all heart. Danny said George had never seen a hanging. George said watching an execution wasn't on his list of things to do in the foreseeable future.

At the White Cockade the manager introduced himself as Jimmy Carstairs. Red-nosed, flabby and soft-handed, he said he was delighted to welcome three paying guests on a Sunday night. Business was less than brisk, he said. It was the war. It was the weather. It was petrol rationing. Then, fixing his eyes on Danny, he said: 'I remember you from before… four or five years since. Never forget a face in this line of business. Stayed the night and went down to the ferry first thing in the morning.

'Aye, you're the one… polis… three of you were here to collect that Fenian that was hanged in Glasgow. Killed a bank teller, he did. In Paisley. Good for you. I hope the sod suffered.'

'No question on that count,' Danny said, looking directly into the eyes of the manager. It was a look of undisguised contempt.

'The sod suffered alright,' Danny added. 'You could smell the fear when his arms and legs were tied just before he was hooded and the rope went round his neck. Then a big thud when the trapdoor opened. He swung for a while, twitched all over. Smelled like a public urinal when they cut him down... I can talk you through the whole execution if you like. I've only told you the nice bits.'

'Oh, no, that won't be necessary,' the manager said. He seemed shocked by Danny's offer of a full account of a judicial killing. 'I could do without the fine details.'

Danny had no time for the likes of Jimmy Carstairs. The well-heeled, well-padded burghers who, from a safe distance, cheered on the hangman without ever having seen the hangman's handiwork close up.

'So you'd be down for this other IRA man that got shot down there by the ferry earlier today. His pal ran away, so they say,' the manager said. 'Talk of the town. It's all the gossip, you know. People getting shot in Stranraer. What's the world coming to? It's like the front lines.'

Danny said that from personal experience he could assure Mister Carstairs that Stranraer was nothing like the front lines.

George cut in. He asked: 'This gossip about the two men being IRA... Do you know something we don't?'

The manager shook his head. Oh, no. Certainly not. He didn't know a thing. It was just, well, you know, Irishmen and guns made people think of the IRA. His voice trailed off.

He cleared his throat and suggested sandwiches in the guest sitting room. Or perhaps a dram. A nice soft island malt. On the house. It would be getting late soon. Perhaps the guests were a bit tired. Glasgow was a fair way away. The fire was on in the sitting room. It was still a bit sharp even for this time of year.

'Sandwiches and a dram sound fine,' George said. 'Maybe later, though. For now, myself and Sergeant Inglis have some official business. But Miss Fraser might want to make herself at home. Perhaps you'd be kind enough to give me a key. We could be gone for two or three hours.'

Finola's unspoken and fleeting inclination was to suggest she might accompany George and Danny on their official business. She knew, however, that long-standing workplace friendships and informal cooperation aside, neither George nor Danny would accommodate her presence. Official Military Intelligence business was official Military Intelligence business. Some lines were best left uncrossed at least for the time being.

Finola said George and Danny wouldn't need a key. She'd be fine letting them in. Anyhow, she knew and they knew she'd buttonhole them the moment they returned.

The Stranraer Police Station was three streets away from the White Cockade. It was a short distance but George and Danny drove. A moist fog was rolling in from the Irish Sea. It was the sort of fog that dampened overcoats and chilled their wearers to the bone. The weather-blackened sandstone station was deserted save for an inspector and a constable on the front desk. The Inspector raised his eyes from the newspaper he'd been reading when George and Danny entered.

'You'd be the Cloak and Dagger Boys from Glasgow,' the Inspector said, nodding. 'I was told you were on the way. Somebody called Rudder... Rutter...? Rubber...? Some English name like that phoned a couple of hours ago. Said to expect you. Recognise your type anywhere. Shifty buggers.' There was a wry, old-style copper's smile on his face as he spoke. It was a face that had not been left unmarked by a lifetime of mingling with too many of the bad and the ugly and too few of the good. The nose was not quite straight. Above each eye, where eyebrow cushioned bone, there was scar tissue.

George and Danny introduced themselves. The Inspector, square-shouldered and broad-chested like an Ayrshire coal miner or a tidy middleweight boxer, extended a hand. His handshake marked him to George and Danny as a Freemason, a Cautious Man of the Craft, a Protestant.

Even without the handshake, George and Danny would have picked him as a Freemason. Catholics never got above the rank of sergeant in any police force in Scotland. He introduced himself as Inspector Willie Macbride, ushered George and Danny into his office and, from a top drawer, produced a bottle of Ardbeg – the prince of Islay whiskies, he said – and three glasses.

Any time was the right time for a nip, Willie Macbride asserted. The assertion went unchallenged, as did the Inspector's warning that if George or Danny harboured the thought of asking for a splash of water in the Ardbeg they could leave the premises right away. Inspector Willie Macbride had the look and manner of a man unused to accommodating contrary views.

George remarked on the obvious lack of activity and officers in the police station.

'Aye,' the Inspector said. 'There's just me and the young constable there. Everybody else is out at the roadblocks or looking under every rock for the waster that got away. We've even pulled in men from Ayr and Kilmarnock and Paisley. We'll get the bugger, though.'

The inspector outlined the events of that afternoon. His men had been checking the identity of passengers due to board the Belfast ferry. They'd had word from Glasgow to lift anybody by the name of Tommy Duthie or Tommy MacSherry.

'My lads were walking towards two men. One of them was MacSherry as it turned out,' the Inspector said. 'At least that was the name on a ration book we found on him. A good forgery it is, too. Anyhow, MacSherry pulled a revolver and fired at my boys. They returned fire and MacSherry went down. All my lads down at the dock carry revolvers these days. Anyhow, MacSherry took two bullets in the leg. The other bugger ran into a group of passengers so we couldn't take a shot… and he just disappeared. He can't be far. We'll get him… the MacSherry cove is up at the Infirmary. He's not in the best shape. Fifty-fifty chance so I'm told. His leg's buggered even if he does pull through. The surgeon says the patient lost a lot of blood. He's full of morphine. Out for the count. I've got two men in the room with him at the Infirmary and two outside the door. Not that he'll be making a run for it. But there's always a chance with the likes of MacSherry that somebody – one of his own, maybe – will have a crack at him. Depends on what he knows and who he knows.'

There was one other thing, the Inspector said, opening a folder and pushing a scrap of lined paper towards George and Danny. The paper had been in MacSherry's wallet. Scrawled on the paper was the Partick address of the late Billy Dalgleish.

'Does this mean anything?' he asked.

George nodded.

'Not really my business,' the Inspector said, 'but what exactly were these Duthie and MacSherry characters up to?'

George thought for a moment and said: 'A bit of rough stuff in Glasgow that left a wee man with a broken neck.'

The Inspector said Glasgow rough stuff and a wee man with a broken neck didn't usually interest the likes of George and Danny. Maybe, after all, there was an IRA connection.

'We're starting to suspect that MacSherry and Duthie have sympathies that don't exactly lie with King and Country. A reasonable guess is that they're IRA. Does that answer the question?' George said.

That was all the Inspector needed to know. George and Danny would get all the help they needed from Willie Macbride and his men.

'That help,' George said, 'can start with telling us where the infirmary is.' The Inspector waved the suggestion away. 'Tell you what,' he said. 'You drive, and I'll come right along with you.'

***

There were two Uniform men, built like Ayrshire pit ponies, outside the door of the room where Tommy MacSherry lay. Two other Uniform men, just as strongly built, and a red-haired and fair-skinned nursing sister were in the room. The nursing sister was filling in a chart clipped to the end of her patient's bed. She looked at George, Danny and the Inspector.

'You won't get a peep out of this one if that's what you're here for,' she said, 'not for a while yet. Even when he comes to, with all the morphine, he won't know what day it is. He'll be lucky if he knows his own name.'

She said the patient had a moderately steady pulse. He'd probably lost two pints of blood. His breathing wasn't the best but that would have something to do with the morphine. His temperature was a bit on the high side. She'd be back in half an hour. The surgeon, Doctor Roddy Campbell, would be back first thing in the morning, before breakfast. He was an early starter, was the doctor. The visitors were more than welcome to stay at the hospital although she thought they might have better ways of passing their time. Wasn't there somebody else out there, on the run?

The nursing sister left, but the scent of her bleached and starched uniform remained in the room.

George and Danny and the Inspector moved to MacSherry's bedside. A half-moon wire cage ensured that neither sheet nor blanket touched the patient's heavily bandaged upper left thigh. The bandage was blood-stained in the two places where police bullets had torn into flesh.

Danny slid a hand onto the bloodstains and pressed, hard.

There was no response from MacSherry.

'He's out for the count right enough,' Danny said. Turning to George and the Inspector, he added: 'You have a push. See if you get anything.'

George and the Inspector said they'd accept Danny's

word that MacSherry was, indeed, out for the count. George said there was no point in staying by the bedside when there was supper and a dram and a fire and a bed waiting for himself and Danny at the White Cockade.

'If there's any change overnight,' George said to the Uniform men guarding the patient, 'let the Inspector know and he'll let me know.'

'As good as done,' the Inspector said. 'They'll tell me and you'll be the next to know,' he said. 'You'll be kept posted. The same goes for any sign of Tommy Duthie.'

For now, a lift back to the police station would do the trick, the Inspector said. Another quick dram or two to keep out the damp was proposed. Willie Macbride would be spending the night at the station. The cells were quite comfortable.

'Too good for some of the riff-raff and local tinkers and chancers we get in there on Friday nights,' he said.

It was midnight when George and Danny returned to the White Cockade. Finola opened the door. She'd heard the car as it came to a halt.

'Come away through,' she said. 'The manager left sandwiches and a bottle down the hall in the guest sitting room. The local version of supper, apparently. Now, you two get comfortable and warm and you can give me your verdict on the mystery Mister MacSherry up at the hospital.'

George winked at Danny and bit into a corned beef and relish sandwich. Danny did likewise. Both chewed and swallowed slowly. Then George poured two tumblers of whisky. It was Raasay cream; a respectable Skye malt.

George and Danny sipped slowly, deliberately.

'This drop quite hits the spot on a damp night,' George said.

'So there is hope,' Danny said, 'that we'll get you off that gin rubbish.'

Finola, impatient, her neck reddening, asked: 'Come on, come on you two. What's the verdict?'

'The jury remains out,' Danny said, holding his tumbler at eye level. 'It could take two or three refills before the verdict is in. My initial inclination is that it's not quite in the same peaty league as Inspector Willie Macbride's Ardbeg. But it's still a sound drop.'

Both looked at Finola.

George offered her a sandwich. She shook her head. She wouldn't have a dram, either. George was sorry he had no Muscat to offer. What about a cigarette? Of course, he'd forgotten. Finola wasn't a smoker. Was she really sure she didn't want a sandwich? The redness of Finola's neck spread and deepened by the half-second.

George and Danny had savoured their few minutes of fun, but decided it was time to stop teasing the terrier.

George said they were a bit further forward – 'a fair bit,' he suggested – than they were when they'd arrived in town. 'When the police emptied MacSherry's wallet they found a bit of paper. Billy's name and the address of his digs were on the paper. So we've got a connection between Billy getting on the bevvy and getting himself killed because he stumbled on something.'

George motioned to Danny to take up the story.

'The bit of paper puts Billy's unexpected end down to MacSherry or Duthie, or maybe both,' Danny said. 'And it bears out Billy's idea that his drinking pal had something to hide – something to do with being a Mick and trying to pass himself off as a Prod.

'So, wee Billy tells his new best friend that he's inclined to report him to Glasgow's Finest. That maybe there's more to Tommy than meets the eye. Not the cleverest thing to say in the circumstances. The new best pal is battering Billy when Uniform arrives on the scene. The new best pal buggers off. Billy gets lifted. God knows what Billy might tell Uniform. Right away, somebody has a reason to want Billy well out of the way. Billy does the night in the cells… he's taken back to his digs. Enter MacSherry or Duthie or both.'

Finola said the slip of paper was a big step forward. 'It means you know for certain that somebody got the word to the Irish boys that Billy was back in his lodgings,' she said. 'It has to be somebody on the inside. Uniform? Your lot?'

George agreed.

Danny looked at his watch. It was after one in the morning. He'd paid for a bed and he intended to use it. Another quick dram and he'd be gone.

Two minutes later the guest sitting room was deserted. The flames in the fireplace flickered more slowly. The embers turned from red to grey. Outside, the grey and damp mist kept rolling in from the Irish Sea.

***

It was barely eight o'clock when George was wakened from a dreamless sleep by a firm, persistent knocking on his door. It was the manager.

'Mister Maclean, you're wanted on the telephone at the front desk. It's Inspector Macbride calling.'

'Right, right,' George said. 'No need to batter down the door. I'll be there in a minute.'

He dressed quickly.

Down in the lobby, George took the handset and held it to his ear.

'There's blue murder over at the hospital,' the Inspector said. 'I'll meet you there.'

Chapter six: Loose ends

The bearer is authorised to immediately take into custody and to transfer to a secure place the prisoner now detained in the Stranraer Infirmary. The bearer is additionally authorised to take custody of all medical documents relating to the above. Your immediate compliance is required—
Brigadier E. Stuart, MC, Officer Commanding, Military Intelligence, Glasgow/Clyde Sector.

The Bearer in question was Lt. Col. Elphinstone Rutter. George and Danny saw him as they drove into the grounds of the Stranraer Infirmary. He was standing by the open doors of a military ambulance. Two soldiers, their red-topped caps marking them as military policemen, were sliding a stretcher into the rear of the vehicle. Two other military policemen flanked Rutter who stood, expressionless, in the face of a tirade from a gaunt, white-coated man, Doctor Roddy Campbell.

'On your own head be it,' Campbell said, his voice raised. 'He shouldn't be moved anywhere. He's still in shock. He's been bleeding overnight. I'm telling you, the move will kill him. This is an outrage. You're a damned disgrace. You'll get an official complaint within the hour. Mark my words. An official complaint. A damned disgrace, that's what you are.'

Rutter was unmoved. 'Rest assured,' he said, 'that any complaint that goes through the official channels will be properly and quickly dealt with. Now, if you don't mind, there's a job to be done. Perhaps you'd be good enough to let us get on with it. There's a good fellow. I'm sure you have others, far more deserving, in need of your attention.'

The doctor looked at the Inspector. It was a look that

pleaded for police intervention. Macbride raised a hand to calm the doctor. He felt obliged to intercede, to at least make a show of supporting Campbell. After all, the two were in the same Lodge. He knew, of course, the Bearer would not be moved. Decency was always the loser when it confronted authority.

Turning to Rutter, he said: 'Maybe the doctor and a nurse could travel with the patient.'

Rutter shook his head.

'That really won't be possible,' he said. 'There's nothing in the paperwork that will remotely allow consideration of the Inspector's suggestion. Personally, I can't imagine what you're worried about. There's an army medical orderly and an army doctor in the military ambulance.'

Macbride looked from Rutter to the doctor. He raised his eyebrows and shrugged. He'd done his best.

'Now,' Rutter said, 'if the doctor here can just hand over the medical documents, I'll be on my way. The patient is being moved to a more secure facility. He's my property until we reach that location. Surely I don't need to repeat that?' Rutter glanced sideways and saw George and Danny approach. He turned away from the doctor and the Inspector.

'Ah, Maclean and Inglis,' he said. 'Friendly faces. Seventh Cavalry riding to the rescue... appreciated, of course, but not quite needed. All sorted without coming to blows.'

MacSherry's medical file in hand, Rutter climbed into the military police car that followed the military ambulance from the hospital grounds.

'Better be off,' Rutter said to George and Danny in parting. 'I'll tell the Brigadier you rode to the rescue. Expect he'll want to hear from you when you've done whatever still needs doing here. Oh, and let the Good Doctor know where to lodge his official complaint.'

There wasn't, really, much more for George and Danny to do in Stranraer, the Inspector said when the three returned to the police station. Duthie hadn't been found. Uniform had scoured the district for ten miles. Duthie had simply disappeared. 'There was a report that came in before I went up to the hospital, of a stolen car a bit up the road towards Glasgow. No details yet. We'll follow it up and we'll keep looking. But if your man is away, then he's away. As for MacSherry, to tell the truth, it's a bit of a relief to have him out of town. It frees up four of my lads. They're needed up the road, about 20 miles up the road, at Floors Farm.'

'What pressing business might the police have at Floors Farm?' Danny asked.

The inspector said a German twin-engine Messerschmitt came down at the farm at about four in the morning.

'Must have been lost and out of fuel. There's nothing around here that would interest the Jerries, not that I know of. I'm told the pilot parachuted out before the plane belly landed on the ground. Home Guard picked him up. He was just sitting in a field. Not a mark on him. Speaks perfect English. Mad eyes, so they say.'

'So where's the pilot now?' George asked.

'Under lock and key at the Home Guard drill hall until the Army collects him and takes him wherever it is they take German pilots these days. His war's well and truly over. One less Jerry to do Hitler's dirty work. Personally I would have preferred it if his parachute hadn't opened.'

'So why do they need your lot up at Floors Farm if the German is in Home Guard custody?' Danny asked.

'The Home Guard major needs somebody to watch the plane while his lads get off to their day jobs,' the Inspector said. 'If there's nobody up there, the local tinkers will steal the lot. In ten minutes flat you wouldn't know there was ever a plane there.'

Through the Inspector's window, George and Danny looked out on a picture of bleakness. The town was one of those countless places in Scotland where the seasons changed every few hours.

The mist of the night before had turned to rain, great

stabbing lances of rain. George and Danny, the Inspector said, might want to wait until the rain eased before they returned to Glasgow. The rain, the Inspector said, came and went in squalls. Why didn't they have a nip to keep out the damp and then they might be on their way.

A nip, Danny said, wouldn't go astray.

Talk turned to the war, the Clydebank Blitz, rationing, how the Inspector had planned to retire two years earlier, how he'd been prevailed on to stay for the duration and then retire.

'I can just see me in a wee white cottage up by Loch Tay,' he said. 'A bit of fly fishing. A nice big fire in winter when the nights are drawing in. Well, that's the dream if this war ever ends. I can't see that happening for a fair while.'

Danny Inglis said he might do the Police Commissioned Officers' exam. He could see himself as the Inspector who replaced Willie Macbride at Stranraer.

'The sooner the better as far as I'm concerned,' the Inspector said.

George said it would probably be straight back to The Herald after the war. But you never knew.

Australia could be on the cards. There were one or two good newspapers there – he'd heard about The Sydney Morning Herald. There was The Age, too. That was in Melbourne. All that sunshine, blue skies, beaches. It was never winter in Australia, that's what people said. A place where it was never winter, imagine that.

The rain was easing. George wrote his Room 21A telephone number on a page torn from his pocket notebook. He'd appreciate a call from the Inspector if Duthie happened to be lifted by the Stranraer lads. If that happened, George and Danny would be straight back down to have a word or two. For now, though, George or Danny would keep the Inspector posted if Duthie was lifted on their patch.

'We better make a start for Glasgow,' he said. First stop, though, would be the White Cockade.

They saw Finola as they pulled into the driveway. She was on the steps that led to the hotel's big double doors. Her clothes were dripping wet. She turned at the sound of rubber on gravel.

'Well, if it isn't The Lost Boys,' she said as Danny parked the car. 'I'm just back. It's amazing what you can find out on a wee walk around here. No need to buy a newspaper here or listen to the wireless. Just walk into a shop and they'll tell you the news. Go on, ask me anything you want to know.'

George said whatever he and Danny wanted to know would keep for ten minutes. Unless Finola had a desperate wish to die of pneumonia, it might be an idea if she changed into dry clothes. After that, they'd settle the bill and be on their way.

The manager saw them off with a handshake that intimated he was not a Cautious Man. The three were welcome at the White Cockade any time, night or day. Their comings and goings would be strictly confidential. Unlike many in Stranraer he was not one for gossip.

'I picked that up straight away,' Danny said.

As their vehicle rolled along the coast north towards Ayr, Finola told George and Danny there had been a shouting match at the hospital. A Doctor Roddy Campbell had gone hammer and tongs with some bigwig in uniform. The doctor was beside himself, so people said. It wasn't often that Doctor Roddy lost his rag. Apparently the shouting match was over the shot Irishman being taken away in an army ambulance.

And there was more. A German plane came down in the middle of the night near some local farm. The German pilot landed by parachute. He spoke perfect English, and looked quite mad.

Danny resisted the temptation to tell Finola she should save her breath; that the stoush at the hospital and the downed German plane were old news. Instead he asked where, exactly, had Finola collected her pearls of information?

'In the local post office,' she said. 'I got talking with the woman behind the counter. I said I was looking for directions. Always a good way to start a conversation. Act lost. Damsel in distress. Then she started telling me about the trouble down at the ferry. The next thing she says is that her husband was up half the night in the Home Guard after this German plane came down and they captured the pilot. Spoke to them in English, he did. The pilot, not the husband.'

Danny, driving, tilted his head towards George. 'Who needs us when Her Ladyship in the back seat there is on the job? Maybe we should have her on the payroll,' he said. George said the pay was better at The Glasgow Herald. Finola would be a mug to move.

On the long, curved stretch of road that led into Paisley, their car was overtaken by two Military Police vehicles. The vehicles accelerated then slowed sharply, stopping behind half a dozen cars at a police checkpoint. Four Uniform men walked along the line of halted cars. Drivers and passengers were ordered to step from their vehicles and produce identification.

Two Military Police officers, a sergeant and a lance corporal, pulled a handcuffed man from the back seat of one of the vehicles. The handcuffed man was wearing a flying suit. He glared at the Uniform man who asked the Redcaps: 'And who might this be? One of Adolf's wee pals by the look of it.'

The taller of the Redcaps, the lance corporal, nodded: 'German pilot. Came down in the middle of the night. We're taking him up to Glasgow, up to the Maryhill Barracks. But that's between you and me.'

The Uniform man leaned into the German's face and spat. 'That's for Clydebank. Dirty German swine,' he said, 'and this is for Clydebank as well.' His fist thudded into the man's stomach. The blow was delivered with considerable and calculated force. The handcuffed man doubled up and crumpled, gasping, to the ground. The Uniform man stepped back from the prisoner, perfectly positioned to knee the German in the face.

The lance corporal, said: 'I'm not stopping you. Have another whack if you feel like it. Have as many as you like. Have one for me and another one for my late Granny.'

The Redcap sergeant intervened, stepping between the Uniform man and the groaning prisoner.

'Right, enough is enough. We'll have no more of this,' he said. Then, turning to his lance corporal, he added: 'Our orders are to deliver the prisoner to Glasgow in working condition. He's a Jerry swine right enough, but he's a prisoner of war.

'There's rules about prisoners of war. Nobody has to like the rules. You just have to follow them. Do we understand? Are we all on the same page?'

The Uniform man and the lance corporal nodded. They understood.

'Fine,' the sergeant said. 'Now, we'll get this sod back into the vehicle.'

They pulled the German to his feet. Spit slid down the prisoner's face.

George produced his Military Intelligence identity card as the Uniform man approached. 'That's fine, Major Maclean,' the Uniform man said. 'And your passengers? You can vouch for them?'

George nodded and asked what the Uniform men might be looking for.

An Irishman on the run from Stranraer, really?

'We've just come from down there,' George said. 'We did hear a bit of gossip to that effect... something about an Irishman being shot near the ferry and his companion going on the run. Heading for Glasgow, seemingly.'

'Probably in a stolen car,' the Uniform said. 'We had a report to that effect. Mind you, God alone knows how many reports we've had. Reports about an Irishman trying to row a stolen boat to Belfast... passing himself off as a priest.' He believed the Irish were troublemakers. 'Them and their bloody bombs. And them saying they were neutral in the war. A pack of lies, if you ask me. Everybody knows about the German submarines hiding in Irish waters, just waiting for the convoys from Canada. They need hanging.'

Danny, of course, thought otherwise. Anybody who'd seen a hanging thought otherwise. Not even the Irish needed hanging. He didn't mention his view to the Uniform.

George, Danny and Finola were waved through the checkpoint and arrived back in Glasgow within the hour. Rural green gave way to grey. The fringes of the city were like the slowly turning edge of a great whirlpool. Glasgow lured and sucked people into its heart.

Finola took her leave in George Square, a two-minute walk to The Glasgow Herald Office. They'd catch up, maybe for a drink, at the Clachan. Later in the week would be fine. Between now and then she'd telephone George if she heard any whispers. And, yes, before George mentioned it, she wouldn't tell another soul about the Billy business. Lips were sealed.

★★★

In Room 21A at Glasgow City Police Headquarters George leaned forwards in his swivel chair and reached for the telephone. He called the Brigadier.

'We'll need a word or two with MacSherry,' he said. 'Can you—'

The Brigadier cut in. 'As good as done. I'll have Rutter arrange the necessary.'

'Good,' George said. 'And we'll make sure Uniform knows that if they pick up Duthie, he's ours. Body and soul.'

Chapter seven: Star gazer

Inside the cave were all manner of precious goods.
This was no ordinary place. Here there were no
mere baubles. Each object was a treasure in itself.
Aladdin's eyes were dazzled. What manner of person,
he wondered, had hidden such things —?
    The Story of Aladdin, Children's Library Press,
Finchley.

At Maryhill Barracks, three miles away from Room 21A,
the handcuffed German pilot with dried spit on his face was
signed over to the custody of two privates and a sergeant. The
prisoner was led to a room where he was stripped. One private
stood by the door of the small room. The other pulled on a pair
of black rubber gloves.

The body search was slow and deliberate. Rough fingers
ruffled hair and prodded cavities. Mouth open. Legs spread.
Squat. Stand up. Don't look at me. Eyes down. Look at the floor.
Look at the bloody floor. Are you deaf or just stupid? Do exactly as
you're told, German pig.

It was the same with every prisoner. The process was
designed to humiliate and intimidate. It never hurt to show
who had the power. What followed the body search wasn't
Geneva Convention. Not by a mile.

Standing there naked, the prisoner glared at the army
custody sergeant. The prisoner's eyes were wide, dark as pitch.
He gave his name as Rudolf Hess. He said he was Hitler's
Deputy.

The army custody sergeant was not favourably disposed
towards Germans, glaring, dark-eyed, or otherwise. A year
earlier at Narvik in Norway, a German bullet in the stomach

sidelined him from what he called 'real soldiering' into a desk job. It wasn't a job he warmed to. He was a regular soldier. His World War One ribbons showed he'd seen action in the trenches. Now he was reduced to this: Maryhill Barracks and body searches.

He jabbed a finger into the prisoner's chest. 'Hitler's Deputy. Is that a fact? Lovely to meet you. I'm the bloody Duke of Windsor.' Then, turning to the private who stood by the door, he snapped: 'Better follow the rules and get the duty doctor. We might have a head injury here. Hitler's Deputy in Maryhill... God almighty, I'm in a lunatic asylum.'

The naked prisoner raised his voice. 'I demand...'

Speaking was a mistake.

The sergeant was not well disposed to demands by anyone in his custody. Then again, he'd never, even before Narvik, been particularly well disposed towards anybody – with or without demands.

The words had barely left the prisoner's lips when the sergeant sent him sprawling with a fast, hard, backhanded blow that drew trickles of blood from his nose and a corner of his mouth.

'No,' the sergeant said, 'you demand nothing. I demand you shut your bloody German mouth. Right now. Murdering swine. Shut it or you're on the next bus to Clydebank. You'll last five minutes there. That's if you're really lucky. They'll skin you alive. Back up on your feet. Get up.'

When the prisoner stood, there was another fast, hard, backhanded blow. This time, perhaps prepared, the prisoner remained on his feet.

'Pigs, the lot of you. Animals. Savages,' the sergeant said, his face within an inch of the prisoner's face. 'You turned Clydebank into an open grave.'

The prisoner said nothing.

He maintained this silence until the army doctor, a captain in his early thirties, arrived twenty minutes later. The doctor pointed to the blood on the naked prisoner's face and asked: 'How did he come by these injuries?'

'He was a bit lippy,' the sergeant said, 'and I had to quieten him down. He speaks English. You can ask him yourself.'

The doctor ordered the removal of the handcuffs and the return of the prisoner's clothes. There was a nod of thanks from the prisoner. A chair was brought in. The prisoner sat, hands clasped on his thighs.

'We'll start with your name,' the doctor said.

The sergeant cut in: 'He says he's Hitler's Deputy. That's why I had you fetched in. He must've banged his head. Concussion, maybe.'

The doctor raised his hand, silencing the sergeant. For the briefest fraction of a second the sergeant wondered if the doctor was offering a Nazi salute. You never knew with doctors. They were all toffs. Full of themselves. Born-to-rule University boys.

'We'll let the prisoner speak for himself,' the doctor said, 'unless you have some profound medical insights you might care to offer. Or perhaps you have some personal experience with head injuries.'

The prisoner cleared his throat. His English was perfect. It was spoken with confidence: 'I am Rudolf Walter Richard Hess. I am Adolf Hitler's Deputy. My identity will not be difficult to confirm. A photograph will serve that purpose. And there are those in your Diplomatic Service and within Mister Churchill's government who have had personal dealings with me in less hostile times.'

The doctor nodded, scribbled some notes and asked: 'Apart from your mention of friends in high places, is there any other reason for coming to Scotland at this time of year? Some might say it's a bit early for the grouse and a bit late for the salmon.'

The prisoner shrugged. He knew he was being assessed rather than patronised. His comprehension of language and his capacity to understand questions were being tested. The prisoner said he had better to do than follow the seasonal activities of the British landed classes although they could be enjoyable company at times.

'Are you familiar with horoscopes? With astrology? With star signs and their profound and well-established influence on individuals?' the prisoner said. The doctor shook his head. The prisoner continued: 'For example, I was born in Alexandria, Egypt, at 3.46 am on 26 April, 1894. This means I am a Taurus. My exact time and place of birth and my Taurus sign exert that profound influence. Do you understand that?'

The doctor shook his head again. He looked sideways and saw the sergeant roll his eyes.

The prisoner went on: 'Astrology is an exact science. Medicine is an inexact science. Astrology predicts the events in an individual life. Medical science merely suggests courses of action and possible or probable results of those suggested actions. In Germany we have a learned institution that is dedicated to the exact science. It is the Astrological Lodge of the Theosophical Lodge of Greater Germany. It is led by Professor Karl Ernst Krafft, a brilliant man. He is my personal astrologer in much the same way as an important personage, a person of rank and standing, might have a personal physician. I am here on the advice of Professor Krafft.'

The prisoner paused, indicating he didn't intend to elaborate.

The sergeant, unseen by the army doctor, tapped his temple with a forefinger. Voice lowered a whisper, he said to the two privates: 'Away with the fairies. A right headcase.'

One private winked. The other nodded. It never hurt to agree with the sergeant. Keep the sergeant happy, that was rule number one. Rule number two was the same as rule number one. And, no two ways about it, the German did sound like a right headcase.

The doctor ignored the sergeant's whisper and nodded to the prisoner. 'Please continue,' he said.

The prisoner shook his head. The exact details of that advice from Professor Krafft were neither the business of the doctor, whose attention he appreciated, nor of the sergeant, whose attention was less welcome. What brought him to Scotland would be revealed only when the prisoner had spoken with a senior officer who, in turn, would advise those in the highest places of the presence of Rudolf Hess.

'When my presence is known, those in the highest places will wish to speak with me without a delay of any sort. Now, I would be obliged if you would be good enough to initiate a meeting with a senior officer. It will not go well for you if you do not see to this immediately.'

The doctor said a prisoner of such importance was right to expect the attention of a senior officer. However, there were channels. A captain in the Medical Corps couldn't simply make direct contact with the top brass. He was sure the prisoner, being German, understood all about channels and pecking orders. 'Nevertheless, I'll see what I can do,' the doctor said. 'You have my word on it.'

Rising to his feet, the doctor motioned for the sergeant to follow him from the room. They closed the door behind them. The doctor said the prisoner was obviously confused. He might be mildly concussed or seriously fatigued. Both conditions presented similar symptoms. On the other hand, the prisoner might be utterly and profoundly roaring mad. But for now, the prisoner should be placed in a custody cell under observation at all times.

The doctor would return. One or two hours, probably. Some time to let the prisoner settle down. The doctor said there would be no additional cuts or sundry marks on the prisoner when he returned. The sergeant nodded. He understood perfectly. He resolved that should he have occasion or inclination to strike the prisoner again, he would leave no marks.

'What about this Hitler's Deputy business?' the sergeant asked.

The doctor shrugged. He'd see how the prisoner was when he returned. He'd make a decision then.

'What name will I put on the prisoner's documents?' the sergeant asked.

The doctor suggested: 'Rudolph Walter Richard Hess seems as good as anything for the moment.'

The sergeant shot back: 'I'll write it in pencil. You never know, we might have to change it to Robert Burns or John-the-bloody-Baptist. Or what about the Moderator of the General Assembly of the Church of Scotland... Berlin congregation...' There was a guttural, rasping, Glasgow sharpness in the sergeant's tone. His words stopped just short of ending in spit.

***

There was no such sharpness of tone in the canteen on the fourth floor of The Glasgow Herald building where Finola Fraser sat opposite Andy Auld, a soft-spoken Caithness man. He'd been the newspaper's Chief Reporter for the better part of twenty years.

'So, what news of great import have you brought from your travels?' he said. There was a father-daughter warmth between the two. He'd interviewed her when she applied for her first reporting job and he helped find her 'respectable digs' when she arrived in Glasgow.

In her greenstick junior reporter days he'd been her mentor. Having the approval of Andy was no small thing at the paper. If he gave you the nod it meant you were in with the bricks.

By reputation he had the best contacts list in Scotland. There wasn't a top-shelf private telephone number he didn't have and there was, so the story went, not a door that was closed to Andy.

Ruefully, he eyed a plate of overcooked chips and a reheated corned beef pie.

Prodding the pie with his fork, he lamented: 'The field kitchens in Belgium dished up better than this.'

Like many of his generation, he had volunteered in 1914 and had seen action in the King's Own Scottish Borderers for the best part of two years until a Blighty wound – a mortar fragment in his left knee – had secured his departure from the front lines.

He said Finola had shown considerable wisdom in settling for tea rather than canteen food.

He listened to Finola's grapevine account of the failed attempt by two Irishmen to board the ferry. As an old hand in the listening and asking business, he sensed Finola was holding something back. He said nothing. When she had more to say, she'd say it. All in her own good time; that was Finola Fraser for you. Cards close to the chest.

'The local police put a fair bit of stock in there being an IRA connection,' Finola said. 'I think they're right. So, now there's one on the run and there's another one that was shot and spirited away from the hospital down there. He'll be well tucked away somewhere. Wherever the shot one is, there's not a chance in a million we'll get near him.

'By the way, coming back there was a police roadblock near Paisley. Obviously they were looking for the Irishman. Everybody had to step out of their cars and identify themselves. The Military Police in front of us stepped out with a German, a pilot by the look of what he was wearing.'

Wasn't that a coincidence, Andy said. A while earlier he'd had a call from a contact about a German plane coming down near Stranraer. Probably lost or low on fuel, that seems to be the story. Worth page one, though. The sub-editors would come up with a two-line 18 point, single column headline, too. Something like:

Nazi airman
in custody

That would do the trick.

The business of the shooting, that was another sure thing for page one, but in the next day's paper, probably above the fold on column eight, the final column on the broadsheet.

Nothing too alarming, though. Just a to-the-point description of the incident. Police challenge two men boarding the ferry. Mention Irish but not the IRA. Well, not for now. One man shot and taken into police custody. Second man on the run. Not to be approached. May be armed, that style of thing. Roadblocks set up. Vehicles searched. Six or seven paragraphs.

Pushing the plate of half-eaten chips and reheated corned beef pie towards a corner of the canteen table, Andy stood. 'The paper won't bring itself out,' he said. 'We'd better get back to it. No work, no wages. Sadly, that's the way of the world.'

★★★

Not ten minutes away, in the secure ward at the Glasgow Western Infirmary, a stone's throw from the Clachan in Byres Road, a doctor and two nurses worked to MacSherry's wounds. Elphinstone Rutter was impassive as the doctor said the patient should never have been moved. Blood pressure was falling. The pulse was weak. MacSherry was in shock. It was touch-and-go, the doctor said. Could Rutter please leave?

'Certainly,' Rutter said. 'I'll have a couple of chaps take a seat just outside the door where they won't get in the way, and someone else by the bedside.'

He said he was sure the doctor could be relied upon to do his very best for the patient. Much appreciated. Nobody wanted a death in custody. So much paperwork. Always some poor doctor or nurse getting the blame. Quite unfair, of course. Mind you, there wasn't a lot of fairness going around.

'Well, I'll leave you to the task in hand. I'm sure you'll do your very best for the patient. That's what doctors and nurses are here for, isn't it. I've written down my number on this slip of paper. Any change in circumstances and you'll make sure I'm the very first to know.'

★★★

Rutter arrived back at his Lochard House office as,two doors away, a signals clerk handed a message to the Brigadier. The message was from the Duty Officer/Radio Transmissions Interception/Military Intelligence/Glasgow/Clyde Sector. The Brigadier read and reread the message. It said:

> *Intercepts – two.*
> *Outgoing – one.*
> *Incoming – one.*
> *Outgoing source triangulated to Randall Street, Clydebank.*
> *Incoming identity: Abwehr Branch, Der Geheime Funkmel-*
> *dedienst des OKW, Ausland/Intelligence code Ab/271/GX.*
> *Decoded outgoing:*
> *TM injured/ detained. Sender safe for now. Immediate*
> *advice necessary. TD.*
> *Decoded incoming:*
> *Proceed to Chrysalis for instructions.*

The Brigadier told the signals clerk: 'Get Maclean and Inglis out here right now,' he said. 'And I want to see Rutter on the double. He should be back by now.'

★★★

Before Rutter had even closed the door after entering the Brigadier's office, his superior started talking. Brisk, straight to the point. 'I've a job for you, Rutter. Take six Redcaps and get down to Randall Street, Clydebank. Don't have a street number. Wireless fellows have intercepted a couple of transmissions. I'll get Maclean and Inglis to meet you there.

They're on their way here. I'll brief them and send them to Randall Street. *Sans* delay. Chop-chop. Any rough stuff at Clydebank, step back and leave it to the Redcaps. No heroics, Rutter, just secure anything or anybody you find.'

The tone of the no heroics order was borderline sarcastic, contemptuous. As far as the Brigadier was concerned, he couldn't think of anybody less disposed towards heroics than Rutter. A bloody pen-pusher, a bean counter in a uniform he didn't deserve to wear. That's what he was.

The Brigadier passed the decoded intercept to Rutter.

'TM and TD… Tommy MacSherry and Tommy Duthie. I'd say the late little Billy Dalgleish of Partick really was onto something,' Rutter said. 'A life not entirely without worth after all. Fate plays some odd tricks. I'll round up the Redcaps and be on my way.'

***

Duthie had been on his way from his Clydebank hiding place an hour before two Redcaps, watched by Rutter, battered down a green door on the ground floor of a sandstone tenement in Randall Street. Four other Redcaps positioned themselves, front and rear, outside the building. They were still there, when George and Danny, briefed by the Brigadier, arrived one hour later.

It wasn't difficult for Rutter and the Redcaps to pinpoint the source of the clandestine radio transmission. Only one building in Randall Street had survived the two nights of bombing. And only one flat in the building was obviously in use. The doors of the other five flats were boarded shut.

***

Duthie knew sending the message to Berlin would be risky. It would be even more risky keeping the transmitter open for the time it took for Berlin to send its instructions. Since the raids on Clydebank, Royal Signals' wireless detector vans had been operating night and day.

But Duthie needed instructions and they'd have to be issued from the highest level in Berlin. That took time. He'd have to take the risk. Then he'd make himself scarce.

Under cover of dusk Duthie made his way from Randall Street. He hid himself in the rubble of what had been the Clydebank Ambulance Depot. German bombs had destroyed four ambulances even before they could be deployed on the first night of the bombing. The initial target list drawn up by the Luftwaffe Central Command in Berlin included the ambulance depot, four fire stations, the Clydebank Infirmary and schools that might be used as makeshift medical facilities or assembly points for civilians.

The destruction of such targets meant Clydebank and its people and its industries would be on their own, isolated in the eye of a firestorm. Buildings became shells and, in some places, humans became pools of melted fat. And the noise. The noise of it all. The thunder and roar of the flames. The terrible screams.

Clydebank, in the two nights of bombing, became an image of hell and vileness. An image from Goya's Black Paintings.

Duthie waited in the rubble until daylight faded before he made his move. He walked at a brisk pace, constantly looking over his shoulder, along unlit and bombed-out streets. Weeks and then months had passed since the raids but there was still, in the air, a smell of smoke and damp and the dust of destruction. Here and there was the waft of dead flesh rotted deep in the rubble. It was the smell of war. Total war, Hitler called it. To those on the receiving end it was, simply, cold-blooded murder.

Within minutes Tommy was in the kitchen of a neat, modest house that adjoined the Clydebank Seafarers' Mission.

It was one of the few undamaged buildings in the town. He was safe there. The house was occupied by the Reverend Martin Lang. He was above suspicion. A Lutheran pastor at the Hamburg Seafarers' Hostel, he fled Germany four years earlier. He stowed away – that was what he said – in a rusting Baltic trader that regularly plied the waters between Hamburg and the Clyde.

The authorities in Clydebank were impressed by his story of how he refused to serve in a Lutheran Church that had become subservient to the Religious Affairs Directorate of the Nazi Party. The refusal, the Reverend Martin Lang told the authorities, made him a Nazi target in Hamburg. His telephone calls were monitored. He heard mysterious clicks on the line. His mail was being opened and read and resealed. The Lutheran Church hierarchy advised him to be more circumspect in his sermons. Otherwise, he might, he was told, find himself stripped of his State-issued licence to preach. He'd received, so he said, written and telephoned threats of physical violence because of his 'un-German sentiments.' Several times he'd been jostled by Nazi bully boys in broad daylight outside his church. Members of his congregation had been advised to worship elsewhere.

With permission to remain in Scotland as a clergyman at risk of persecution, and perhaps death or imprisonment, in Germany, the Reverend Martin Lang easily secured a position at the Clydebank Seafarers' Mission.

There was a vacancy for a chaplain and the Reverend Martin Lang fitted like a glove. He was comfortable with seafarers and they were comfortable with him. He was a good listener. The chaplaincy allowed him the run of the shipyards and the docks. Night or day, rain or shine, the Reverend Martin Lang did his pastoral rounds in the heavy engineering workshops, on the quayside and in the factory canteens.

He'd ask how things were going. How was the family? Wasn't it busy? The yards seemed to be working overtime, didn't they? Lots of patching up and repairs. Isn't the weather awful?

The boys out there on the convoys must be getting tossed about all over the place, musn't they?

Everybody in the workshops or on the docks had a good word for the Reverend Martin. And at the top levels of the Abwehr Overseas Communications Directorate in Berlin there were those who thought very highly of the chaplain at the Clydebank Seafarers' Mission, too.

Of course, his name was never mentioned in Berlin. They simply referred to him as Chrysalis.

In late September 1939, just a few weeks after the war began, Berlin assigned Chrysalis a pair of subordinates; IRA men Tommy Duthie and Tommy MacSherry, sent – on the recommendation of the IRA Army Council – first to Germany for radio and encoding training and then to the Clyde shipyards as undercover agents.

Certainly, the Abwehr Overseas Communications Directorate had no doubts that Duthie and MacSherry, the names on their perfectly forged documents, would prove to be useful for any dirty work and for gathering nuggets of information and gossip. But Chrysalis was the jewel in the crown.

He was a singularly valuable asset. He'd been a Party man since his theology student days in the late 1920s. To the eager and earnest student, Martin Lang, Hitler was a Christ-like figure. The Fuhrer was an ordinary man of modest origins. He had risen above the welts of social insignificance and a deeply personal sense of humiliation after Germany's surrender in 1918 and the punitive terms of the Armistice that came with the surrender. He had risen as a single-minded saviour, casting the Jews and their intellectual Pharisees from their temples of power in the professions.

After ordination, Martin Lang was the Party's eyes and ears in the Lutheran churches in Hamburg. Carefully, gradually, he was encouraged by the Party to craft a reputation as a pastor becoming less and less comfortable with the relationship between his church and the Nazi state. A word here and there, a veiled criticism of Party intrusion into the pulpit. It was not uncommon, some in the church felt, for people like Martin Lang to simply disappear. In fact, several of those in the Lutheran community who had quietly told Lang they shared his views had already disappeared, taken away to Dachau in the night.

Clearly, it suited the Abwehr to assist the Reverend Martin Lang, troublemaker, to disappear to Clydebank. He could be of considerable value in enemy territory. He would be seen as a 'Good German' who had fled persecution and National Socialism. He would be trusted as a man of conscience and courage.

His subsequent coded reports from Clydebank disclosed a level of attention to detail that delighted his Abwehr masters. The reports listed arrival and departure times of merchant ships, their origins and destinations, their cargoes, their armaments. Reports on Royal Navy vessels were similarly detailed. Some included names of captains and first officers. Then there were the reports on what was being built or repaired in the dry docks and how many shifts were operating at every shipyard.

***

In the kitchen of his neat, modest dwelling, the Reverend Martin Lang was attentive as Tommy Duthie detailed the despatching of Billy Dalgleish.

MacSherry had been 'in a right state' after police arrested Dalgleish. He'd returned to Randall Street where he told Duthie how he'd watched, sheltering in a tenement doorway, the arrest of Billy. He couldn't be sure what Billy might tell the police.

'He said he would telephone you. There's a phone box still standing near the bombed-out ambulance station in Clydebank,' Duthie said.

Chrysalis interrupted: 'I told MacSherry I had been advised by an impeccable source where Dalgleish was to be located. I said both of you were to silence Dalgleish and make for the Stranraer ferry on the train.'

Duthie continued: 'That's what we did. We went down to Partick. Tommy gave the door a push with his shoulder and it opened, just like that. Billy didn't have time to make a sound. I waited by the door and Tommy took four steps inside and snapped Billy's neck like a matchstick. Start to finish, it wouldn't have taken three seconds. Tommy was always good with his hands. He could crack walnuts with his fingers.

'Then we went down to Stranraer. There was hardly anybody on the train.'

Duthie recounted the subsequent events that had left him shaken – the shooting at Stranraer, the wounding of MacSherry, the heart-in-mouth escape through bog and field, how he'd waved down and stolen a car just north of the town, how he'd gone to Randall Street and sent his message to Berlin, how he'd waited for what seemed like a lifetime before being ordered to contact Chrysalis.

'God knows where Tommy is,' he said.

Chrysalis said MacSherry could well be dead. 'That might be better for all concerned,' he added. 'If he is alive we have to assume he will cooperate with our enemies. They will offer him the choice of hanging or talking,' he said. 'And when he has done everything they demand of him, told them everything they want to know, he will be hanged. The British have a ruthless and brutal streak. They didn't build their Empire by being soft. Ruthlessness and brutality are perhaps the only two characteristics I admire in our enemy.'

Duthie said MacSherry would never betray his comrades. Chrysalis smiled. MacSherry might well be prepared to hang for Ireland, he said, but hanging for Hitler was another matter entirely.

'I will speak plainly. MacSherry is a man of small horizons, unlike you, Tommy. We are men cut from the same cloth, you and me. We can see the bigger scheme of things. MacSherry is an unthinking foot soldier. Surely you know this?'

Chrysalis was a gifted dissembler. Men of the cloth often were. Their calling demanded an ability to persuade others of the veracity of stories that, to the rational mind, could not possibly be true – stories of loaves and fishes and walking on water and raising the dead and virgin birth and eternal life beyond the cold and damp of the grave.

Chrysalis' observations did not sit comfortably with Duthie. He and MacSherry had been comrades in the same Belfast IRA active service unit. They had shared danger and, together, had shed the blood of others. However, he said nothing. There and then Chrysalis was his lifeline away from this mess.

Chrysalis cleared his throat. Enough, for now, of MacSherry. Other matters had come to light since his shooting and capture. Exact details of those other matters would come from Berlin overnight. They related to the capture of a German pilot not far from Stranraer.

Chrysalis said he knew no more than that. He would listen to Radio Berlin's English-language wireless propaganda broadcast, the nightly rant from William Joyce, Lord Haw-Haw, who, in time, would hang in Wandsworth Prison, London, as a reviled war criminal and collaborator.

Chrysalis would listen for the words 'star gazer.' If these words were used by Haw Haw, they indicated Berlin was sending a message to Chrysalis.

Five minutes after he heard those words he would activate his wireless transceiver in the attic, and tune in to the frequency used by his superiors – he pronounced the word 'zooperiors' – in Berlin. He would, in that message, receive his orders.

But for now, Chrysalis said, Duthie should relax. He was safe.

'I am above suspicion,' Chrysalis said. 'I am the German

pastor who turned his back on Hitler. Soon we will be gone from here. A plan is already in place.'

Duthie was in a deep and motionless sleep – the sleep of an exhausted man – when Chrysalis received the wireless message from his 'zooperiors.' It was a jaw-dropping transmission. The coded message came in seven second bursts at two and three minute intervals.

The message advised that Deputy Fuhrer Hess had flown a stolen Luftwaffe plane to Scotland. He was now in British custody, possibly in Glasgow although his exact whereabouts were unknown. When they were known, further instructions would be issued to Chrysalis. These instructions would come directly from the Fuhrer. They would be followed to the letter.

Chrysalis read and reread the message he had decoded. Hess, Hitler's Deputy, in Scotland. It was beyond belief. Surely not? Hess, the man who had been by Hitler's side from the early days of the Party, who had served time in prison with Hitler. Hess had stolen a plane and flown to Scotland. This was the same Hess whose radio speeches had stirred in the student Martin Lang something approaching euphoria when he spoke of Greater Germany and the purging of inferior and anti-German elements... when he spoke of how the Party would scrub away the dark stain of the 1918 Armistice.

Chrysalis cast aside his initial doubts on the veracity of the message. It was a message from Berlin. And Berlin did not make mistakes. Most certainly, it did not make mistakes when it said orders would follow from the Fuhrer.

Chrysalis thought of his one brief meeting with Hess at the Party's most secret training centre near the Dachau prison and punishment camp not far from Munich. At the centre, agents like Chrysalis were schooled and re-schooled in wireless operation, in field craft, in avoiding surveillance.

It was the place where agents like Chrysalis were blooded, taught how to kill with bullet and knife and bare hands. Inmates from Dachau – usually Communists and critics of the Party –

were used as teaching aids in these killing sessions. The inmates were not in short supply.

On one of four eight-day periods of instruction at the training establishment, Chrysalis had been introduced to the visiting Hess. The introduction came after Hess and his uniformed entourage watched and then applauded as Chrysalis snapped the neck of a terrified handcuffed prisoner after punching him unconscious. Chrysalis remembered Hess for his iron handshake, his square jaw and his dark, staring eyes. He remembered the words Hess had said during their long, strong handshake.

'Ours is not an easy task,' the Deputy Fuhrer said. 'We must be strong and firm enough to set aside pity. Greater Germany will not be built by men whose tears blind them to their moral obligations. We have been chosen – perhaps by history or perhaps by God – to assert our racial supremacy and, without a second thought, to cast into the furnace of irrelevance those who lack our purity of blood and manifest destiny. This is our right, our duty and our obligation.'

The man standing by the side of Hess nodded but said nothing. Chrysalis recognised the man as Heinrich Himmler, Chief of the then recently merged German Police and the SS. He would never forget Himmler's gimlet eyes. They were the eyes of a man without pity or empathy. Just the sort of man Hitler needed to accomplish his vision of a pure and great Germany.

It had been such a day, that day near Dachau. An encounter with Hess and a nod from Himmler. Such men. Such men. Chrysalis could follow them into the searing fires of hell. They simply had to issue the order.

And now this; the news that the Deputy Fuhrer had flown to Scotland in a stolen plane. Chrysalis shook his head in bewilderment then encoded his response to Berlin:

Chrysalis received. Moving to secure location. Further contact at earliest opportunity. Within 12 hours if possible.

***

While Duthie slept like a child in Lang's lodgings, George and Danny looked on as two of Rutter's Redcaps removed the last of the floorboards in the two-room groundfloor flat in the Randall Street tenement. Rutter watched, too, saying nothing.

The search was fruitful. It took several hours. The Redcaps found two German Luger pistols and close to 200 rounds of ammunition. There were seven detailed plans of Clydebank shipyards. A small knapsack contained a wad of ration books – food, clothing, petrol coupons. A pocket notebook contained single-line strings of numbers and letters. There was a miniature Leitz camera and two rolls of exposed microfilm. There was a small suitcase radio transceiver.

'Aladdin's cave,' Danny said. George agreed. It was a treasure trove.

Rutter broke his silence. 'We'll get our specialist and technical chaps at Lochard House to have a good look at everything. I'll make sure they get a move on. I'd want a report to put on the Brigadier's desk by mid-morning.'

George nodded and looked at what had been uncovered by the search.

'Well then, nothing for us to do here. We'll stand down for a few hours – some shut-eye, a shave, a tub and a clean shirt should see me right. We'll be out at Lochard House in the morning – see what your boffins have to say about this lot. And we need to have a talk with MacSherry. You'll fix that, won't you? Point us in the right direction, that sort of thing.'

'MacSherry is in rather a bad way,' Rutter said. 'I doubt you'd get much – if anything – out of him at present. He could very easily shuffle off this mortal coil at the drop of a hat. That would be something of a loss, a very great loss, given he might be persuaded to tell us a thing or two.' George said that was all the more reason to question MacSherry as soon as possible. 'Anything he says, anything. A word, a nod, a scribble on paper might lead us to Duthie… and God alone knows who else.'

Chapter eight: Talkative Tommy

Materials retrieved Randall Street, Clydebank, confirm existence of active German cell. Probable IRA connection. Investigating further. Will advise soonest. Stuart, E. (Brig.), Glasgow/Clyde Sector— Telex message to O/C, Central Sector, London

Mid-morning at Lochard House. The Brigadier, over tea and Macgregor's Digestive Biscuits, briefed George and Danny on MacSherry's condition in the secure unit of the Western Infirmary and on what had been revealed by the examination of the Randall Street treasure trove.

'The doctors at the Western tell us the patient is all over the place,' the Brigadier said. 'He's drifting in and out of consciousness. Blood pressure up one minute and then dangerously low the next. He's a mess. Shock. Blood loss. The quacks aren't prepared to give us any odds on MacSherry's survival. Damned doctors. Reading between the lines, though, I'd have to say it isn't promising at all.'

Much more promising, however, was the haul from Randall Street. 'The rolls of exposed film found with the Leitz camera have been developed,' the Brigadier said. 'Not a pretty sight. Just about curled my hair. About half a dozen pictures show external views of Lochard House. And there are dozens of prints of rebuilding work on the Clydebank shipyards and factories and dry docks. One roll is nothing but Royal Navy and Merchant Navy ships berthed on the Govan reach of the River Clyde. Jerry would love this.'

The ration books and coupons were forgeries that only expert eyes could fully discredit. The radio was a beautifully engineered S108/10 model issued by the Abwehr in Berlin.

It had three compact elements – a power unit, a receiver and a transmitter.

'Our boffins say you've got to hand it to the Hun when it comes to quality. Personally, the only thing I'd hand the Hun would be a quick and noisy lead injection behind the ear.'

'What about the pocket notebook that was found, the one with the strings of numbers?' George asked.

'These codebreaker fellows,' the Brigadier said. 'Great ones for stating the obvious. They told me that the numbers could refer to agents – but whether those agents are in Clydebank or Berlin is another matter entirely. Then again, the numbers might refer to targets. Or they might refer to persons of use to the Germans. Or even spies on British soil. It's also possible, they say, that these numbers might refer to contact points or radio frequencies or meeting places. They could refer to the Man in the Moon for all the eggheads know. One of them had the absolute gall to tell me that they thought decoding these numbers might be tricky.'

The Brigadier sighed and rolled his eyes. 'I told them, in no uncertain terms, that they weren't there to do the easy tasks, so would they be kind enough to just get on with the damned job? *Tout de suite*. Of course it's a tough nut to crack. If it was easy they'd be out of a job. Cadging drinks off Major Maclean and doing cryptic crosswords with him in some dreary lounge bar.'

George ignored the reference to cryptic crosswords. With the Brigadier's permission, he said, he'd run through the facts as they seemed to be unfolding. The Brigadier said that seemed reasonable. Always handy to recap, to lay things out and try to join the dots. Have everybody on the same page. Singing from the same song sheet.

It was now beyond doubt that a German espionage cell was operating in Clydebank. What before had been strongly suspected was now confirmed. The cell, George was sure, had been behind the pinpoint accuracy of the second night of the Clydebank Blitz.

'Duthie and MacSherry were working together. They were working for the Germans,' George continued. 'Somebody let them know where to find Billy Dalgleish – and it has to be somebody on the inside. Either somebody in the police or somebody who knew Dalgleish had been lifted, kept in overnight, interviewed by myself and Danny and then taken back to his digs in Partick.'

George took a deep breath, as though considering the implications of what he had said. The Brigadier nodded, indicating George should continue.

'So what else do we know? MacSherry is still under lock and key in the secure ward of the Western Infirmary and he's not getting any better. We know from that intercepted signal that Duthie is probably back in Glasgow or Clydebank. Someone is hiding him. Myself and Danny need to talk with MacSherry. Without delay.'

Danny cut in: 'Even if it kills him.'

The Brigadier said he'd prefer, for the time being, if any questioning left MacSherry alive. 'Don't want to do the hangman out of his twenty guineas, do we?' he said.

George pressed for a direct answer on immediate access to MacSherry. 'So, you'll give us the all-clear on getting over to the Western Infirmary and getting into the secure unit?'

The Brigadier said Rutter would advise the hospital and the Redcaps guarding MacSherry's room to expect Major Maclean and Sergeant Inglis within fifteen minutes.

'So, you'd better get going.'

***

It took just under fifteen minutes to drive from Lochard House to the Western Infirmary. George and Danny parked their vehicle on the cobbled concourse close to the main entry to the building. The secure unit, four single rooms, was behind swing doors at the end of a long, antiseptic-smelling corridor.

Two Military Police officers sat on a backless bench at the door of MacSherry's room. They stood and saluted. Major Maclean and Sergeant Inglis were expected.

'Identity cards and a signature, please, gentlemen,' the taller of the two Military Police officers said, handing a clipboard to George. 'Just a formality. If you could sign here, please. Lovely. Thank you. In you go. We're here if you need us.'

Inside MacSherry's room, the duty doctor who had attended to the patient since his admission said MacSherry's life was hanging in the balance. 'And, no, in answer to your next question, I'm not prepared to offer odds. Even raised voices could tip him into heart failure. Perhaps you can keep that in mind. If I had my way, nobody apart from medical staff would be speaking to a patient in this condition.'

There was MacSherry's blood loss to consider. The severe damage to one limb. The shock. The transfer to Glasgow certainly hadn't helped, either.

'In fact, moving the patient was barely short of criminal,' the doctor admonished. 'He regained consciousness for a few minutes before he lapsed back into unconsciousness. He said nothing that made any sense. Just babble. Mumbling something about a minister or a pastor. Maybe he wants the last rites or something like that. Haven't a clue. I just tend to the body, not the spirit. And I have more than a few bodies to tend to right now.'

The doctor initialled MacSherry's temperature and blood pressure chart. If the worst came to the worst it was at least evidence that MacSherry was alive when he was left with George and Danny.

As he opened the door to leave, the doctor made glaring, unblinking eye contact with George and Danny. 'Keep your voices down. Don't pressure or threaten. At best, you'll just make him worse and at worst, you'll kill him. There's a nurses' station at the end of the corridor and I'll be around somewhere if the patient is experiencing difficulties.'

'Perfectly understood,' Danny said. 'We'll do nothing to upset him. Rest assured of that. Now we'll let you get on with your work and we'll get on with ours.'

When the doctor left, George and Danny stood by MacSherry's bedside. His pillow was wet with sweat. His breathing was shallow. His eyes opened. His tongue brushed his dry lips.

'God Almighty,' Danny said, startled, stepping back, 'he gave me a right fright.'

He stepped forward again, and leaned over the patient. 'Hello there Tommy,' he said. 'You wouldn't remember us. You were out for the count when we dropped in at the Stranraer Infirmary the other day. Terrible state you were in. Terrible. You look worse now.

'Terrible about that leg, too. Well and truly buggered, so the doctor says. He says you've been asking for a minister or a priest. Is that right? Close to the end, is it? And not a sign of your pal, Tommy Duthie. The same Tommy Duthie that ran away and left you when you got shot. Just ran away and left you there lying in your own blood. Some friend he is.'

MacSherry groaned. His lips moved but no words came. His eyes moved from Danny to George, and then back to Danny.

George leaned over MacSherry. 'Don't you worry about Danny here,' George said. 'He just gets very agitated when he thinks about poor wee Billy Dalgleish lying there in Partick with his neck broken. You remember Billy? How could you forget, though? Are you the one that broke his neck? Or was it your toerag pal? Danny gets very upset just thinking about it. And you know what? He gets just as upset when he thinks about Billy's address being found in your pocket in Stranraer. But you'll come to no harm from Danny. He wants you well enough to hang. Mind you, the doctor says it's fifty-fifty, maybe less. And I'd put my last shilling on the doctor knowing more than Danny here.'

Maybe this was a good time for Tommy to get things off his chest.

'Going with a bad conscience is an awful way to go,' George said. 'A powerful creature, the human conscience. You think it's long gone and there it is, right there beside you, right next to your deathbed, whispering in your ear. Tommy, Tommy, it says, tell the truth or burn in Hell. I'm told you can smell its breath. I'm told it smells like bad meat. Is that what you can smell, Tommy?'

MacSherry's breathing quickened. He might even have sniffed the air. George couldn't be sure. The patient raised a hand from the bed. Again, his lips moved, but there were no words.

'I'll do the talking and you just nod or shake your head if it's too much trouble to speak. How does that sound?' George said. 'And Danny here can write down the answers.'

The patient nodded and gripped George Maclean's hand with surprising strength. It was the grip of a man holding onto life with his every fibre.

'So you and Duthie were in this together – this terrible Billy Dalgleish business. Poor wee Billy, and him a family man. You and Duthie went to Partick when you were told where to find him. That's right, is it?' George asked.

MacSherry nodded.

'And you both did for wee Billy? Is that right?' George said.

Another nod.

'And you got orders to kill him. You didn't want to, but orders are orders. Is that right?' MacSherry nodded again. Danny doubted the patient had been a reluctant killer. He'd seen too many like MacSherry over the years. They'd lie on their deathbed rather than own up to what they'd done.

George continued: 'You and Tommy were chummed up with the Germans. We know there's Germans, spies, in Clydebank. You and Tommy were right in with them, isn't that right? And you were giving them all the chit-chat from the shipyards? You probably gave them all the information they needed for the second night of the Clydebank Blitz. That was a fine night's work, Tommy. You filled a few thousand graves, so you did. You'd be right proud of yourself. Women and bairns burned beyond recognition. They could make a medal for the likes of you. They could call it The Bastards' Cross.'

'I quite like that,' Danny said. 'It has a nice ring to it. "The Bastards' Cross".'

This time there was no nodded response from MacSherry.

'Oh, Tommy, don't be daft. Get it off your chest,' George cajoled. 'We already know a fair bit. We know that you and Duthie have a bit to do with Chrysalis. Maybe you could tell us about Chrysalis – he's a German, that's right, isn't it? And maybe tell us a wee bit about how you came by the address where Billy Dalgleish had his digs. Who was it that told you where to find him? Will you do that, Tommy?'

The patient nodded.

'That's very good, Tommy. I think you're sorry for doing some really bad things,' George said, 'and you want them cleared up. Is that right, is that why you want to tell us the truth?'

The effort was almost superhuman, but MacSherry spoke. 'Yes.'

'You're doing the right thing,' George said, 'We'll make sure people know you did the right thing. Look, we're all just soldiers in a war. Sometimes soldiers do terrible things they don't want to do.'

Danny looked up from his notebook, raising an eyebrow. George was playing the prisoner like a fly fisher plays a brown trout.

MacSherry coughed. His superhuman effort resumed. He was speaking. Slowly. With difficulty. He was sweating profusely. But he was speaking

He would speak for the best part of an hour. He wanted to speak. There was no deathbed stoicism here. He was not a man who wished to take his secrets to the grave. He was a man who had many burdens to cast aside. There were the ordered killings. The standover tactics. The savage beatings delivered to anyone suspected of betraying the Republican cause.

MacSherry spoke in bursts. There would be a few laboured sentences and then long, sometimes wheezing, pauses. Sometimes he was lucid. Other times he lapsed into rambling, mumbling, disjointed strings of words.

George learned that MacSherry and Duthie had been brothers-in-arms in the IRA. Highly recommended to the Abwehr by the IRA Army Council, they went to Berlin. There they completed, with flying colours, their cipher and radio training. Three months before the outbreak of war they were sent to Clydebank.

They were placed at the disposal of Chrysalis. They would act on his direct orders. He was, they were told, well connected.

It was one of these connections, MacSherry rasped, who told Chrysalis where to find Dalgleish. The connection was known by the code name Kingfisher. Neither Duthie nor MacSherry knew who Kingfisher was.

'High up,' MacSherry said. 'Very high up.'

Apart from the location of Dalgleish, Kingfisher told Chrysalis that Robbie Kirkness was a police informant and it was information from Robbie that put Military Intelligence on the trail of Duthie and MacSherry. Chrysalis intended to take care of Robbie Kirkness. He was a marked man.

'This Chrysalis contact of yours,' George said, 'what's his real name…? Where do we find him…?'

Without warning, MacSherry's breathing quickened again. He was making a gurgling sound. His face was ashen grey. He was convulsing.

In an instant, Danny was on his feet, heading for the door. In the trenches and on the no-man's-land wire he'd seen countless men die. Some he'd killed with bayonet and rifle butt and bullet. Some he'd comforted as they breathed their last. Others he'd stepped over without a downwards glance.

He knew what impending death looked like. And MacSherry looked like a dying man.

'Get a doctor, any doctor,' Danny ordered the Redcaps guarding the room. 'Now. Right now. Anybody in a white coat.'

The doctor, who'd left George and Danny with the patient was by MacSherry's bedside within half a minute. Two nurses were on his heels. The patient's eyes were rolling and his limbs were rigid, like steel. The doctor swore loudly. An oxygen mask was placed over the patient's nose and mouth. A syringe of colourless liquid was injected directly into the patient's heart.

'Just you two get out of here,' the doctor shouted at Danny and George. 'What, in the name of God, have you done? This is a hospital, not a police cell!'

George and Danny waited with the Redcaps. They waited for forty minutes.

The doctor emerged, his face red with anger. His tone was barely restrained. 'He's alive. Just. No thanks to you two. The initial signs are that he's had a major heart attack, possibly even a stroke. Whether or not he survives beyond the next few hours is really the toss of a coin. And even if he does pull through – if it's a stroke – he could lose speech or sight or hearing, or all three. I haven't a clue how much damage has been done. We'll need to get a couple of specialists on the job.' He paused. Unable to fully contain his anger any more, he glared at George and Danny and said dismissively: 'Go on. Go away. I hope you're delighted. You've near killed him.'

George shook his head slowly, deliberately. No, they hadn't near killed the patient. 'Let's be very clear about that,' George insisted.

MacSherry had been talking, answering questions in his own time. Then he seized up. No warning. Nothing. His breathing changed and then he seemed to be having a fit.

Danny cut in. 'That's right. And, by the way, the man in there is a murderer. You're saving him for the gallows. If you want, I'll get you an invite to watch him swing.'

The doctor said he wasn't remotely interested in whatever the two cared to say. 'I don't know who you are and what you do away from here. But in this place you don't count for anything.'

'That's as may be,' George said. 'But we'll need to be kept informed of the patient's condition. I'll write down my telephone number.'

'That won't be necessary,' the doctor said. 'I've been instructed to ensure a Lt. Col. Elphinstone Rutter is kept informed of the well-being of the patient. I'm sure he'll keep you informed if he thinks you need to be informed.'

'Fine,' Danny said, sharply. 'We'll be on our way. We might drop in for a small libation at the Clachan just up the road. You're most welcome to join us, Doctor. We're convivial company. You can even bring MacSherry along. He could probably do with a heart starter. We could give him a lift, plenty of room in the back seat. Mind you, walking would probably do the patient here a bit of good. It would help the circulation.'

The doctor said nothing. He pointed to the door.

***

Leaving the hospital, George and Danny paused at the kiosk just inside the main entry. Their attention was caught by a newspaper billboard. It said: *Latest news – Nazi pilot in custody.*

George reached for coins in his pocket and bought a copy of The Glasgow Evening Times, the sister paper of The Glasgow Herald. The smell of the ink was strong. The paper felt moist. It couldn't have been more than an hour off the presses.

A brief page-one story reported:

In news just to hand, Authorities have confirmed that a German pilot who parachuted to safety south-

west of Glasgow has been taken into custody. It is understood the pilot abandoned his aircraft when it ran out of fuel. There is speculation that the pilot may have been lost or off course.

It is understood the aircraft took off from Augsburg in Germany and flew over the North Sea before coming down on a farm north of Stranraer. It is further understood the pilot was taken into custody by a local unit of the Home Guard. The pilot, according to Authorities, offered no resistance on being taken into custody. After an initial medical examination, the pilot was reported as uninjured.

George passed the newspaper to Danny. 'That must be the bugger we saw the other day,' he said. 'Shifty sod. Mad eyes.'

Danny said their intended immediate destination, the Clachan, was full of shifty sods with mad eyes. Anyhow, they wouldn't stay too long. A quiet drink – a gin or two for George and a nip and a pint, or two, for Danny – would be just the ticket. They deserved a wee break. They'd park the vehicle in Great George Street, just round the corner from the Clachan. They'd call Lochard House later.

Chapter nine: The winged messenger

Professor Karl Ernst Krafft/Astrological Lodge/ Theosophical Lodge of Greater Germany: Nazi Party member/January 1927/Germanic/Occult Studies PhD Berlin/1912/Captain Deutsches Reichsheer/garrison duty Munich/no active service/ 1914-1918. Personal Astrologer/Confidante of Rudolf Hess. Known to Hitler. Chronic alcoholic. Narcissistic/ grandiose tendencies/delusional—
    British Army Intelligence Records, file note, London, May, 1941.

The quiet couple of drinks at the Clachan had become a quiet four drinks when George felt a hand on his shoulder. It was the Brigadier's driver, Private John Morrison.

'A matter of some urgency,' Morrison said. 'The Brigadier requires a word. You're to report to him without delay.'

The softness of the accent said Morrison was a Western Isles man. Perhaps Lewis or Harris or North Uist. Certainly, he'd be a Gaelic speaker.

George said Private Morrison might enjoy a quick dram before departing the Clachan.

'Thank you, no,' Morrison said. 'The Brigadier, with all due respect Major, has no wish to be kept waiting.'

'Well,' George said, 'if you won't join us you could at least indicate how you found us.'

'The Brigadier told me to telephone you at the secure ward at the infirmary,' Morrison said. 'The doctor there said you'd left and come up here for a drink. I told the Brigadier, and he sent me to fetch you.' Morrison's tone was abrupt. The Western Isles disposition towards patronising directness was on display. It annoyed Danny. There he was, enjoying a quiet drink, and in comes this bloody sheepdog in uniform rounding people up.

'You strike me as a Gaelic Bolshie type, would I be correct? Are you a Bolshie, Morrison?' Danny said.

Morrison stiffened. Fixing his green, piercing eyes on Danny, he shot back, 'No, Sir, Free Church of Scotland. Can't say I've noticed any Bolshies in my place of worship lately. We should be going. My vehicle is round the corner.'

Danny smiled.

'So is ours. We'll lead. You follow.'

He was never one to surrender the last word.

★★★

Approaching Lochard House, there was no sign of the Redcaps who usually manned the gates. They'd been replaced by heavily armed Royal Marines. Within the grounds, their presence was even more obvious. They patrolled in pairs, armed with automatic weapons and carrying grenade and ammunition pouches. Four were clearly visible on the blue-grey slate roof. Two sand-bagged machine gun pits were being dug by the main doors of Lochard House.

The Brigadier was waiting by the main doors. The Marines guarding the front gate had alerted him to the arrival of George and Danny.

George looked around. 'Some late spring gardening?' he said.

The Brigadier ignored the question. 'Apart from your good selves, we have another visitor. A rather important German house guest,' he said. 'He's upstairs, confined to comfortable quarters. He arrived from Maryhill Barracks not so long ago. That's when I sent Morrison to track you down.' He nodded towards the Marines. 'Fearsome-looking lads. Whitehall insisted on them. They started setting up shop before we took delivery of our guest. Come inside. You need to be in on this, all of it. And there's somebody you need to meet – although meet probably isn't the right word.'

The Brigadier opened the heavy wooden door to his office. Ushering George and Danny inside, he pointed to a figure, a small suitcase in one hand, standing by the bay windows.

The figure turned to face the Major and the Sergeant. 'George. Danny. Fancy meeting you here, of all places,' Finola Fraser said.

George and Danny exchanged wide-eyed glances.

'Obviously, you had no idea,' the Brigadier said. 'That's good, very good. I'm pleased. Nothing like running a tight ship.'

'No idea of what?' George said.

The Brigadier said it might be more comfortable if everybody sat down. Private Morrison was called in and despatched to organise tea.

'A Free Church man,' the Brigadier said after Morrison left the room, 'very much at home with the gloomy view of life. I don't think he'll meet his Maker with a grin on his face. Hard to know what to make of these island fellows. They're either roaring drunkards or they're carrying the banners for the Temperance League. Dour to their backbones, some of them. Generally good soldiers, though. Saw them in action in France during the last dust-up. Not a sight for the squeamish. Anyhow, where were we? Yes. Miss Fraser here.' Finola, the Brigadier revealed, had been part of the team after being recruited – 'a most willing and able recruit, if I may say so' –18 months earlier. She held the army rank of Captain.

George raised his eyes towards the ceiling.

'Well,' he said, 'Miss Fraser here can certainly keep a secret.'

Danny said nothing. In silence, he resolved he would face a firing squad before he saluted Captain Fraser. Finola sensed Danny's discomfort. She smiled.

'Don't upset yourself, Danny,' she said. 'I won't insist on a salute.'

The Brigadier said Finola had been particularly valuable since her recruitment.

'Our Captain Fraser is rather a good watcher and a listener,' he explained. 'And some of those Fourth Estate scribblers could do with watching and listening to, but I won't go into details. Anyhow, now that Miss Fraser's little secret is out, you'll be pleased to know the three of you will be working together.'

It was, the Brigadier said, a very special job. 'I want you to babysit our German guest upstairs for the brief period we'll have charge of him. He's a singularly important fellow and he doesn't pose any obvious physical threat, so it's all smiles and small talk and making him feel comfortable until we pass him up the line.

'Miss Fraser, by the way, won't be back at The Glasgow Herald for several days, possibly a week. We've decided there's a sudden illness at the manse, and the dutiful daughter here has had to race back to tend to an unwell father.

'I'm sure you'll work famously together.'

He smiled at Finola. 'Miss Fraser is quite a warrior, you know. She came through the Spean Bridge course with flying colours. Did it in her holiday time so she wouldn't arouse suspicions.'

George and Danny were immediately impressed. The Spean Bridge course, first designed to test the mettle of aspiring Royal Marines, was the brutal, notoriously tough two-week rite of passage for anybody of active service age and ranked Major or below, recruited by Military Intelligence. The only exceptions were the boffins and the 'Cipher Johnnies.'

The course involved night and day marches over moor and mountain in full kit. It involved small arms instruction and sleep deprivation. The hand-to-hand combat training crippled some for life. For every ten who attempted the Spean Bridge course, seven would fall, literally, by the wayside.

George and Danny had completed the course themselves – barely.

'It just about killed me,' Danny said. 'I had three days in the sick bay when it was over. I couldn't see my feet for the blisters. They were the size of eggs.'

George hadn't fared much better. 'There wasn't a muscle that didn't feel like it was on fire,' he said. That Finola had come through with flying colours... well, what else was there to say? Except that if there was to be any rough stuff on future assignments, he and Danny would delegate the task to Finola.

'First things first,' the Brigadier said. 'The Major here might like to give an account of his meeting with MacSherry, and then we'll get down to tin tacks. You'll be here for a few days. Rutter will get somebody to organise shirts, undergarments, socks, shaving kits, those sorts of things. Miss Fraser arrived well prepared.' He pointed to her small suitcase.

George outlined what had been learned during the time spent with MacSherry. 'All things considered, he was very forthcoming,' George said. 'It was a big effort for a man in such a bad way. We were right on the verge of getting the name of his German contact in Clydebank, when he had a seizure and the doctor told us to get off the premises.

'MacSherry might have had a stroke. But if he comes through he'll be worth his weight in gold. He wants to talk, clear his conscience, get things squared away. He could be our key to collaring God knows how many people. There could be quite a few playing for the other side.'

Nobody could argue with that. It was beyond doubt, the Brigadier said, that the time spent with MacSherry had been time well spent. The mysterious Chrysalis and Kingfisher seemed to be at the centre of events under investigation.

Obviously, they were in the service of the grubby Mister Hitler and, certainly, Kirkness, was in grave danger of going the way of Dalgleish since his exposure as a police informant.

'Of course,' the Brigadier said, 'not that Kirkness is of any further use to us now that he has been identified. However, he is also the worm on our hook. We'll track him down and put some Plain Clothes Redcaps on his tail around the clock. I'd wager ten bob that Chrysalis will find Kirkness and make a move on him. If that unfolds the way I think it will, the Plain Clothes men will pounce. With Chrysalis in the bag it won't be long before Duthie is reeled in. I'll personally and privately attend to the questioning of both of them.'

Danny said Kirkness wouldn't be too hard to find. He'd either be in the Slipway Bar in Clydebank or somewhere not too far from a knocking shop.

The Brigadier picked up the telephone. Rutter should – '*sans delay*' – organise the finding and watching of Kirkness round the clock.

'And,' he told Rutter, 'we don't move on Kirkness unless somebody else is making a move on him first. Whoever has a go at the little snitch, I want that person alive. And nobody speaks to him before I do. If there's a rat in the ranks, I'm the first to know... understood?' Replacing the telephone handset, the Brigadier reached under the blotting pad on his desk and produced a fawn-coloured file. It was stamped *Most Secret – Winged Messenger*.

He slid the file towards George, Danny and Finola. There was a photograph clipped to the inside cover of the file.

'Open the folder. Take a very good look,' the Brigadier said. 'You'll recognise the face straight away. Rudolph Hess, Hitler's Deputy. The madman's biggest admirer. He's upstairs.'

There was a brief stunned silence from George, Danny and Finola before all three spoke at once. Rudolf Hess, Hitler's Deputy in Glasgow? Upstairs at Lochard House? Never... Rudolph Hess...? That was the German airman they'd seen at the police roadblock on the journey north from Stranraer? The one who'd been spat on and punched?

The Brigadier said the file might be the most interesting document the three would ever read. 'It was put together by a couple of our Whitehall chaps who came straight up here – very hush-hush – after our visitor was brought to Maryhill Barracks. They've confirmed beyond any doubt the identity of our guest... photographs, family history, childhood, contacts with various people here before the war. I can tell you – and what I tell you doesn't go beyond this room – Hess had some very high level meetings over here when he visited London on official business before this latest how's-your-father with the Hun. Our Whitehall chaps are back in London giving a face-to-face report to Churchill.' The Brigadier paused, watching the astonished expressions on the faces of George, Danny and Finola.

Danny exhaled, almost whistled, through pursed lips. 'Winston Churchill,' he said. 'A direct report to Churchill?'

Yes, it was as top level as that, a face-to-face with Winnie himself. The Brigadier said the doctor who first examined Hess thought he was 'bonkers.' He pushed it up the line. 'Maryhill passed it straight to Army Lowland Command in Edinburgh. From there it came to Lochard House and that's when I called Whitehall. The London fellows who came up and said that even if our visitor has several very large screws loose, he's a real catch. A lunatic, but one of the highest-ranking lunatics in the gaggle of gangsters running Germany,' the Brigadier said.

The Whitehall men had been thorough in preparing their fawn-coloured file. It said Rudolf Walter Richard Hess, Deputy to Adolf Hitler, was born to German parents in Alexandria, Egypt, in April, 1894. His father was a well-to-do German businessman. The family returned to Germany in 1908.

Hess, at age 20 in 1914, initially served with the Bavarian infantry in the Great War. Wounded, and awarded a bravery medal, he transferred to the German Imperial Air Corps where he showed himself to be a fast learner and a skilled pilot.

After the war, Hess studied politics and history and economics in Munich and it was there, in 1920, where Hess first heard Adolf Hitler address a beer hall gathering. He was captivated. There and then he became one of the earliest members of Hitler's Nazi party. Their political activism saw both Hess and Hitler serve sentences in Landsberg Prison.

The file detailed the rise of Hess in the Hitler hierarchy and the ruthlessness of both men. It described the abiding interest of Hess in flying and his success as a competitor in air races.

It noted, in the final three paragraphs, the Hess fascination with astrology and the Hess friendship with Professor Karl Ernst Krafft. The Professor was believed to have been retained by Hess as his personal astrologer. The file observed that Krafft was probably an alcoholic and a charlatan of the first order.

The Brigadier rose from his desk and walked to the bay windows. Then he turned and spoke, 'Our visitor upstairs is only passing through Lochard House. Perhaps three or four days at the most, then we'll move him to a more out-of-the-way place,' he said. 'While he's here you'll keep him company. The Whitehall chaps will be back up here after they've briefed Winnie and worked their way through whatever it is our visitor told them.'

Finola asked where the more out-of-the-way place might be.

'We'll shift him up to Lord Dunolly's place in Perthshire, Altskeith Estate. It's close to Loch Ard, near Aberfoyle, utterly lovely part of the world by all accounts. Apparently, before the current to-do, Dunolly often used the place as a country retreat for his set of people... industrialists, bankers from all over the place, the big money brigade, the ones who dine at the Savoy three times a week when they're in town,' the Brigadier said.

'You'll be escorting our guest to the Altskeith Estate when we're ready to move him. The Whitehall chaps will do the detailed interrogation up there. But while he's here you'll take it in shifts – eight hours each, round-the-clock in his room upstairs. If he wants to talk, let him talk. But make a note of anything he says and we'll pass it on to Whitehall. Nothing to it, really. We'll have one of the Royal Marines inside with you and two on the door outside. Curtains are to be closed at all times.'

It was beyond doubt, the Brigadier said, that Hess would be an information gold mine for Whitehall. He'd been by Hitler's side since the early days. He knew Berlin's secrets and scandals and he probably had a thing or two to say about matters closer to home, matters of interest to Whitehall. 'When Hitler was on the up-and-up there were more than a few over here – and not just Oswald Mosley and his home-grown Blackshirts in London – who didn't make too much of a secret of their fondness for the Nazi way of doing things. That treacherous waster, the Duke of Windsor, and his tart of an American fancy woman, Mrs Simpson, were very cosy with the powers-that-be in Berlin. Idiots.

'They weren't the only ones, of course, being wined and dined and God knows what else by that cabal of crooks. There's a few big names in Burke's Peerage that also supped with the Devil. Hess would know every one of them, and Berlin would have a very big interest in keeping him quiet.'

The Brigadier said decoded intercepts of short, high-speed Abwehr wireless traffic showed Berlin knew Hess had been picked up near Stranraer. So far, the Germans didn't seem to have a clue where Hess was being held. But it was clear the Germans wanted Hess dead. Berlin had said exactly that in a four word wireless order to Chrysalis. It ordered: *Find/ eliminate Winged Messenger.*

'You don't have to be a genius to work out that Winged Messenger and Hess are one and the same,' the Brigadier said. 'It all points to the inside job we've talked about.'

George speculated: 'Kingfisher might be that insider?'

The Brigadier nodded. 'I'll take care of that line of inquiry. If Kingfisher knew Hess was in custody, there's a better than even chance Kingfisher would also know where Hess is right now... and that information would be passed on to Chrysalis,' he said. 'That's why you'll be issued with side-arms, just in case somebody has a go at Hess while he's here. I'll have Private Morrison attend to that. Pop them somewhere out of sight. We don't want our guest to be alarmed and hiding under the bed. Softly, softly at least for the time being.'

As a reassuring afterthought he added: 'Doubt you'll need the sidearms. Not much gets past the Royal Marines. Now, about the babysitting shifts. We'll have the Major as our opening batsman. Your sleeping quarters are on the first floor. They're rather well appointed. Easily the standard of a very good hotel – private facilities in each room, drinks cabinet too. Make a note of anything you drink. Rutter likes to keep a tally of those things.'

Danny winked at George. The Brigadier asked: 'Some little secret I should know about?'

George shook his head.

'Fine,' the Brigadier said. 'If you'll allow me to carry on. Thank you. With the Royal Marines being here we'll have the kitchen open all hours. Pop down if you're peckish. I'll have Morrison settle you in. If the Major can be back in here – let's say twenty minutes – I'll do the introductions. You might even find something to chat about, Major… you know, those summer visits to Germany in your Edinburgh University days, that place you used to stay in Berlin… quite close to Lehrte Station, wasn't it?'

The Brigadier, clearly, had been revisiting the fine detail in George's personal file. The Whitehall people would have seen the file, too. Obviously, the Major had been handpicked for the Hess assignment. And, just as obviously, Whitehall had been involved in the hand-picking.

The Brigadier as good as confirmed this Whitehall involvement when he said: 'You're just the chap for this, Major. And that's not just my view. Fluent in German, familiar with Berlin. Our visitor will feel quite at home. And you and the Sergeant seem to be a good team… no sense in breaking up a good team.

'As for Captain Fraser... well, the Spean Bridge results speak for themselves. And you all know each other. I think that's always a good thing, don't you? Chums tend to work well together, that's my view.'

The Brigadier really could be a patronising sod of the first order.

Chapter ten: Hitler's little helper

Prime Minister Churchill said he was to be fully advised of the progress of the Hess interrogation. He expressed the view that Hess was insane, he used the word imbecile, but useful—
Security briefing minute 104 MI/PM.

The briefing in the War Cabinet bunker deep below Whitehall lasted for close to two hours.

The stenographer, a young Royal Signals Lance Corporal, took notes. The briefing was provided by intelligence officers Eric Villiers and Ralph Charteris. They had returned to London after their initial identification and preliminary interrogation of Hess.

Villiers and Charteris were two years apart at Eton. Both attended Sandhurst, the Royal Military Academy. Both were commissioned into the Household Division – Villiers into the Blues and Royals and Charteris into the Coldstreams – and both were seconded to clandestine work with Military Intelligence during the Irish Republican Army's infamous 'S Plan' that unleashed a wave of bombings across England in 1938 and 1939.

When war between Britain and Germany broke out in September 1939, Villiers and Charteris were told they would remain with Military Intelligence for the duration of hostilities. They were viewed, by their superiors, as being tailor-made for top secret operations. They were observant, perceptive, persuasive, and, when required, displayed a capacity for utter ruthlessness. The latter was a product of lessons learned on the playing fields of Eton.

The talents of Villiers and Charteris, it was decided,

should be deployed against the Germans and any friends they might have in Britain.

The two completed five months of intensive German language training at 'The School' – a top secret Foreign Office facility near Cheltenham. The consensus within the highest echelons of Military Intelligence was that Villiers and Charteris had been something of a find.

Less than a year later they were briefing Churchill.

He was advised that Hess was being held in a secure location on the outskirts of Glasgow. Arrangements were being made to transfer him to Altskeith Estate, a Perthshire property owned by Lord Dunolly, a senior member of the War Cabinet.

Hess was being guarded by Royal Marines and three officers from the Glasgow/Clyde sector of Military Intelligence. The senior of the three officers was Major George Maclean. He was an Edinburgh University man, fluent in German, who had spent some of his student summers in Berlin.

Hess would be comfortable with Maclean, his fluency in German and his familiarity with Germany and German history. And, if push came to shove and there was an attempt on the life of the prisoner, Maclean and his colleagues – Captain Finola Fraser and Sergeant Danny Inglis – could, by all accounts, be relied on to take any bullet meant for Hess. It would, of course, be unfortunate if this happened. But there was a war to be fought and won. Sacrifices were often unavoidable. It was a pity, but there it was.

Churchill said little while Charteris and Villiers outlined the rise of Hess through the ranks of the Nazi Party. They spoke of Hess' infatuation with Hitler and the relationships between Hess and other top Nazis and the pre-war official contacts – in London and Berlin – between Hess and Britain's great and powerful, Britain's industrialists, Britain's captains of capital and commerce.

Some of the great and powerful, Churchill noted, had looked rather fondly on Hitler's transformation of a bankrupt and defeated Germany into a place of full employment, national pride and ruthless suppression of dissenting voices. Hitler, some said with admiration, knew how to run a country. They said Britain could do with the likes of Hitler. He'd fix the Bolshies and the unions quick smart.

Churchill was particularly taken by Hess' opinions, expressed to Villiers and Charteris, on SS chiefs Heinrich Himmler and Reinhardt Heydrich, propaganda supremo Joseph Goebbels, and Luftwaffe commander Hermann Goring and, of course, Adolf Hitler.

The Fuhrer's Deputy was dismissive of Himmler as a weedy chicken farmer who had risen well above his station, a limited and cowardly little man with an unlimited capacity for duplicity in pursuit of self-interest.

Hess told Charteris and Villiers that Himmler was a man of low breeding and lower intellect. A rodent in a well-tailored uniform. Hess believed Himmler could be bought and sold. If the tide ever turned against Germany, there should be no doubt that the Judas Himmler would sell his soul and his knowledge to the highest bidder. Hess wouldn't be at all surprised if Himmler was not the ethnically pure German he professed to be.

Hess said Heydrich, on the other hand, was cultured, well-bred, methodical and a devoted servant of Germany, its destiny and its supreme leader. Heydrich could never be turned. Heydrich believed Hitler was on a divinely inspired mission. Hess believed there was much to admire in Heydrich. He was racially and ideologically beyond reproach. He had purged pity from his soul. In several respects, Heydrich represented the ideal, the almost mythical, son of Germany: the warrior scholar.

Hess' views on Goebbels and Goring were searing. Propaganda Minister Goebbels was a half-cripple… a 'poor specimen' of Aryan manhood. He was a calculating sycophant. He was a womaniser, a serial adulterer, an abuser of the young actresses who appeared in his propaganda films. His wife, Magda, admired Hitler beyond words. Given a chance, she would be Hitler's whore.

As for Goring... the supreme commander of the Luftwaffe was a 'fat, gorging obscenity' who was 'addled with morphine.' Goring was an 'incompetent and a pathological liar.' His greed and grandiosity were well known. Worse, he was a grasping degenerate who exploited young men.

Hess' gushing observations on Hitler were unsurprising, quite predictable.

The Fuhrer was a genius, one of history's great men. Only Hitler could have inspired and then led Germany's rise from the ashes of the Great War, from years of domestic political instability and hyper-inflation and mass unemployment in the 1920s and early 1930s. Only Hitler could ensure Germany became Greater Germany, that Jewish and Communist conspirators were exposed and brought to account for their crimes against the German people.

Hess claimed it was a foul lie to suggest that Hitler had set out to manufacture conflict. The Fuhrer wanted nothing more than an end to the humiliation that followed the 1918 armistice and the return of territories stolen from the German people.

Hitler had never wanted war with Britain and there were many in Britain – in the highest places – who had no quarrel with Hitler. It was, Hess said, the position of many right-thinking Germans that Britain and Germany should unite against the Jews and the Communists. Britain and Germany were natural allies.

The absolute correctness of this position, Hess told Villiers and Charteris, was confirmed by Professor Karl Ernst Krafft, a man of staggering intellect and insight. Krafft had spent several weeks compiling a most detailed horoscope for Hess. That horoscope had been the basis for the course of action that saw Hess commandeer a Luftwaffe plane, take off from Augsburg, north of Munich, and fly to Scotland.

Hess would say no more of his mission to his Whitehall interrogators. What he had to say would only be said to those in the highest places. Hess said Villiers and Charteris should initiate contact with these people without delay.

A transcript of notes taken by Villiers and Charteris during their initial session with Hess was handed to Churchill during the briefing in the War Cabinet room.

Several times Churchill read and reread the transcript where it touched on Hess' explanation of the reason for his flight to Scotland. Each time Churchill read the transcript he shook his head. At one point in the briefing Churchill read the transcript aloud. It said:

The prisoner Hess, in his initial interview with officers Villiers and Charteris (MI/Central Sector/London) several times asserted that he had been acting on advice in making the journey from Augsburg. This advice had been contained in a horoscope compiled by Professor Karl Ernst Krafft of the Astrological Lodge of the Theosophical Lodge of Greater Germany. The Prisoner Hess said Professor Krafft was a paramount scholar of the Astrological Sciences. The Prisoner Hess said the horoscope prepared by Professor Krafft indicated there were six planets in The House of Danger and that the star of the planet Algol was in an auspicious orbit. The Professor said there were indications that Hitler's meteoric career was about to falter. If this faltering was to be avoided, decisive action was immediately necessary. That action necessitated the commencement of discussions with Germany's natural racial allies.

Churchill inhaled on his cigar and raised his eyes to the reinforced concrete ceiling. He asked Villiers and Charteris: 'And he actually said all this... this gibberish?'

The two nodded. The transcript was an accurate account of what the prisoner Hess had said. Churchill was beaming, rubbing his hands like a gleeful schoolboy, a cat with the cream. Hitler's little helper was in the bag.

'I think the fellow is utterly crackers. Barking mad,' Churchill said. 'I used to think he was just a grubby little Hun. Now I think he's a lunatic grubby little Hun. So, when are you two chaps heading back up to Scotland?'

Villiers and Charteris would travel north within two days. There wasn't much more they could do with Hess until they'd thoroughly gone through any files on the prisoner's pre-war contacts during visits to Britain or visits to Germany by British politicians or industrialists. The files were in London. That's where Villiers and Charteris would remain in the short term.

'Good, good,' Churchill said. 'Better get on with it.' Then he added, still beaming: 'Well done. Well done… what a damned imbecile.'

Villiers and Charteris left the War Cabinet room. The stenographer looked at his notes in copperplate shorthand. The word imbecile made rather an attractive Pitman's script outline on the page.

★★★

Four hundred miles north of the War Cabinet room, the Brigadier, on the first night of the prisoner's well-appointed custody at Lochard House, introduced Major George Maclean – 'an Edinburgh University man and a scholar of Germany and the German language. He spent several of his wayward student summers in Berlin' – to Hess.

A Royal Marine lance corporal looked on, silent, from beside the curtained windows of the prisoner's comfortable room with its rich carpets, writing desk, canopied double bed and adjoining bathroom. There were three bottles of spirits – gin, brandy, malt whisky – and two Caithness Crystal glasses on the silver drinks tray on the writing desk. There was a soda siphon and an ice bucket.

George nodded at the sinewy, dark-eyed, hollow-cheeked Hess and introduced himself in German. Hess responded in perfect English, praising the Major's flawless Berlin accent.

Then he inquired: 'Tell me, Major, are you a student of the science of astrology and the first class work of Professor Ernst Krafft?'

It was an unexpected start to the conversation.

George, trying to hide his surprise at this blunt opening gambit, said he was not familiar with the work of Professor Krafft. But, then again, Germany had produced more than its fair share of scholars. Perhaps Herr Hess might offer some guidance on how best to engage with the work of Professor Krafft.

Or perhaps Herr Hess and George might exchange memories of earlier, younger times in Berlin?

Hess' response was rambling, animated. He spoke of the genius of Professor Krafft, the scientific validity of astrology and the undoubted worth of well-cast horoscopes. He spoke, too, of the purity and destiny of the German people.

'That purity and destiny,' Hess said, 'is revealed beyond doubt in the great work of ancient scholar and historian Tacitus. It is all there in his work *Germania* when he writes of the racial purity, the superiority of the great German tribes of those ancient times. The destiny of those tribes is spelled out. Only a fool would fail, or refuse, to recognise that destiny.'

George said nothing. As an undergraduate in Edinburgh he had read Tacitus. He was familiar with Germania. It had long since been exposed, by Oxford's top classical historians, as a fiction, a fantasy. Some had even described the Tacitus work as drivel.

George gestured for Hess to continue.

Hess obliged, talking of Germany and his younger days and his initial involvement with the embryonic Nazi Party and his ringside seat during the reconstruction of his devastated and defeated homeland.

He spoke with enthusiasm for the utter brilliance of Hitler. Maybe, George thought, Hess was simply deluded rather than out-and-out mad. Maybe madness and delusion were two sides of the same coin.

Enthusiasm aside, Hess was an attentive and inquisitive listener, too, offering drinks and engaging George in conversations on the Major's student summers in Berlin.

George accepted a glass of gin. He had acquired his liking of gin in Berlin. It was cheap and, for a young man raised in the drabness of Edinburgh's Cowgate, gin was rather bohemian, almost exotic. Quite daring, even. He admitted to many fond memories of Berlin and his lodgings near the Lehrte Station close to the Invaliden Strasse, an easy stroll to the Reichstag building.

'You were there in Berlin at a most important time,' Hess observed. His dark eyes flashed, lit up as he spoke. Berlin had been another world in those early 1930s days. Ordinary patriotic Germans were increasingly supportive of Hitler. After more than a decade of hardship and desolation and shame, Hitler was promising Germans a new world. It was a world they deserved.

There would be *lebensraum*, living space, in a Greater Germany. The Communists and the Jews and the *untermenschen* – the Slavs and the Poles and the Soviets – would be pushed to the furthest fringes of this Greater Germany. If needs be, they would be pushed off the edge of the Earth or sent to end their days in Madagascar.

'They will be quite at home on an island filled with natives and monkeys,' Hess said.

This new Greater Germany would be sunny and prosperous, a place where national pride and dignity had been restored. The shame and venality of the 1918 Armistice would be redressed. There would be employment and unity and the half-wits and the deformed and the lazy would be weeded out. There would be no exceptions. Decadent music and art would be consigned to the pig sty. Iron discipline would once again fashion and inspire an iron-hard people. Spirit and will would triumph over any adversity, any setback, and any resistance.

To be German, to be a National Socialist German, in those important times was, Hess said, to be a standard-bearer, a keeper of the light of all that was good and all that was deserved – a pure bloodline that subscribed to pure, scientific truths. To be a National Socialist German in those times was to recognise and embrace manifest destiny.

'We had the world at our feet,' Hess said, leaning forward towards George over the writing desk. 'Nothing could stop us. Nothing could prevail against us. We had a certainty of purpose that was beyond description, beyond challenge. Fist was met with fist, club with club, bullet with bullet. We showed no weakness and we despised weakness in others. There was only one truth and it was ours. Have you any idea of the power that flows from defining truth?'

'Not really,' George said. 'I can't even begin to imagine it. However, my Edinburgh education tended towards the modest proposition that our efforts should be directed towards uncovering truth. Defining that elusive beast seems to me to be another matter entirely, something best suited to greater intellects than mine. Your country, as everybody in the civilised world knows, has never been short of great intellects. Professor Krafft, surely, is testament to this?'

Hess agreed. Now, perhaps the Major would care to share his memories of his student summers in Berlin?

George sipped from his Caithness Crystal tumbler of gin. Berlin in those student summers was… it was… George was briefly silent. His memories were mixed. He was remembering the smell of diesel fuel and trucks laden to overflowing with uniformed men who almost foamed with rage. Hate-filled Storm Trooper brutes, and bullies with their armbands and flags and stupid, stupid songs. He was remembering Jewish shop windows dripping with phlegm. Jewish women and old men pushed from pavements.

He remembered the street fights and the swaggering parades of Hitler Youth. They were nothing more than children in uniform. Hate-filled children with their drums and bugles. He was remembering the rallies and the mad spit-laden ranting of Joseph Goebbels and Hitler. They raged and roared and spoke nonsense, while scores of thousands cheered. He was remembering how he wondered, in the Berlin days, if he was watching a nation – a civilised and cultured nation – going mad. And he remembered whispered stories of the German students – the 'Jazz Boys and Girls' – who simply disappeared or who were taken to Dachau and who returned to their studies, months later, pale as bone china, empty-eyed and subdued.

He thought of Ilse Grichting, his pretty, outspoken, lively companion during his last student summer in Germany. Their shared interest in literature had brought them together, initially, in the bookshops and coffee shops around the Berlin University campus and later in his clean, cheap, comfortable lodgings.

Alone, walking home from an evening lecture, Ilse was set upon by brown-shirted hooligans and battered into a coma from which she never emerged. She was attacked because she was carrying a copy of Erich Maria Remarque's banned book *All Quiet on the Western Front*.

These were not memories George intended to share with the man who sat opposite. But, of course, there were other memories that could be more easily, prudently, shared.

'There remain so many recollections,' he said. 'Where to begin? Where to begin? I was younger, an eager student of your language and history, a bystander on destiny's doorstep. But there were the distractions of youth... the gin, the companionship, the coffee, the earnest arguments, the girls. Berlin had an energy, a vitality, all of its own. To have come from Edinburgh to Berlin... well, you can imagine. I was in another world.'

Hess nodded and nodded again. He was keen to hear more. George obliged.

'My rooms were comfortable and cheap. I remember with great fondness the slow walks from these lodgings down to and then beyond the Reichstag building and on to the Foreign Office in Wilhelm Strasse where, as a foreign student, I was issued with cheap or no cost tickets for admission to Berlin's museums and galleries and travel on local trains and tramcars. From the Foreign Office I would meander past the Reich Chancellery and along Potzdammer Platz to where it met Bellevue Strasse.

'Occasionally, when funds permitted, I allowed myself an extra special treat. Coffee and cakes in the Hotel Esplanade. Such a place. The service. The silver. The perfect sugar cubes. The starched shirts of the waiters.'

Hess listened, almost hypnotised as memories were rekindled of a time when he was in the vanguard of the standard-bearers of his shared, self-defined truth. He delighted in George's descriptions of the buildings, the hotels, the coffee shops, the parks and the tree-lined avenues. George was a man who understood Germany.

Hess said the early 1930s in Berlin had been times beyond dreams, times when a humbled Germany was rising from its knees, times when the Jews and the Communists would be 'cast from the temple of a new Reich.' He said George, in his old age, would reflect on his great good fortune to have seen, first-hand, the secular miracle of National Socialism.

'You have stood in the waiting room of history,' he said.

★★★

At their second meeting, Hess told George: 'Hearing your Berlin accent yesterday, I might well have been in Berlin, recalling old times with comrades. We have much in common, Major Maclean.'

George shrugged, a polite non-committal slow movement of the shoulders and a slight tilting of the head. He said nothing. What could he say? That he had nothing in common with Hess or what he represented? That, for all his intelligence and education, Hess worshipped at the altar of a false and cruel god? That Hess and his like were blood-soaked criminals and psychopaths? People like Hess had punched and kicked and clubbed the life from Ilse Grichting. 'There are those in the highest places here in your country,' Hess said, 'who will be pleased to see me on British soil. They will make contact with me soon. My time in this comfortable custody will end shortly. I will be invited to sit at the high tables of your country's innermost circles. Be assured, Major Maclean, that I will advise them of my high opinion of you.'

George smiled patiently and nodded. That was all he needed – an employment reference from Hitler's star-gazing chum. That would really impress everybody. Jesus, how he wished this babysitting job would end quickly. There was real work to do.

Duthie was still at large. Chrysalis remained a mystery as was the identity of Kingfisher. Then there was MacSherry. He had suffered a severe stroke. He was drifting in and out of consciousness. His life hung by a thread.

Advised, by Rutter, of MacSherry's parlous condition, the Brigadier had observed, almost jovially, there was nothing in the rule book that said a chap couldn't be hanged just because he'd had a stroke. He wouldn't be the first miscreant to be hanged tied to a chair although the trapdoor on the gallows might have to be widened.

'We'll cross that bridge when we come to it,' he told George over breakfast. 'The main thing is that we'll have Hess off our hands within a day or so. One or two more Lochard House sleeps, at most, for Hitler's little helper and we'll have done our job. Rutter is making the arrangements for the transfer to Altskeith Estate.'

Chapter eleven: Chasing shadows

Reports are being examined relating to a seven-day visit, by a party of British industrialists, to German Ruhr Valley coal mining and steel-producing areas in 1937. The prisoner, Hess, was the official German host of this visit. Will advise soonest—

> *Villiers/Charteris/Security Briefing note 110, MI/PM.*

MacSherry never lived long enough to swing on the gallows. Nor did he talk again with George Maclean.

While Hess slept soundly at Lochard House, MacSherry drew his last breath in the secure unit of the Glasgow Western Infirmary.

Two Redcaps, a lance corporal and a private, were guarding the door to MacSherry's room when the visitor arrived. It was after midnight. The hospital was silent. The scent of formaldehyde and carbolic soap was pervasive.

The Redcaps stood, yawning, as the visitor, one hand deep in a raincoat pocket and the other hand holding a leather-bound book, a Bible, approached the door.

He introduced himself as the hospital chaplain. He understood the patient had asked to see a priest. He should have been there hours earlier but there had been others to comfort. There were too few hours in the day. Now that he was here, perhaps the Redcaps could leave him alone with the patient. Confession was a most private matter.

The lance corporal said MacSherry was not to be left alone with anybody. There would be no exceptions. The chaplain could enter the room, he could hear the patient's Confession, but the Redcaps would have to be present.

'Well, rules are rules and these are unusual times,' the visitor said. 'Please show me in.'

The door was opened. The Redcaps stepped inside, moving towards the patient's bed. The visitor drew an automatic pistol from his pocket and fired two silenced shots into the back of the head of each guard. One. Two. The Redcaps died instantly. Blood and slivers of bone spattered the walls and the bedding. The visitor moved quickly to the bedside. Three quick steps.

MacSherry was unconscious, breathing heavily, perspiring profusely. One shot to the head and one to the heart. The whole killing business, from the moment the visitor entered the room to the moment he pocketed the pistol, had taken no more than twelve seconds. It was a very tidy piece of work. Textbook.

The visitor turned, stepped over the bodies of the Redcaps and left the room, closing the door behind him. His footsteps echoed along the long corridor that led from the secure unit to the main part of the hospital. Then he was gone into the night.

He walked quickly to a vehicle parked in the shadows beyond the hospital gates. He looked at his watch, started the engine and drove off towards Clydebank. There was one other matter to attend to before daylight. That matter was the informant: Robbie Kirkness.

***

It was just before six in the morning when the visitor's swift, tidy piece of work at the Western Infirmary was discovered. The night matron was making her final rounds in the company of a staff nurse and the junior duty doctor. The secure ward was the last stop on these rounds. Emergencies aside, the secure ward was visited by the night matron twice during her shift – at ten pm and at six am. Regular as clockwork.

MacSherry's medical chart listed Rutter as the point of contact should there be any change in the patient's condition. Bullets to the head and the heart indicated there had been such a change.

A telephone call from the night matron roused Rutter from sleep in his tidy, almost monastic, first floor room at Lochard House. There were no books or personal effects in the room. No photographs. No trophies. Nothing that suggested a life beyond Lochard House. Nothing, really, that suggested a life. There was a single bed, a bedside table, a bedside lamp, a wardrobe, a chest of drawers and a chest of drawers that contained ironed shirts and underwear. There were no pyjamas in the chest of drawers. Rutter slept naked.

'Just repeat that,' he ordered the night matron. 'Stone dead, you say. Three of them. Gunshot wounds. And nobody saw or heard anything. Who else is there with you? Right, listen very carefully. Do exactly as I say. Don't touch anything, don't move anything, and don't say anything to anybody. Not a word. Nobody in or out. I'll attend to getting somebody over there.'

Rutter shaved and dressed quickly. A few minutes before seven am, he briefed the Brigadier on the killings. The Brigadier was taking his day's first meal – black tea, toast and boiled eggs – in his quarters. The eggs were a shade soft for his taste and the toast was overdone. Somebody should have a word with the below stairs staff. He'd see to it.

The Brigadier listened to Rutter and pushed his breakfast plate away. 'Get Maclean, Inglis and Miss Fraser down here,' he said. 'God Almighty... shot dead in the secure unit.'

★★★

Five minutes later, George and Danny, unshaven, and Finola, tousled, were in the Brigadier's quarters.

'It's a mess,' the Brigadier said. 'MacSherry and two of our Redcaps have gone the way of all flesh – shot dead at the hospital in the middle of the night - and nobody saw or heard a thing. From Rutter's account, it was a most professional affair. Between the night matron's first and last ward rounds.'

'The timing is the thing,' Danny said. 'Whoever did for MacSherry and the Redcaps would have to know the routine at the Infirmary. I doubt Duthie and Chrysalis would be familiar with that sort of detail... when it was quiet, when nurses and doctors were doing their rounds.'

'So it has to be somebody who was a regular at the hospital,' Finola said. 'Like a cleaner, an ambulance man, a tradesman.'

'It doesn't even have to be a regular,' George said, 'just somebody who wouldn't be out of place there at any time of the day or night. Anybody wearing a white coat could do it. Or maybe an undertaker? A chaplain?'

The speculation was cut short by the ring of the telephone on the Brigadier's desk. He lifted the handset, listened and said: 'Get him here right away.'

'That was the duty Inspector down at Clydebank,' the Brigadier said. 'A certain Robbie Kirkness has sought sanctuary at the local police station. Seems that he has been rather knocked about. Babbling away about escaping the clutches of death. Prattling on about needing to see Sergeant Inglis and the Major. He mentioned Lochard House. We may as well put a big sign on the front gate.

'Clydebank is bringing Kirkness over. Find out what he has to say. I'll deal with whatever you come up with. You've other things to see to... like taking our Mister Hess on a tour of the delights of our native heath as soon as Rutter sorts matters out with the people up at Altskeith Estate. I'd say sometime later today or first thing tomorrow.'

***

When Kirkness arrived under escort at the Brigadier's office, it was obvious he'd had a belting. There was bruising on his neck. One eye was almost closed. His nose was swollen. His knuckles were scraped raw. His shirt was ripped from neck to waist and one shoe was missing.

Danny looked him up and down. 'You're a bit the worse for wear,' he said.

'Gave the bastard as good as I got,' Robbie said, full of bravado, puffing up his chest and immediately wincing from the pain of battered ribs.

'Highland Light Infantry training to the fore. Fight hard and dirty. You never forget, do you? There's a few German prisoners felt the toe of my boot up their behinds in the last war and the point of my bayonet in their ribs. Isn't that right, Sergeant Inglis? You'd remember how we battered some of the bastards when they surrendered.'

Danny shook his head: 'Aye, aye, aye. Anything you say, Robbie. But before we go any further, you just remember this... not a word about this place and anybody you see here to another soul for as long as you live... and who knows how long that might be.

'One word, one whisper, and you're a goner – there's the Official Secrets Act, the War Precautions Act, the Thieving Wee Sods Act, the Loud-Mouthed Wee Buggers Act and a dozen other Acts we can come up with to make sure you'll either swing or rot away in solitary at Barlinnie. Mutton stew and white bread twice a day for the rest of your natural, and a chamber pot that gets slopped out every two days. Nothing classy about that place, Robbie, you'll probably fit right in with all the chancers and Conshies and a few of what we call enemies of the Realm.'

Robbie was offended by Danny's tone and he made this known.

'I'm a lot of things, Sergeant,' he said. 'But I'll not hear or do a thing against King and Country. Not me. Not Robbie Kirkness. I'm black affronted you think otherwise.'

George, smiling, said no offence was intended. Robbie was, indeed, many things but none could doubt his loyalty. When it came to loyalty, Robbie Kirkness was the salt of the earth. King and Country were blessed to have men of the calibre of Robbie

Kirkness. Now, enough of the flannel, perhaps Robbie would care to share whatever it was he had to tell.

'Well,' Robbie said, 'it was after midnight. I was delivering some nylons and lipstick and perfumes at the knocking shop just off Broddick Lane.

'Flora Boyce is the Madam there. Fine, handsome woman. A right smasher in her day, I'd say. She runs a very proper place with some lovely girls, very well spoken. Probably Edinburgh lassies. Right wee charmers, better than the usual Clydebank street tarts and desperates that look like they got killed in the bombing and dug up. My dead Granny, dead these last ten years, would be a better looker than the Clydebank tarts. Mind you, Granny would probably need some lipstick and a dab of rouge.'

Robbie made regular deliveries, once or twice a week, to Flora Boyce and her lovely girls. The deliveries were always in the small hours and always via the back door. Two loud taps and two gentle taps secured entry to the premises. Entry to the lovely lassies was, Robbie said, a matter for private negotiation.

Danny rolled his eyes.

'So there's me dropped off what was to be dropped off,' Robbie said, 'and I'm on my way down Carlyle Close. Dark as a bloody coal mine with the blackout and everything. I hear these footsteps. I'm being followed so I ducked quick smart into Angus Lane and gave whoever it was the slip. Then it's back to the digs two streets down.

'It's pitch black. I can't see my hand in front of me. I'm fumbling with the keys and somebody steps out of the shadows, and then there's this grip around my neck. Strong. Tight as a vice. God Almighty I just about wet myself. But there's no flies on Robbie Kirkness. I jerked my head back, right into his face. Whoever it was gave out a right shout. Cursing and swearing... not in English, though. It was German, the same as the prisoners yabbered in the last war. He spat away blood and then he hit me as hard as anybody ever has. He wasn't going to leave me alive, that's a fact. Do or die; that was it. I landed a good punch fair on his mouth and split his lips. He got me a good one in the face. Then I got him a few good ones in the stomach. I got my hands round his throat. He's wheezing like a coal miner but then he manages to get his hands round my throat. Jesus, he was strong. Honest to God, I thought I was finished.

'I knew I had one good punch left and I gave it everything. Smackeroo, right into his face and down he goes. Sack of potatoes. Bam. Jesus, it was a hard hit. I can't see his face for the blood. Anyhow, he's trying to get up off the ground to have another crack at me. I know that if he gets up, I'm finished. I've nothing left to throw at him.

'Well, I'm not that daft that I'll give him a second chance. So, I slip him two right good kicks in the ribs as a bit of a cheerio message. It must have been the slowest getaway ever. I could hardly walk let alone run and I hid in the first bomb-damaged place I came to. After about an hour I went to the polis. I mentioned Sergeant Danny's name and Major Maclean here and said I wanted to see you. I said I wouldn't say a word to anybody else. So now I'm here and I want protected.'

First things first, Danny said. What about a description of the attacker? Robbie said it was too dark to get a good look at his attacker. But he did have something. He reached into a pocket and produced a clerical collar. 'It must have come away when I had my hands on his throat. Can you imagine? A minister carrying on like that? It rules out him being Church of Scotland. They're too refined for grabbing people around the throat and trying to choke them. You never know, though.'

George reached towards Robbie and took the collar. He looked at Danny. 'The doctor, remember what that doctor said when we first saw MacSherry up at the Western Infirmary. He said MacSherry had muttered something about a minister, a pastor. And we thought MacSherry wanted the last rites? Did we ever get that wrong! MacSherry was talking about

Chrysalis. He must be a minister or he's passing himself off as one. A minister would have no trouble, would hardly be noticed, visiting the hospital at all hours.'

Danny nodded. George was onto something here. A man wearing a clerical collar and speaking with a German accent had tried to murder Robbie. The same person, wearing a collar, could have murdered MacSherry. That person had to be Chrysalis.

In the space of a few minutes Robbie had gone from being a man threatened with the gallows or an eternity of mutton stew and white bread in Barlinnie Prison to being a treasure.

'Wait a minute, wait you just a wee minute,' he said. 'A minister, you say. There's that minister at the Seafarers' Mission in Clydebank. He's foreign. Been here, so they say, since before the war. He's everybody's pal around the docks and the shipyards. Lang, that's his name. Martin Lang.' He paused, then, remembering. 'Bumped into him once or twice in that pub near the Seaman's Mission, The Pier Inn. He'd drop in there, so they said, for a natter with the convoy men. Never had that much use for a minister myself. But you hear people talk. The Reverend this and the Reverend that... what a nice man he is... always helping and blethering away to people that are on the ships and in the yards. Visiting people up at the Western Infirmary after the bombs. Right enough, maybe it was him that had a go at me. God knows what for. Anyhow, you'll not have any trouble recognising him, if it was him. His face would be black and blue after the belt I gave him.'

Robbie cleared his throat. Then, in a tentative tone, asked: 'I don't suppose there's a wee reward on offer for services rendered? A token of appreciation wouldn't go astray. Me being a treasure as Sergeant Inglis here just said.'

George suggested Robbie might have to content himself with getting his reward in heaven. But for now, he said, Robbie would stay right where he was in Lochard House. The footsteps Robbie heard, George added, belonged to the plain clothes Redcaps who were keeping an eye on him. 'If you hadn't given them the slip, you wouldn't be here right now. You got a battering for nothing. For now you're safer here than out on the streets. There's a good chance your midnight sparring partner would have another crack if he saw you on the loose. We'll get a billet sorted out here for a few days. Free food and drink for the duration. It'll be a lock-and-key job, Robbie. Can't have you wandering around here. You'll be comfortable but you'll be confined.'

'And we better get right on to this Seafarers' Mission place,' the Brigadier said. 'It's a job for the Marines. Let's get cracking.'

★★★

Fifteen minutes later, eight Royal Marines – a Second Lieutenant, a Sergeant and six Privates – were despatched to Clydebank and the lodgings and workplace of the Reverend Martin Lang.

The Brigadier told the second lieutenant on the steps of Lochard House: 'If there's anybody there, get as rough as you need to get. But no permanent damage. Take Rutter with you. He can have a good look around before you bring him back… but leave a couple of your fellows down there.'

The officially sanctioned roughness deployed by the Marines extended only to shouldering open the front doors of the Seafarers' Mission and the Reverend Martin Lang's lodgings.

Rutter's report on his return to Lochard House was matter-of-fact. The premises were deserted. Two beds had been slept in. There was a blood-stained towel on the kitchen floor. The water in the kitchen kettle was lukewarm.

'There was a German radio in the attic, same as the model we uncovered at Clydebank… nothing else, nothing obvious, no papers, money, nothing like that. Nothing like our little treasure trove at Randall Street the other day,' Rutter said. 'But we'll arrange another look, though. A good look. Pull up floorboards, that sort of thing. If there's anything there, we'll find it.'

The Brigadier stood, then paced. The sound of his footsteps was muffled by the finely knotted Turkish carpet that covered most of the floor. He turned to face George, Danny and Finola.

'Well, weighing it all up, I suppose it's more good news than bad news, if you ask me,' he said. 'At least there doesn't seem any reasonable doubt, that our Reverend is the mysterious Chrysalis. But where he and Duthie are right now would appear to be secrets known only to God and Berlin. One thing's for sure... they won't be walking the streets.'

George asked: 'So we'll get Uniform on to railway stations and bus stations? A few questions down at the docks and the yards...?'

The Brigadier shook his head. 'No. No. You've got other things to do. I'll have the looking around arranged from here,' he said. 'Yourself and the Sergeant and Captain Fraser will be having a quiet drive in the country with our upstairs visitor. All under control... isn't that the case, Rutter?'

Rutter nodded. All was indeed under control. Half a dozen Royal Marines would be leaving Lochard House within the hour. They'd join the squad of Royal Marines already at Altskeith.

The Brigadier continued: 'Rutter's going up to Altskeith with you. Needs to be there for the paperwork... signing over the prisoner to the London lads, Villiers and Charteris. They should be there when you arrive. Rutter here knows the estate like the back of his hand... used to get up there quite a bit with Lord Dunolly... making sure the estate books were in order and the silver was well polished, I suppose?'

Rutter nodded again.

'When you get our guest settled in up there, have a bite and then get back here,' the Brigadier instructed.

Turning to George, Danny and Finola, Rutter said, 'The Marines will let us know when they're satisfied Altskeith is watertight. The road's not bad most of the way. We turn right at the main gates here, out through Clydebank then through Dumbarton and Alexandria and then we're in Aberfoyle. It gets a bit bumpy after that on the way out to Altskeith. We'll take three cars. I'll lead the way with a couple of the Marine fellows and you can follow with our guest. We'll have a third vehicle behind you. Marines in that, too. All tickety-boo. Not a word to our chap upstairs until we're ready to move. Leave the rest to me.'

George winked at Danny. He looked directly at Rutter. 'Tickety-boo right enough. You're the boss on this one. We're in safe hands, Danny.'

Rutter shot back: 'Well, Major, they also serve who only stand and wait. Never hurts to remember that. Doesn't hurt to remember, either, where you sit in the order of things. You might recall that a major sits somewhat below a lieutenant-colonel in this man's army. Unless, of course, you've used your obvious and considerable reporter's skills to rewrite King's Regulations?' He turned and left the room.

'Well, well,' the Brigadier said, 'you've really put a bee in his bonnet. Never seen that side of him before... a bit of a touchy streak buried deep down, wouldn't you say?'

George shrugged. Finola said: 'It goes a fair bit beyond touchy. That's a man running on resentment. Behind the smiles and the phoney politeness he's the waiter who wants to strangle the dinner guest.'

Given that the dinner guest was Hitler's Deputy, the Brigadier said, strangling should be avoided at all costs. Nevertheless, as a diner, he'd often thought of strangling a waiter or two. It might not have improved the food but it would have taken much of the pain out of paying the bill.

Chapter twelve: Strange bedfellows

The rolling hills to the east of Loch Lomond offer some fine walking for the enthusiastic tramper. There are no steep pitches although the country is, in places, boggy. Birdlife abounds, making this an area of considerable, if bracing, charm. A steady, four-hour walk will take the outdoors man from Loch Lomondside to the Aberfoyle district—
The Scottish Tramper Field Guide, 1938.

It was early evening when the Brigadier advised Hess he was being moved.

'You're being taken elsewhere,' the Brigadier said. 'Somewhere much more suitable. I guarantee you'll be very comfortable in your new quarters. You'll have all the delights of a country house at your disposal. Not exactly a schloss in the grand German style but something that reflects the importance we place on your arrival. Obviously, there are those in higher places who are at pains to ensure you are made to feel welcome… unlike the ruffians you encountered at the Maryhill Barracks. But let's not dwell on that.'

Hess smiled his approval. The Brigadier's returned smile was forced. He resented having to stroke the ego of this man. However, needs must when the Devil drives.

· ★★★

Four hours later, Rutter's three-car convoy was ready for the journey to Altskeith.

'I'll be glad to have him off our hands,' the Brigadier told Rutter as the two walked towards the vehicles.

'Get him settled in and then it's straight back here. We've

other fish to fry. Duthie and this Chrysalis character have just vanished. They could well have vanished by now.'

★★★

The Brigadier was right. Tommy Duthie and the Reverend Martin Lang were well away.

Lang had made for the relative safety of his lodgings immediately, but not quickly, after the bloody encounter with Kirkness. His face ached from the pounding he'd received. His ribs throbbed. A knee to the groin – a glancing blow – seemed to have done no lasting damage although his testicles felt like half-inflated balloons.

Lang's walking pace to the car he'd parked a hundred yards from Robbie's digs was pained. He walked in the manner of a Hollywood cowboy, legs bowed from too long in the saddle. Driving was no more comfortable than walking. Every gear change brought a stab of pain from his fingertips to his left shoulder.

★★★

Duthie heard the car halt outside the Seafarers' Mission. He waited, pistol in hand, in the darkened living room. Lang entered. He switched on the light.

'Jesus God Almighty, you look a right sight,' Duthie said. 'You look like you fell under a train... or was it ten rounds with that German heavyweight of yours, Max Schmeling?'

Lang offered no answer to Tommy's question. Instead, he said, 'There are canvas bags in the attic. Get them. We have little time to spare.'

The bags contained two compact MP 38 sub-machine guns – tidy weapons for close encounters of the violent kind – as well as two dozen 32-bullet MP 38 magazines, two silenced Luger pistols, 60 rounds of boxed pistol ammunition, eight stick hand grenades, a thick wad of Bank of Scotland small denomination notes, perfectly forged petrol coupons, canvas-backed Ordnance Survey maps, a copy of the 1938 edition of *The Scottish Tramper Field Guide*, one pair of Carl Zeiss binoculars and a torch with four spare batteries. The canvas bags were bulky but not overly heavy for the squarely, strongly-built Tommy Duthie.

While Duthie retrieved the bags, Lang boiled water and then wiped his bloodied face on a towel in the kitchen. He touched his nose and his cheekbones. He looked at his swollen knuckles then gingerly felt his ribs. There were no obvious broken bones. He turned when Duthie entered the kitchen.

Placing the canvas bag on the linoleum floor covering, Duthie pressed his earlier question – how had Lang come by such a hammering?

'An unwelcome encounter with two of Clydebank's countless drunks,' Lang lied. 'I had attended to some matters and I was getting into my vehicle when they set upon me. I put one on the ground and the other ran away and I came back here. This is a country full of savages.'

Duthie agreed.

'It is no longer sensible to remain here,' Lang said. 'We will go to a place where we will be safe. It has everything we need. You will drive and I will give the directions. I cannot drive any more. Not now.'

Lang also had news of MacSherry. 'I have made some inquiries. It seems he is no longer in danger. There have been improvements. The British have been questioning him but he has said nothing. I may have underestimated him. If this is the case, my apologies.'

Duthie nodded again. Not for one minute, did he believe his comrade would have betrayed him. 'We've been shoulder-to-shoulder through things you wouldn't believe. He's never a man to save his own neck if it means throwing others to the dogs. He'd sooner swing.'

Martin Lang barely heard a word. His thoughts were on his destination that day, the safe house near Rowardennan on the north-east shores of Loch Lomond, the safe house with the wireless transceiver that would link him with his 'zooperiors' in Berlin and the instructions that would come directly, so he'd been advised, from the Fuhrer.

Lang's directions to Duthie were uncomplicated. Clydebank to Dumbarton, through Renton and Alexandria to Balloch. On to Buchanan Castle. Left along the eastern shore of Loch Lomond on the road that snaked north and abruptly stopped two miles beyond a cluster of houses and boat sheds and a hotel and a sign that proclaimed this was Rowardennan.

Ironically, the three-car convoy from Lochard House would travel part of that same route several hours later journeying to Aberfoyle and then to Altskeith.

Where the road halted two miles beyond Rowardennan, Duthie followed instructions to turn right onto a track. A board nailed to a tree said the track was private property and that trespassers would be prosecuted. The track continued for close to three miles and stopped by a solidly built stone cottage almost hidden behind a stand of trees. The cottage was well away from any prying eyes that might have ignored the warning not to enter private property.

Chrysalis, pulling a heavy key from his pocket, opened the solid timber door. Duthie followed him inside.

'Cosy,' Duthie said, eyes roaming around every inch of the living room. 'Very comfortable. Lovely and comfortable. A bit on the chilly side even for this time of year. But we can get a fire glowing in the grate in no time.'

Chrysalis informed him there were logs and kindling in the shed behind the cottage. Duthie should get started. There was a cooking range in the kitchen and Tommy should fire that up, too. The cupboards in the kitchen were well stocked with tinned food. There were cups and plates in one of the cupboards. And if Tommy cared to look, he'd find half a case of Ardlui single malt whisky in the cupboard under the kitchen sink. Ardlui was a good drop. It was distilled locally, just across the loch.

The German said he and his companion would benefit from a drink. A cup, or even a few cups, of single malt might just dull the aches from his rough encounter in Carlyle Close.

By the time the lingering dusk faded to black, a second bottle of malt had been opened. Both men were effusive, but not intoxicated in the sense that most Glaswegians meant when they used the word.

For most Glaswegians, intoxicated meant unconscious, blacked out in an alcoholic stupor, lying urine-soaked on the pavement. Chrysalis and Tommy Duthie, sitting in armchairs by the open fire, had merely enjoyed the Glaswegian version of a wee drink.

Duthie wondered aloud if the two might pass the duration of the war there in the secluded cottage on the hills above Loch Lomond. Perhaps he and Chrysalis could lie low until the regiments of the Reich had a victory parade down Sauchiehall Street in Glasgow and working men took to cultivating Hitler-style moustaches and saluting each other.

Duthie laughed. Chrysalis laughed, too, at the thought of legions of short, kilted Scots with ginger moustaches, arms raised in the Nazi salute. But a sharp pain in his ribs ensured his laughter was brief.

Stoking the dancing flames in the grate, Duthie said he and his four brothers and sisters would have killed for a cottage like this. They'd been brought up in a tenement flat by a grey-faced, embittered, mother and a volatile and violent alcoholic father who'd buried two older brothers after the 1916 Republican Easter Uprising in Dublin. MacSherry had been raised in the same damp and dark tenement building. The two were pals long before they became comrades as young Republican volunteers. MacSherry had lost an uncle and an older brother in Dublin, too.

'The English shot them in the yard at Mountjoy Prison,' Duthie said. 'They put the big fish in the Republican movement on trial and then hanged them. Some of the minnows, like my Dad's brothers and MacSherry's uncle and brother didn't even get a trial. They were shot in the middle of the night. The English said they'd tried to escape. Lies. The English are great liars.'

Chrysalis drained his cup. Duthie offered a refill, Chrysalis declined. Another cup would have seen him in that state described by Glaswegians as intoxicated.

'So,' he said his German accent becoming more pronounced as the single malt Ardlui did its work, 'what makes you and your brother-in-arms tick is revenge? Old Testament revenge?'

Duthie, splashing a good measure of Ardlui into his cup, shook his head. 'No, not revenge,' he said. 'I just want the Irish, not the English, to run Ireland. It's nothing more complicated than that. Revenge is messy and it gets in the way of results. Revenge never ends. Payback breeds more payback. It took me a while to learn that.' He prodded the fire again and added: 'That's what makes me tick. But what about you? What makes the Reverend run? And how did you come by this place?'

Chrysalis had no idea who owned the cottage. He knew only that it was safe and out of the way and that, in any wireless communications with Berlin, he was to identify its location as Vienna. There was no need for him to know more.

'I was told of this place before I left Germany. It was at my disposal should unforeseen events make it wise to leave Clydebank,' he said. 'Such events have now unfolded and that is why we are here. Every few months I come here for a day, two days. I make sure it is untouched. Sometimes I stay overnight. Other times I see that all is secure and I return to Clydebank.'

Duthie returned to the first of his two questions. What made the Reverend run?

Chrysalis, his tongue loosened and his physical discomfort eased by the honey softness of the Ardlui, felt the inclination to talk. It was some years since he had talked, openly, with anyone. There was a great weight within. He had carried it for longer than he could remember. He had lived several double lives.

He had been, at once, an outspoken Lutheran pastor and a Party informant in Hamburg. He had been a friendly face in the Clydebank shipyards and factories and a bringer of death and terrible destruction through his wireless reports to Berlin. He had been whatever he had needed to be at any given time. He was a player in a death-dealing repertory company. One day Macbeth, one day Hamlet, one day Othello, one day King Lear.

'I never knew my mother. She died two days after I was born,' Chrysalis said. 'My father was a good man, a good Christian man.'

His father had been an example for Lang to follow. Honest, decent, a real German. He saw active service in the First War and was awarded an Iron Cross, Second Class. After the war he went back to his old job making lithographic plates. He was highly skilled. A true craftsman. He worked most of his life for a printing company. It was owned by rich Jews, the Meyer family.

'When the Great Depression came, the company threw my father and hundreds of workers like him onto the streets like used rags,' Lang said. 'I was at university studying theology when this happened. The Word of God would change the world. I believed that, you know.'

He paused and shook his head. He spat into the fireplace. 'God would change the world? What a fool I was. I should have remembered that Jesus was a Jew. Losing his job left my father a broken man. He worked all his life. He risked that life in the trenches... and there he was, cast aside by the Jews; the usurpers in the Temple.

'One evening, the police came to my lodgings at the university. My father had been killed. He was set upon, minding his own business, by a mob of Communists. In those days – before we sorted them out and taught them a lesson – the Jew Communist mobs would take to the streets and cause mayhem.

'My father was out looking for work that didn't exist – washing dishes, collecting rubbish, clearing drains, digging sewers, anything. I identified his body. He was battered to a pulp by Communists, Russian sympathisers. Russia is run by Jews. They are degenerates, these people, animals. They breed like rats and they look like rats.'

Lang had drifted towards the National Socialist Party in the beer halls. He stayed away from lectures for months after the murder of his father. He'd had enough of study. The Word of God would change nothing. Cold steel would change everything. Lang was done with university and theology but the Party persuaded him to finish his studies. The Party said he could be of use within the church. Many traitors in the church opposed the Party. Lang was to spy on them. He was to win their confidence by pretending to support their anti-party views. And this is what he did until it was decided he should be trained to serve Germany beyond Germany.

Chrysalis looked at Duthie. The IRA man had heard nothing. He was fast asleep. Snoring.

'I think we are strange bedfellows, Herr Duthie,' Chrysalis said, his voice slurred. He stood up, and then slumped back down into his chair.

***

The fire was dead when the two awoke in the morning. Condensation dampened every window in the cottage. A cold front had rolled in during the night.

In the hours of darkness, while the two men slept where

they sat, Berlin sent four five-word messages to Chrysalis. The messages from Berlin were relayed via U-boat 502 on patrol off the western approaches to Scotland, under the command of Kriegsmarine Captain Gunther Lohmann.

Kriegsmarine frequencies were only used when the Abwehr in Berlin believed its direct wireless link with an agent in the field had been penetrated by the Allies.

Each message was identical. *Chrysalis report status/ location soonest,* they said. There had been no possibility of any response. The wireless transceiver at the cottage lay wrapped in a blanket under the kitchen floorboards. The batteries were hidden behind the crockery in a kitchen cupboard.

Chapter thirteen: Familiar places

German Minister Hess has returned to Berlin after an eight-day visit to London. Official engagements were cancelled for four days. German Embassy reported Hess confined to bed with a severe chest cold. Surveillance and protection officers not deployed during this period—
   Metropolitan Police Special Branch, file note, 326/21, 1937.

While Duthie and Martin Lang slept their Ardlui Single Malt sleep, the light from the near full moon washed over the three-car convoy from Lochard House. The cars were halted on the shoulder of the narrow road five miles south of Aberfoyle. This was the middle of nowhere.

Elphinstone Rutter walked round the vehicles inspecting the damage. The paperwork would take days, he said. Who hit what, where and when? Who had been driving?

It had been impossible for the first car to avoid thudding into the stag, a big ten-pointer. It just stood there, absolutely still, frozen in the headlights. Thud. Thud. Thud. Car two, driven by Danny, hit car one. Car three, driven by a Royal Marine hit car two.

'Thankfully, no injuries,' Rutter pronounced. 'Damage looks worse than it probably is… popped bonnet, bent bumper, driver's side front tyre punctured on my machine… buggered passenger side front lights, front bumper pushed back on the passenger side tyre on Sergeant Inglis' vehicle… a bit of a ding, front mudguard third car. Shouldn't take long to bend the offending panels back into shape, change the punctured tyre and get on our way.'

Five Royal Marines were tasked to attend to the damage. They went about their work briskly. Two more Royal Marines were detailed to watch over Hess who had stepped from the back seat of the vehicle driven by Danny.

George Maclean sighed theatrically. Where, in the name of God, did Rutter think Hess might abscond to? And why would he abscond in the first place?

George and Hess ambled a few dozen yards from the halted three-car convoy. Two Marines followed, automatic weapons cocked. Danny and Finola leaned on their car, saying nothing, looking up at the pulsing of the stars.

Hess, hands on hips, craned his neck towards the heavens. He pointed to the constellations, naming each one. He spoke in German. 'The stars speak to us,' he told George, 'with great eloquence and clarity. But, of course, it demands great skill and intellect and willingness and open minds to understand the language in which they speak.'

There was no place for closed minds in the emerging Greater Germany. Hitler had lifted Germany from the rubble of a war it had never really lost. Rather, it had been cheated out of victory by an Armistice engineered by Jewish money helped along by Russian treachery. Hitler's success was only possible because the German people were willing to open their minds to the views and visions of perhaps the greatest man who ever lived. Christ had raised Lazarus from the dead but Hitler had raised a nation from the dead.

Hess said Professor Karl Ernst Krafft of the Astrological Lodge of the Theosophical Lodge of Greater Germany was a man of great skill and intellect and willingness to learn. He understood the language of the night skies. Routinely consulted by Hess and sometimes by Hitler himself, the Professor, as a younger man, had been ridiculed and vilified by sections of the German scientific establishment. Scorn had been poured on the papers Krafft submitted to scientific journals. These papers championed the place of astrology in mainstream science.

'In those days,' Hess said, 'much of the scientific establishment was controlled by Jews and infiltrated by Communists. They secretly sold their research to the highest bidder – Moscow and Washington. They were not Germans. They were Yiddish whores and pimps. Thankfully, this is no longer the case. They have been sent packing and Professor Krafft has been recognised and rewarded for his contribution.'

George, in his perfect Berlin-accented German, wondered what that contribution might be.

Hess, almost gushing, said Professor Krafft correctly foretold the rise and rise of the Party with Hitler at its head. Krafft, in his astrological charts, identified Hitler as a star at the pinnacle of German advancement. He also correctly identified the moral threat posed by the perfumed Ernst Julius Gunther Rohm and his brown-shirted Storm Troopers.

'Rohm was a degenerate, a deviate, of the worst type,' Hess said. 'Professor Krafft saw this and we took the only action that was appropriate in the circumstances. Rohm and his cronies were removed, permanently. Hitler was personally involved in the arrest and killing of many Brownshirts. I stood by his side as he pulled the trigger. He was silent and unflinching. An example to all of us. To stand alongside Hitler was to stand alongside a volcano. You could feel the power. The strength. The moral courage of the man.'

Krafft, additionally, had correctly predicted the reluctance, in 1938, of Neville Chamberlain, then the British Prime Minister, to challenge Germany's initial territorial claims and subsequent territorial demands in Europe. Chamberlain had been a fool who played into Germany's hands. He had seen the devastation of the Great War. He did not believe Germany had the appetite or the courage for another conflict on this scale. He had failed to recognise the burning determination within ordinary Germans to reclaim their predestined place at the centre of European power and influence. Germany was the real intellectual and industrial hub that sat at the core of

Europe. Honour demanded that it be fully recognised as such. Nothing less would be accepted by the German people.

The professor predicted, too, there would be no more than a whisper from France, Britain and the United States when Germany's racial purity laws were deployed, with cruel efficiency, against German Jews.

'The big powers knew what we were doing. They did nothing because they knew we were right,' Hess said. 'Britain and France never trusted the Jews – remember the Dreyfus Affair. And the Americans put the Jews in the same basket as the Blacks. Untermenschen. Germany did what Britain and France and America dreamed of doing.'

George said he was most interested to learn of the part played by Professor Krafft in the Hess decision to come to Scotland.

Hess said coming to Scotland had been no small matter. Some at the highest levels of the Party would, he was certain, see his journey as a betrayal. Hess was prepared to suffer such accusations and the denigration that would come with these accusations. When the truth of the mission – and the results from that mission – were known, Hess would be vindicated. There could no doubt of this.

'I will be seen as a man of courage and vision,' Hess said. 'I will be embraced as the man who united the Third Reich and Great Britain in their fight against the Communists. I will be recognised as the man who knew that Moscow and the Jew bankers and elites provoked this war and who knew that unless these forces were destroyed now, the time would come when the civilised and cultured nations of the world would face a wall of Soviet steel on their borders.'

George nodded again. It would be futile, he knew, to challenge the rant from Hess. The man was raving. For a second George thought of howling at the night sky.

Instead, he returned to his question. Might the role of Professor Krafft in the flight to Scotland be explained in more detail? That role, George said to Hess, seemed unclear.

'From time to time,' Hess said, 'I enjoy the pleasure of the Professor's stimulating company at my second residence at Wannsee near Berlin. In recent months the Professor alerted me to some matters that have come to light in his detailed preparation of my revised astrological chart. From his scientific calculations he affirmed a view I have often expressed to him... that the real enemy of Greater Germany – and Britain, for that matter – is Russia... Russia in league with the Jews. Savages in league with degenerates. It is the Professor's view that Germany should not confront this enemy alone. The Professor firmly predicts, on the basis of the scientific evidence he has assembled, that any lone confrontation with Russia will be a disaster.

'Naturally, such views, even though they are firmly grounded in science, would not be well received at the highest levels of the Party. The views would be dismissed as defeatism. It was the Professor's opinion that, based on his calculations, should I undertake a secret mission to encourage Britain to cease hostilities against Germany and unite with Germany against Russia, such a secret mission would enjoy success. I have no doubt that he is correct. I have no doubt of this because I know there are those at the highest levels in your establishment who are sympathetic to an alliance – based on blood and racial purity – between our two countries.'

Rutter interrupted Hess' monologue. George, for once, felt pleased to hear the man's voice. Hess was a boring self-centred sod. The sooner he was signed over to the Whitehall interrogators, Villiers and Charteris, at Altskeith, the better. George would be pleased – no, absolutely delighted – to see the back of him.

'Ready to go. All fixed,' Rutter said, 'everybody back on board. Time to make tracks. Not very far to go. Chop-chop. Tickety-boo.'

George shook his head. *Chop bloody chop. Tickety bloody boo.*

George felt sandwiched between a mad bore and a pompous buffoon. 'Right with you,' George said. 'Quick as a flash.'

There had been no mechanical damage to the vehicles. Each engine spat into life with the first turn of the ignition key. Only one headlight on the vehicle driven by Danny was working. But that didn't matter. There was the moonlight and, in front, there was the beam of Rutter's headlights.

From Aberfoyle, where the vehicles turned left towards Altskeith Estate, the road worsened. It was barely more than a wide, pot-holed, gravel path. The going was slow and bumpy.

Beyond Aberfoyle, the vehicles were stopped in their tracks by blinding lights directly in front and directly behind them. A voice behind the lights demanded: 'Stay where you are. Do not move. Identify yourselves.'

Rutter wound down his window and shouted a response. He could see nothing beyond the brightness of the lights.

'Lt. Col. Elphinstone Rutter, Military Intelligence, Clyde District. We have a delivery for Altskeith Estate. We are expected,' he said.

Eight Marines appeared from behind the blazing lights, front and rear. All were heavily armed. Their faces were streaked with camouflage paint. One of the Royal Marines, a sergeant, stepped towards Rutter's open window. The others peered into the halted vehicles.

The sergeant saluted. He looked at the obvious, though superficial, damage caused by the ten-pointer stag and the concertina collision that had followed.

'Been in the wars?' he said. Rutter made no response. The sergeant waved the vehicles on. 'Straight ahead,' he said. 'Half an hour will do it. I'll radio ahead. They're expecting you. We have some other lads keeping an eye on the road between here and there. They'll see you but you won't see them.'

Hess, next to George in the back seat of the second car, had been impressed by the men who had emerged from the darkness behind the blinding lights.

'I appear to be in very safe hands,' he said. 'But the British Army and the German Army are cut from the same cloth. Discipline, tradition, determination... these are the qualities that set us apart from the rest. We are natural comrades.'

George felt otherwise. He said nothing. His view on Hess was changing. He had been prepared, after their first conversations at Lochard House, to see Hess as a zealot, a delusional German nationalist. He was prepared, even, to settle for the view Hess might simply be evil. Now he was leaning towards the possibility that the man sitting next to him had probably started life as evil and had slithered, over the years, into lunacy. In the Scottish patois, Hess was probably best described as a nutter. A headbanger.

The convoy of three vehicles rolled on to Altskeith.

The house was impressive, clearly visible in all its detail in the moonlight. It was a white-painted granite highland lodge in the grand and ornate Victorian manner with its turrets and slate roofing and big double doors and mock battlements and bay windows.

The Lochard House vehicles halted on the white pebble driveway directly in front of the wide, imposing steps that led to Lord Dunolly's rural, but decidedly not rustic, Perthshire retreat.

The Royal Marines in the front and rear cars stepped out and, wordlessly, formed a protective shield around George and Hess when the two stepped from the car driven by Danny.

Villiers and Charteris, the London men, stood, waiting, by the double doors that opened into the main hall of the lodge.

Hess paused on the ninth of twelve steps. He inhaled deeply, sniffing the scent of the hills. There was a stillness in the night. He looked around, slowly nodding as his eyes flitted from the turrets to the mock battlements, to the terrace that surrounded the building. George sensed in Hess the manner of a man who had returned to a place from his past, the manner of a man remembering.

Touching Hess lightly on the shoulder, George said: 'Perhaps we should get inside. You wouldn't want to catch a chill.'

There was, and Hess knew this, not the most remote chance of catching a chill in the mildness of that night.

For George, the real concern was that, standing on the steps, Hitler's Deputy was an easy target. A gunman concealed in the stand of trees 75 yards in front of Altskeith would have an easy shot. Squeeze. Bang. Bye-bye Herr Hess.

Charteris and Villiers stepped forwards when Hess reached the top step. Both spoke in German. Villiers spoke first.

'Herr Hess,' he said, 'we do hope the last few miles haven't been too bumpy, although we did have a message from the fellows who stopped you down the road that you'd already had a bit of a bump.'

Charteris said: 'Well, no more bumps from now on. You'll be snug as a bug here at Altskeith. Safe from prying eyes. It's a lovely spot. A good place to get things off your chest before we make some longer-term arrangements. Nothing but the best, I imagine... but that's one for the chaps higher up the tree.'

Hess looked impassively at the two London men. Their initial meeting in Glasgow had left him with the view that they were skilled interrogators. Their manner had been polite but not familiar. Their body language had been controlled. They sat upright leaning neither towards nor away from Hess during those first conversations. Both took notes. They had made neither threats nor promises. Their questioning was structured and direct... please tell us about... why do you say this... when and where did this happen... who else was present... who else was aware of this... when did you make this decision...? Their German was more adequate than fluent. However, it lacked the sophistication of the Major's nuanced German.

Herr Major MacLean, Hess had decided, was a cut or two above Villiers and Charteris. George was the product of a great

European University, Edinburgh. He had lived in Germany as a student. He had seen the Phoenix begin to rise. He understood the German soul, the German spirit. He understood Germany. The London men seemed only to understand German. They were the product of a Military Intelligence language school.

Hess was ushered into the entry hall. It was softly lit by two Murano glass chandeliers that filtered the brightness from a dozen bulbs. Wartime entreaties on energy saving had yet to be heard in this part of Perthshire. The entry hall was a postcard picture of what well-to-do Victorian-era industrialists imagined Highland life was like.

The wall panels were oak, lightly stained to give them the colour of honey. Along the panels, on both sides of the hall, were mounted the heads of stags, possibly shot on the estate but more probably bought from Mackenzie and Sons. This Stirling family business, for the best part of seven decades, had done rather nicely from selling 'heirlooms' of questionable antiquity and provenance to wealthy English industrial revolutionaries who fancied themselves as Manchester or Bolton or Liverpool-accented Highland lairds.

Mackenzie and Sons patriarch, Fergus John Mackenzie, after each sale – to the loud and the newly landed – of every stag's head, claymore or sword or brace of pistols would wink at his son, Fergus John Mackenzie Junior, and say: 'It's our way of making them pay for Culloden and the Highland Clearances.'

The polished timber floor of the entry hall was partly covered by the red hues of oriental carpets – more in the rough Beluch style than the intricate Persian or Turkish style. Beyond the hall and to the left was a rather grand breakfast room, similarly carpeted, with a large table that could easily seat 16. Along the walls of the breakfast room were displays of claymores, the great highland cleaving blades that had been more than matched by the stabbing bayonets of the English and their Lowland Scots and German mercenary soldiers in the final battle, in April 1746, of the Jacobite Rising of 1745.

There were other displays, too. Round shields in the fashion of those carried by clansmen during that rising, pikes and muskets and ivory-handled double-edged daggers.

To the right of the entry hall was a book-lined sitting room. It smelled of leather and money. Comfortable and rich. Safe. Secure. Far from the madding common crowd and the hard-handed mill and mine and foundry and factory workers whose toil had enriched the likes of Lord Dunolly.

Heavy curtains were drawn across every window. There was a fire in the big, open grate. At Altskeith it was not uncommon during the late spring and early summer months, when damp mist tumbled down from the hills, for a fire to burn in the sitting room and the breakfast room and the upstairs bedrooms.

Dominating one corner of the sitting room was a long-departed polar bear, stuffed to its full height of seven feet. The years had yellowed its fur. Its unseeing and dull glass eyes stared across the room. There was a melancholy in that dead stare.

Villiers, Charteris and Rutter gestured Hess into the sitting room. George, Danny and Finola followed. Villiers motioned the three to make themselves comfortable. He pointed to a sofa near the sad-eyed polar bear. Hess might care to sit closer to the fire.

Charteris said Hess would shortly be shown upstairs to his quarters. They were comfortable and well-appointed and spacious.

He should stay away from the windows. Curtains would be closed at all times. He should not leave the residence. Dinner would be served within the hour. After that, Villiers said, Hess might rest. Tomorrow would be a busy day.

'Lots to talk about,' Charteris said. 'Lots of things to remember.'

For the moment, though, there was some paperwork to attend to. A signature here and there would confirm Herr Hess had arrived at Altskeith and had been transferred, in sound health, to the care – the word custody was avoided – of Villiers and Charteris. Then, Lt. Col. Elphinstone Rutter, Major George Maclean, Captain Finola Fraser and Sergeant Danny Inglis could be on their way back to Glasgow. They'd done their job. Duty called elsewhere. Thank you very much. Well done. Off you go.

Hess fixed Villiers and Charteris with a stare. His dark eyes blackened and narrowed. The muscles in his jaw tightened. He turned that stare on Rutter. To his credit and to the surprise of George and Danny, Rutter met that stare, unblinking.

Rutter smiled. 'You seem unsettled, Herr Hess,' he said.

Hess pursed his lips, initially saying nothing. He was working to contain his composure. When he spoke, in English, he spoke in the manner of a man well-accustomed to being listened to. He directed his words to Rutter. His words were spoken slowly and quite deliberately in the tone of a prefect making a point to a junior boy.

'It was not my understanding that Major Maclean – and, of course, his subordinates – would depart so soon after my arrival here,' Hess said. 'My preference is that they should remain. I am comfortable in their company – Major Maclean for his conversation and his subordinates for their understanding that I have no desire to engage them in small talk.'

George, Danny and Finola exchanged glances.

'Subordinates, that's a good one,' Danny whispered. George winked and nodded Danny's eyes towards Hess and Rutter. They were staring at each other, unblinking. This would be interesting, George thought. Two vipers coiled, ready to strike.

Rutter smiled again. 'Oh, dear me,' he said. 'Can't imagine what gave you the idea that Major Maclean and Captain Fraser and Sergeant Inglis would be staying on. They've done their little bit. Other tasks beckon now. You're safe in the hands of the London chaps and our rather fierce-looking Royal Marines.

Nothing to worry about with His Majesty's Royal Marines on duty. Now, we'll just settle the paperwork and be on our way.'

Hess shook his head slowly. He pursed his lips again. The tone of the prefect addressing the junior boy was more pronounced when he said: 'You have heard my preference. I expect you to act on it. I am not some nobody.'

Villiers and Charteris said nothing. They watched the confrontation, expressionless.

Rutter, still holding his smile, said: 'Herr Hess, with all due respect, your preferences do not come into it. You have placed yourself in our care. Your position should be perfectly clear to you. You are not, as you must know, in a position to…'

Hess exploded with unbridled anger. 'You are quite correct,' he shouted. 'My position is, indeed, perfectly clear. I am the deputy to the leader of the Third Reich and you are a butler in uniform. I am here in Scotland to speak with people in high places and you are not a man in high places. Major Maclean and his subordinates will remain here because unless they do there will be no conversations tomorrow, or any other day, with your Mister Villiers and Mister Charteris.'

Rutter was, visibly at least, unaffected by the tirade. His face gave nothing away. George was impressed, albeit reluctantly, by the man's composure.

Rutter smiled again. 'I had no idea how attached you had become to Major Maclean, Captain Fraser and Sergeant Inglis,' he said. 'The last thing we'd want is to see you upset. Of course, I'll need to have a few words with people elsewhere. I suppose you'd describe them as people in high places. Let's see how they feel about it. I'll make a telephone call. This very minute. Then, in the morning, I'd say, we can have another chat. But no raised voices next time. That would be more appropriate. The British way. Very civil. I wouldn't be at all surprised, Herr Hess, if you are feeling a smidgin fatigued. You've had a few rather big days when you think about it. A nice relax and a rest and I imagine you'll feel tip-top.'

Rutter nodded to Villiers and Charteris. They should escort Herr Hess to his quarters. Herr Hess might wish to freshen up before dinner was delivered. It had been quite a long day. He'd find daywear and nightwear in his rooms. Mister Villiers and Mister Charteris, if they would be so kind, could possibly return downstairs after Herr Hess had been settled in. There were boxes to tick.

For the night, at least, Major Maclean and his subordinates would remain. Rutter was sure comfortable rooms for the three could be made ready in a jiffy.

Hess appeared calm. He turned to Charteris and Villiers and then to George. 'So, to my quarters,' he said. 'I will bathe and change my clothes. The Major will be enjoyable company with dinner. And Mister Villiers and Mister Charteris will, I am sure, be able to occupy themselves elsewhere. I am not sure I would enjoy their company this evening.'

Hess was attempting to set the agenda. He was asserting himself. He was no ordinary detainee. He would decide who he spoke to.

Rutter smiled. He understood, of course. Major Maclean and Mister Hess no doubt had fond Berlin memories to share. It always lifted the spirits and gladdened the heart to recall – what might we call them? – the days of wine and roses… or even the days of sausage and sauerkraut?

Villiers and Charteris took their leave when Hess reached his rooms.

Hess stripped and ran his bath, leaving the bathroom door open. The Germans, George recalled from his student summers in Berlin, seemed to take some odd pleasure in parading their nudity. There was an exhibitionism about that pleasure. It was an exhibitionism that, to Edinburgh eyes, seemed beyond understanding.

The prisoner washed and soaked, and washed and soaked again for more than an hour. Between long silences, he whistled. It sounded like some Wagner dirge.

George had never thought of Nazis as whistlers. Whistling didn't seem to sit comfortably with the street posters he remembered from his Berlin summers as a student. The posters were everywhere. They projected the Nazi image of square-jawed, hard-eyed, muscled, straight-backed, unsmiling, determined men and Rubenesque blonde women who would bear a generation of supermen and broad-hipped girls whose sole purpose would be to serve on the carnal assembly line of the Master Race.

George conjured up a picture of Hess and Hitler, side-by-side at some mass rally, whistling the German national anthem, *Deutschland Uber Alles*, before a sea, an ocean, of open-mouthed, child-like adoring faces. He imagined a great communal gasp. 'Our Fuhrer can whistle... he has saved Germany and he can whistle... such a man... he can do anything.'

He thought of the tale of the Pied Piper of Hamelin. Hitler and Hess had much in common with that fabled character. They attracted a following of rats and children. Nazism was an absurdity... master race, living space, Jewish plots. Germany was a nation gone mad. Germany was Alice in Wonderland come to life. How, in the name of God, could a cultured people slide into collective insanity?

When Hess stepped from the tub he said in a raised voice: 'Ha, ha, Major Maclean. Did you see your Mister Rutter's face when I said he was nothing but a butler in uniform?'

George nodded to the sinewy figure then looked away. Hess did not cut a trim and taut figure of racially pure manhood. He merely appeared overly hirsute and slightly stooped. This was no Michelangelo's David.

George scanned the room. The quarters allocated to Hess were, by any standard, well-appointed. The bedroom was large enough to also serve as a comfortable sitting room with two red leather sofas, a low coffee table, a writing desk and an upholstered swivel chair.

The adjoining bathroom was big. Its centrepiece was a

deep, claw-footed bath. There was a large gold-leaf framed mirror above a hand-basin. By the side of the hand-basin was a wall cabinet that contained towels, soap, a toothbrush, tooth powder, a safety razor and cologne. A towel dressing gown hung on an ornate polished brass hook by the bathroom door. An important guest had been expected and ample provision had been made for that important guest.

Hess emerged from the bathroom wearing the towel dressing gown. He looked closely at the furnishings, the carpets, the half dozen oil paintings of clan chiefs in full Highland dress: kilts, plaids, bonnets, dirks, thick hose and Badger sporrans.

'Has much changed?' George asked.

Hess seemed puzzled. George suspected the puzzlement was feigned.

'I'm sorry,' Hess said, 'what did you say?'

George repeated the question: 'I asked if much had changed since the last time you were here.'

'Why would you ask that, Major Maclean,' Hess said. 'You have me at a disadvantage.'

'The way you paused on the steps outside when we arrived,' George said. 'The way you seemed at ease when you came inside... the way you have just looked around this room... you seemed to be remembering how it was before. How it might have changed.'

Hess shrugged and commended George for his powers of imagination.

'Imagination is not something one usually associates with the Scots. One usually sees the Scots as a rather pedestrian people, given more to practicality than imagination and speculation,' he said. Clearly, if Hess had visited Altskeith before, he was not about to share his recollections of that visit or its circumstances.

Instead, he shared dinner in the room with George. He ate just as he bathed, slowly.

For more than two hours, Hess speculated on what might

have happened had Britain and Germany reached agreement on the Reich's perfectly reasonable territorial ambitions on *lebensraum* and an expanded Greater Germany.

'There would have been no conflict between our countries,' he said. 'Perhaps we would have joined together, marched together, to confront our real enemies... the Jews and the bankers and the Communists.'

The speculation was interrupted by a knock at the door. Danny appeared. George excused himself and left the room. In the corridor, Danny said: 'I'll take over for the rest of the night. Rutter has organised rooms. You're in the room at the end of the corridor, the last one on the left. I'm next door, the second last room. Finola is opposite you, the last one on the right. Breakfast at eight, that's the word.'

Then he added: 'The Brigadier is downstairs. He arrived not five minutes ago. He must have driven like the clappers. Seems that Rutter telephoned him in a bit of a flap about Hess saying he wanted us to stay on with him. The Brigadier called Whitehall and the Big Shots down there told him to get up here and sort it out. He wants a word.'

George found the Brigadier alone and sipping port in the grand sitting room.

'Ah, Major Maclean,' the senior officer said, 'had to dash up to sort this and that out. Now, a few words before you turn in. How are things with our guest? Still getting along famously, I expect.'

George, the merest sliver of sarcasm in his tone, said he and Hess were getting along like old chums. Two peas in a pod. But there was one thing.

'Out with it, then,' the Brigadier said.

'It's nothing I can pin down,' George said, 'but I get the sense that Hess has been here before... the way he looks around. It's almost as if he's remembering a previous visit.'

The Brigadier drained his glass.

'Can't see it. Not without us knowing about it,' he said.

'He was in London on official business once or twice before this war. That's all on the record. But London is 460 miles from here. Don't see how he could have slithered up unnoticed. Can't quite see why, either.'

George said perhaps Lord Dunolly had extended a private invitation.

Dunolly was an industrial hardman. He'd won his spurs, and his peerage, after the 1926 general strike and the Great Depression years that followed.

'Wouldn't surprise me if he was a quiet admirer of the Nazi style of getting things done,' George added. 'A personal invitation to Hess when he was in London on German government business wouldn't be such a surprise. Hush hush, nothing on the record. But Rutter, as Dunolly's factotum, would know. He probably knows Dunolly's inside leg measurement.'

The Brigadier had his doubts. Not about the inside leg measurement, but rather the notion that Rutter was familiar with every detail of Dunolly's affairs. Dunolly, like every powerful man, would have his secrets. Having secrets was part and parcel of being powerful.

'Can't see Rutter being in on everything,' the Brigadier said. 'He's a fetch-and-carry man, believe me. A good idea to keep your thoughts to yourself and myself. *Entre nous*, as they say. We wouldn't want to find ourselves rubbing Dunolly the wrong way. Let's stick to the job in hand. Always the best way when we're answering to Whitehall. They've got the bigger picture. We've just got a few parts of the jigsaw.'

In the meantime, George might want to catch up on some shut-eye.

'Another snort of this rather fine port,' the Brigadier said, 'and I'll be ready for forty winks myself... Dunolly does seem to keep an impressive cellar.'

George indicated he was inclined to join the Brigadier in a snort. 'It'll give me a taste of how the other half lives,' he said.

Chapter fourteen: Orders from Berlin

The unseasonal cold and wet front moving west
from the North Atlantic has brought dense localised
inland fog. This is expected to give way to widespread
and heavy rain within 48 hours. The rain is expected
to persist for several days—
Aberfoyle Times, weekly weather notes.

The morning was dour and overcast. The Scots had a word for
it: *Dreich*. Villiers returned from an inspection of the defensive
perimeter the Marines established around Altskeith. His
overcoat was damp.

'Out there it's what we English call a real pea-souper.
Weather forecast on the BBC Home Service said we're in for
fog and heavy rain for a few days yet,' Villiers said, entering the
breakfast room.

'Up here, I suppose you'd call it Scotch Mist?' Charteris
said.

'Scotch is a drink,' Danny said, not even looking at
Charteris, 'and, no, we don't call it Scotch Mist. We call it
the weather. We get weather all the time in Scotland, clement
weather and inclement weather. I've never really been able to
tell the difference. Then again, I don't have your eagle eye for
detail. I'm just a run-of-the-mill Glasgow polis… I suppose
down there you'd call me a Copper or a Bobby. Or a Peeler.
You're a bit fancier than we are up here.'

George suppressed a smile. Danny yawned. The yawn
said he was disinterested in any response from the London
Men. It also said he was tired. The tiredness showed on his face.
He'd have breakfast and then get some shut-eye. He'd spent
the night watching Hitler's Deputy sleeping like a baby until a

Marine arrived to tell Danny that breakfast was being served downstairs. Rutter, at the head of the breakfast table, advised Danny, George and Finola that they'd be enjoying the charms – that was the word he used – of Altskeith for a few days more.

'Not half an hour ago, London advised the Brigadier, and the Brigadier advised my good self, that it would be better all-round if you three remained here,' he said. 'It's a relatively minor concession and we don't want to upset our upstairs chap.'

Rutter said George would be present when Charteris and Villiers interviewed Hess. This had been suggested by London. And London always prevailed.

'The feeling down there in Whitehall, as expressed through our Brigadier, was that since Major Maclean seemed, for some reason, to have found favour with Hess,' Rutter said, 'his presence during interviews might be of value, set the chap at ease, that sort of thing. Presence, not participation.'

George had to understand, naturally, that whatever he heard during the interviews was not to be repeated to anyone, ever.

'If you're unsure of my meaning,' Rutter added, 'just brush up on the Official Secrets Act.'

'Anything else we might need to know?' George asked.

'Nothing that springs to mind,' Rutter said. 'I'll defer to Mister Villiers and Mister Charteris, through the Brigadier, on the matter of time to be spent at Altskeith.'

Villiers said the time spent at Altskeith depended, really, on more than the weather. 'Our job over the next few days is to find out exactly what Hess is really doing here. Once we know that, Whitehall will make the decisions. When we had our first chat with our guest in Glasgow he gave us the clear message that he has some people on our side he particularly wants to chat with. People in high places, that's what he called them. He is adamant that he won't reveal any names to us. We're equally adamant that he will.

'We'll be telling him that until we know why he's here and who he wants to talk with, well, he won't be going anywhere and he certainly won't be speaking with his mystery people in high places. Of course, our man upstairs might have nothing worthwhile in the way of names. All this horoscope nonsense. He might be utterly crackers. We don't know yet. The whole exercise could be a complete waste of time. We could end up calling in a headshrinker who will probably declare him barking and have him tucked away in an asylum.'

Charteris cut in: 'In the meantime we're sealed in here, tight as a drum. The Marines have round-the-clock foot patrols on our perimeter and they have men front and back here as well as the two on our visitor's door. There's only one road in from Aberfoyle and that's well covered.'

Then he rose from the breakfast table and drew back the heavy curtains that covered a bay window. Visibility was barely twenty yards.

'If we could see through the fog,' he said, 'we'd have a drab view of some rather grim peat bogs and Ben Lomond away in the distance. Can't see anybody traipsing across that lot to get here. It's heavy going out there. Anyhow, even if somebody got close, they'd be picked up by our foot patrols.'

***

The heavy going that morning wasn't confined to the rolling hills and slurping bogs around Altskeith.

In the bleakest, darkest of seas in the 24-mile strait between Cushendun, County Antrim, and Machrihanish on the Mull of Kintyre, Kriegsmarine veteran Captain Gunther Lohmann snapped the order for U-502 to surface. It was the sixth time in the last ten hours he'd issued that command.

Four times during the night, Lohmann and his crew had spent 25 anxious minutes on the surface. Their relayed messages from Abwehr communications in Berlin – *Chrysalis report status/location soonest* – had drawn no response. The fifth message, sent in the newness of the day, was answered. The answer advised: *Wireless now open. Chrysalis and companion comfortable in Vienna. Await instructions.*

There was an immediate response from Berlin: *Instructions in one hour.*

Lohmann gave the order to dive to 40 metres. One hour later he issued the order to surface for the sixth time. He didn't like issuing the order any more than the crew liked hearing it. These were dangerous waters when the cloak of night was pulled back.

Surfacing during the hours of darkness was relatively safe. Surfacing during daylight hours meant possible exposure to the RAF Coastal Command Bristol Beaufort aircraft that patrolled the strait. Their pilots and crews called themselves 'Beaufort Boys' and their fierce reputation as U-boat hunters and killers was well-deserved.

A U-boat on the surface was easy prey. It had no real defence against a low-flying Beaufort that could drop four 200-pound bombs, climb out of harm's way and quickly circle to inspect the results of its handiwork.

It wasn't uncommon, U-boat crews knew, for Beauforts to machine gun anything that was left on the surface after a successful bombing run. Then again, U-boats had been known to machine gun survivors of torpedoed merchant ships in the North Atlantic. No quarter was given in this theatre of war. Sitting defenceless on the surface, everybody on board U-502 knew, was madness. But the Abwehr in Berlin was calling the shots and that was that, Lohmann said. They were an insistent and unforgiving lot, these bastards sitting comfortably and safe as houses back in Berlin. He doubted any of them had ever fired a shot in anger. The sooner U-502 did what it was told, the sooner it could get back to the real business of sinking enemy ships.

The coded Abwehr instructions that came one hour

after contact with Chrysalis was reestablished were 'from the highest authority.' They were relayed instantly from U-502. Hess was being held at a location, Altskeith, sixteen kilometres from Vienna. He was being guarded by a detachment of Royal Marines. He could be moved at any time. Chrysalis should ensure Hess did not reach any intended destination. It was imperative that Hess was eliminated before—

The message stopped mid-sentence.

★★★

The RAF Beaufort emerged from the coastal mist. Its tell-tale engine noise signalled immediate danger to the defenceless U-boat. Lohmann, too late, barked the order to clear the bridge and crash dive. The Beaufort came in at no more than three hundred feet then climbed sharply in the few seconds between the release of four bombs and their impact on U-502. Then the Beaufort banked and turned back towards the target. The surface was slicked with oil. Bullseye. U-502 was sinking like a stone. It was making its last dive. The Beaufort radio operator tapped a Morse message to RAF Machrihanish: *U-boat engaged. Destroyed. No identification. No survivors.*

Over the Beaufort intercom the pilot told his crew of three: 'Heading home for a nice cup of tea. Well done. Top shot.'

It was all very gung-ho, very removed from the reality of the destruction of 35 lives. Sailors who would never come home from the sea. Sailors whose resting place would never be visited by wives, mothers, sweethearts, sons, daughters.

★★★

In the kitchen of the cottage in the hills above Loch Lomond, Chrysalis began decoding the message that ended without warning. While he worked, Duthie restoked the fire in the living room. He cleared away two bottles that had, a few hours earlier, been coloured by the single malt Ardlui. Neither man mentioned the night before.

It took ten minutes for Chrysalis to decode the message. When he was finished he read and reread the words, lips moving as he read. He was silent until Duthie asked: 'So, what do they say? What happens now? Time to go home, is it? We've done our bit. Helped them flatten Clydebank. Time for a welcome fit for heroes. Isn't that what they say?'

The effortless lies began.

There was some news of MacSherry, Chrysalis said. Berlin understood, through channels, he was making a steady recovery. There was the possibility of the IRA exchanging MacSherry for two British agents kidnapped and held secretly in Ireland. Such accommodations between sworn enemies were not unknown. Chrysalis said, too, that while a welcome fit for heroes could not be fully guaranteed, Berlin was making arrangements for the two to be spirited out of harm's way.

Duthie, cheered by both the news of MacSherry and the prospect of leaving enemy territory, said the sooner they were away, the better. When, he asked, might they be on the move?

Soon, Chrysalis said. However, chance appeared to have intervened in the immediate timing of the departure.

'We find ourselves a few kilometres from a matter that needs to be attended to. The winds of war blow us in unexpected directions.'

From the bag the two had brought from Clydebank, Chrysalis extracted an Ordnance Survey Map and a copy of *The Scottish Tramper Field Guide* – 1938. He spread the map on the kitchen table. The map covered the area from Rowardennan to Aberfoyle. Chrysalis stabbed a finger at two locations on the cloth-backed map. Tap. Tap.

'We are exactly here,' he said, 'and there, a place called Altskeith, is where we have business to attend to. When that is done, we will be away from here.'

Duthie said Chrysalis might care to share the exact nature

of the business to be done. 'A German, a high-ranking prisoner, is being held at this place,' he said, 'and our instructions from the highest authority are to silence the prisoner without delay. Before you ask, you do not need to know the identity of the prisoner. He is known to me and that is enough.'

Duthie shrugged. 'I've always found it easier to kill strangers than people I know,' he said, his words laced with sarcasm. 'It's probably an Irish thing. We're a sentimental people. So, tell me the plan even if you won't tell me the name of the target.'

Clearly, the single malt Ardlui consumed the night before had failed to cement any real bonds of comradeship between the two. The enemy of his enemy wasn't Duthie's friend. He was an arrogant, self-satisfied Nazi.

But, there and then, the enemy of his enemy was Duthie's escape hatch. No more. No less. Without Chrysalis and his Berlin connections, Duthie knew he had no chance of ever seeing Ireland again unless, of course, he could swim the freezing and watery miles between the Mull of Kintyre and County Antrim – after he learned to swim. Belfast was not a place where aquatic skills were fostered. In Belfast, you only swam if the boat went down. And, the Titanic aside, Belfast-built boats – like Clyde-built boats – rarely sank.

Folding the Ordnance Survey map, Chrysalis flicked through the pages of *The Scottish Tramper Field Guide* – 1938. On page 40 was a description of the track and the terrain between Rowardennan and Altskeith. He passed the open book to Duthie. 'We should cover the ground between here and there in three or four hours,' he said. 'When we are in position we will watch and wait for our opportunity. And when this is done we will return here and await instructions for our departure.'

Duthie drew the curtain back from the kitchen window. He wiped the condensation from the panes. He nodded towards the fog. 'Three or four hours? It might take a bit longer in this,' he said. 'And a man could die of the damp, so he could.'

Chrysalis said in that case, perhaps they should walk faster. As for dampness, Duthie would find oilskins on the hooks behind the kitchen door. There was a sharpness, almost a rebuke, in his tone. Duthie was a tiresome man. Beyond the immediate mission he had no value.

'We'll each carry an MP38 submachine gun, extra 32-shot magazines, the silenced Luger pistols and the stick grenades we brought from Clydebank,' Chrysalis said.

'So it's a close-up killing,' Duthie said. 'They can get very messy.'

Chrysalis ignored the remark.

★★★

Away through the mist and over the sodden country that surrounded Altskeith like a moat, Hess bathed and ate breakfast. He nodded when Villiers and Charteris and George entered his quarters. He rose from his chair by the writing desk and smiled. He hoped they had slept well. He had been most comfortable, he told them.

He said they might care to order a pot of coffee. Although he had only recently eaten breakfast and taken tea, he did so very much enjoy a morning coffee. In fact, he enjoyed morning coffee all the more with biscuits. His preference was for shortbread biscuits.

'I tasted your Scottish shortbread,' he said, 'when I visited London before this war of ours. Just a few would do. Perhaps this can be arranged while I make some suggestions on how we might proceed. The sooner we can finish here, the sooner I may conduct my business with those in higher places in Whitehall.'

Hess said he believed they should limit the length of their meetings to two hours. He was perfectly happy to oblige Villiers, Charteris and George by conducting the conversations in English. However, he found that lengthy conversations in

English caused some mental fatigue – 'even for one with my degree of fluency,' he said.

A break every two hours, he felt sure, would be acceptable to all concerned. There would, too, be meal breaks. He would welcome the company of Major Maclean for these.

The Major, Hess said, had a wealth of fond memories of his summer visits to Berlin during his student years. He said the Major's German was flawless. It was a distinct pleasure to hear his recollections of those student years in a perfect Berlin accent.

Then he added: 'I am sure your Whitehall people could make much more use of the Major's high skills and his affable manner. I will tell them this personally when we meet. They will appreciate my observations as a man well used to commanding other men.'

Villiers, concealing his annoyance with the arrogance of Hess and his effusive, provocative praise of George, replied in German. He said Herr Hess might find it less fatiguing to converse in his native tongue. How might that suit? Hess smiled and shook his head. He wouldn't hear of such an arrangement. When in England he should do as the English did.

In mock embarrassment, Hess looked at George and apologised. 'Oh, I had rather overlooked the fact we are in Scotland,' he said. 'I do so hope I have not upset the Major here. I am aware of the historical sensitivities in your barely United Kingdom. The Stuart line deposed and restored and ultimately replaced by the Dutch and the Germans… the crushing of Scotland on Culloden Moor and the shabby treatment of the Scots by the English for almost two centuries.'

George strained every facial muscle to avoid a smile. Hess was working to gain the upper hand and Villiers and Charteris knew it. He was, as before, attempting to set the rules of engagement… times when he would engage in conversation, times when he would eat, times when he would rest. Hess was, beyond doubt, a master manipulator. Such skills had obviously paid dividends in the past. He was, after all, Hitler's Deputy.

Charteris was less inclined to completely conceal his rising rancour. He was polite but there was no mistaking the resolve and the implied threats contained in his response.

He appreciated the prisoner's concern that lengthy conversations in English might be the cause of fatigue. He and Mister Villiers would certainly not wish to fatigue Herr Hess. However, Herr Hess, for his part, might care to guard against misunderstanding his current position.

He had come to Scotland where he had the status of a prisoner of war with all the entitlements to the protection of the Geneva Convention. There was no question of this. However, he had no entitlement to dictate the conditions of his detention or who he might choose to speak with.

'In relation to your desire to meet certain people in Whitehall, Herr Hess,' Charteris said, 'as far as you are concerned, myself and Mister Villiers are Whitehall. If you are to be taken to London it will be when we decide you are to be taken to London.'

Hess opened his mouth to speak. Charteris raised a finger to his lips.

'Please listen, Herr Hess. You will be going to London, if you go to London, when we are satisfied you have something worth saying. Until we are satisfied, you will remain here. Your ability, here and now, to make decisions is severely limited. You can decide how many times you brush your teeth or take a bath. And you are free to decide which biscuits you eat. But, you are not free to decide where you will go and under what conditions this will happen.'

George watched as Hess clenched his teeth. He saw the jaw muscles tighten and dark eyes widening. He fully expected an eruption of explosive rage from Hitler's Deputy. It did not come immediately. Hess sat perfectly still.

Charteris said there were some cards still to be laid on the table. 'Your flight from Augsburg to Scotland some days ago has rendered you, without our protection, a dead man. You know how your people work. You know that an order for your execution will already have been given. As far as they are concerned you are a turncoat, a traitor. We know Berlin has agents in Scotland who will make it their sole business to find and kill you.'

Hess, face reddening and voice raised, told Charteris: 'You know nothing. The success of my mission here will see me return to Berlin as a hero.'

Charteris said he was delighted to hear this. Now, the sooner Herr Hess cared to explain the precise nature of that mission and provide the names of those he wished to meet, the better it would be for all concerned.

By the way, Charteris added after a moment's pause, if Hess felt so sure he would be such a hero of the Third Reich why did he have to steal an aircraft and secretly leave Germany? One could only assume the theft of the aircraft and the secret flight were elements of a plan of such complexity and genius that the plan baffled all who were unfortunate enough not to have been born into the Master Race.

The tables were turning. Hess was no longer dictating the terms of the exchanges between himself and Villiers and Charteris.

Villiers wondered aloud if he might lay some other cards on the table. Charteris nodded.

'Herr Hess, we mentioned the Geneva Convention,' Villiers said. 'It contains provision for the exchange of prisoners or, in some cases, the repatriation of prisoners who might be unwell. In your case we might come to the conclusion that you are of no value to us and we could simply shunt you back to Berlin either directly or through a third country. We would probably say that we thought you were crackers, barking bonkers. Imagine how much fun your Gestapo thugs would have with you. Toenails and fingernails pulled out for starters. Then the teeth. Or an eye poked out. Terrible thoughts, terrible thoughts.'

Hess shrugged. He said Villiers was bluffing.

Villiers met shrug with shrug. Hess was perfectly at liberty to believe whatever he wanted to believe.

Hess erupted with a volcanic rage. He was Hitler's Deputy. He would have nothing more to do with underlings of no consequence. He said his patience had been exhausted. He demanded to be taken to London. His interrogators should make immediate arrangements for him to travel to Whitehall.

Hess stood, glaring, hands on hips. Villiers motioned for Hess to sit down.

'There's a good chap,' he said. 'Just settle down or I'll ask our Marines outside to help settle you down. It wouldn't take much, and they do enjoy a bit of biff. Rough-and-tumble chaps to a man. Quite muscular when they set their minds to it.'

Hess regained control over his anger. He sat down. The transition from fury to an almost feline calmness was seamless. It happened in half the blink of an eye. Villiers smiled as if the Hess outburst had never taken place.

He continued: 'Arrangements for repatriation are usually made through the Red Cross. The exchange or the repatriation is invariably done in a third country. We've lots to choose from... Switzerland, Portugal, Spain, Argentina... lots and lots of choices. What happens then is that the neutral country just ships you back to Germany... and according to you, that wouldn't bother you in the slightest. You'd be, as you say, welcomed as a hero.'

Charteris said he had an even better idea. 'Our RAF fellows have regular nightly flights over Berlin,' he said. 'We could kit Herr Hess out in a parachute and one of those fleecy flying suits the Lancaster boys wear and pop him out just above the Reichstag. All his pals would be there, arms wide open to watch him drift down for his hero's welcome.'

Villiers and Charteris stood up. They motioned George to follow them.

As they left, Charteris said Herr Hess might care to have

some quiet time. Some time to reflect on his position. 'I'll have one of the Marines bring you up that coffee and those biscuits you mentioned,' Villiers said.

Outside, in the corridor, he said to George: 'Let the bugger stew for a while.'

Behind those plummy private school accents, George knew, Villiers and Charteris were as tough as tungsten.

Chapter fifteen: The lion's den

Augsburg matter, initial progress note: The guards on duty during the unauthorised departure of an aircraft are being interrogated. We will determine if the pilot, now held by the enemy, acted alone or in concert. Extreme action to eliminate the pilot has been initiated—

Heinrich Himmler, Reichsfuhrer SS.

Berlin. Flags and men in uniform. The aroma of coffee and fresh bread from bakeries. Newspaper billboards proclaim another victory somewhere in North Africa. Germany is on the march. The call of destiny is being answered.

The Jews and the gypsies and the homosexuals and the frail-minded and the Jehovah's Witnesses are being attended to. They have no place in Greater Germany's destiny. Soon, the Communists in the east will be crushed beyond recognition and resurrection. All that will remain of the Reds will be their red bloodstains in the gutters. The Third Reich will last for one thousand years. The Hitler Youth columns march and sing the Horst Wessel Song. In nurseries, cradles are rocked by blonde mothers who hum 'Tomorrow belongs to me.' Nobody could possibly think otherwise. *Zieg heil. Zieg Heil.* Germany has risen from the ashes. Never again will Germany be humiliated.

Wide-eyed madness is everywhere.

In the Reich Chancellery, Hitler rose from his elaborately carved, high-backed chair, crumpled a typewritten note and threw it across his marble-topped desk. Sitting opposite, the rat-faced Himmler said nothing while Hitler paced the room, roaring like a caged lion. This was the safest option. Hitler was not a man to be interrupted. Ever.

The Fuhrer's anger was white hot. Pointing at the crumpled paper he screamed at his security chief: 'And this is the best you can do?'

Hitler's two black-uniformed bodyguards stood by the door of the room hearing and seeing nothing.

Spit flew from Hitler's thin, bloodless lips as he raged. Expressionless, Himmler wondered what might happen if the Fuhrer screamed himself into a heart attack. Hitler's Deputy, Hess, would not be there to fill the breach. Perhaps destiny had singled out Himmler for... He pushed the thought aside. Thinking could be as dangerous as speaking. He had seen the deepest, most hidden thoughts of many seemingly loyal Germans revealed under vigorous questioning.

Hitler's tirade continued. 'You are telling me that Hess arrived at the airstrip on his own, then commandeered an aeroplane and took off and flew to Scotland? Well, I am telling you that Hess could not have done this alone. Names! I want names. Treacherous scum. I hold you responsible. You let this happen. We can easily find you a place in Dachau. Perhaps a small room you can share with a Jew and no view. Where are your spies, your informers? The people you said told you of every cowardly whisper of treason? Tell me.'

Himmler sat perfectly still, unblinking, staring straight ahead.

Hitler smacked the marble desk top. 'Tell me,' he demanded, leaning into Himmler's face.

Himmler cleared his throat. He would not, there and then, tell Hitler that four of the arrested Augsburg guards had died under interrogation. All had insisted that Hess acted alone. The interrogators insisted he had not.

Nor would Himmler say he believed Hess was insane and should have been despatched, long since, to a special SS medical clinic where the lunatic and the imperfect were extracted from the German gene pool.

Other candidates for extraction, Himmler secretly believed, should be the club-footed Propaganda Minister Goebbels and the morphine-addicted bisexual Luftwaffe supremo Goering.

The Reichsfuhrer SS would not say, either, that Hess appeared to be in the thrall of Professor Krafft, a common confidence trickster. Krafft and Hess were close. Hess was a member of Hitler's inner circle. Thus, any criticism of Krafft was a criticism of Hess and, by extension, called into question's Hitler's choice of confidantes.

Hess, in one conversation with Himmler, had described Krafft as a genius, a man of science and great perceptiveness, a man who saw clearly what others could not. Himmler, however, saw Krafft differently.

In Himmler's eyes, Krafft was an alcoholic charlatan. He was a moral weakling who marched under a flag of personal convenience. Himmler's view of Hess was no less scathing.

Himmler, the son of a school teacher, never liked Hess, the son of a wealthy mercantile family. Even in his earliest activist days with the Party, Himmler viewed Hess with a well-concealed measure of loathing. Hess was a rich boy. He had never suffered as ordinary Germans had suffered through the crushing mass unemployment and the Communist street violence of the 1920s. Hess was an opportunist. The pity was that Hitler, for all his brilliance, had never seen this. However, even the greatest of great men can have their blind spots. Hess was an opportunist. As such, he was a stain on the purity of National Socialism.

Himmler cleared his throat again.

The Reichsfuhrer SS said matters relating to Hess were in hand. The Fuhrer's instructions that Hess should be eliminated were, even as they spoke, being attended to.

Through channels the Abwehr had been informed, by a 'highly placed and impeccable' source in Britain, that Hess was being held at a country estate in Scotland. The highly placed source – whose Abwehr code name was Kingfisher –might, even as they spoke, be at the Scottish country estate. Kingfisher would advise Berlin when Hess had been eliminated.

Himmler offered the assurance that Hess would never leave the Scottish estate alive. 'We have two agents, the very best, who will see to this,' he said. 'They have your orders. They may already have the Scottish estate under observation. They will strike at the first opportunity.'

Drumming his fingers on his marble-topped desk, Hitler demanded: 'And where will your Herr Kingfisher be when all this is happening. Tell me. Will he be opening the door to let your agents in?'

Adopting a formal manner of speech, Himmler said: 'Fuhrer, allow me to suggest that you should not trouble yourself with the details of the pending demise of the traitor Hess. You have higher matters that require your undivided attention. The destiny of Greater Germany is in your hands.'

Himmler knew Hitler, vain and self-satisfied beyond words, felt flattered when a formal tone was adopted. It signified a speaker's deference to the Leader. And deference to authority – through fear of that authority – was the adhesive that held this Third Reich together.

Hitler nodded and waved Himmler away. The Reichsfuhrer SS returned the nod. He was relieved to be leaving the Lion's Den. He was intact in rank and he had not been consigned to Dachau. These were no small matters. For some, meetings with Hitler could end very badly indeed. They could be fraught with danger.

★★★

In sharp contrast, deep under Whitehall, Churchill was beaming. His war room was thick with blue cigar smoke. He sniffed his brandy balloon, leaned back in his leather swivel chair and held the white telephone handset against his ear, nodding as he listened. 'Good. Excellent. Fine,' he said.

The telephone briefing was provided by Brigadier Ewan Stuart. He was 'keeping tabs on things personally at Altskeith.'

One of his men, a Major Maclean – 'unconventional type… but a wizard in all things German… speaks the lingo like a native' – appeared to be on sound terms with the prisoner. Which was just as well since Hess hadn't quite warmed to the Whitehall chaps, Villiers and Charteris.

The Brigadier said Hess had insisted Maclean be present during chats with the two. And, by the way, Hess had also insisted on being taken to London before revealing any details of his mission.

Of course, the Brigadier ventured, surrendering to any demand from Hess was probably out of the question. But, then again, it might not hurt to have Hess under lock and key in London rather than have him 'cooped up at the back of beyond.' It was a matter for the top brass, the Brigadier said, volunteering the obvious.

'Not a question of surrendering to demands,' Churchill said. 'More a case of how best to play the fish. This fellow of yours… Maclean, you said… might have a clue or two if he's the wizard you say he is. Good idea if I have a word with him… never hurts to speak with our boys down the line… get it straight from the horse's mouth. No flannel. Get him on the blower, there's a good fellow.'

***

Less than a minute later, George, called from the kitchen where he was playing cards with two Marines, was speaking with the Prime Minister.

The Brigadier, walking George towards the telephone in the empty Altskeith Lodge sitting room, said, voice lowered: 'It's Churchill on the line. Says he wants a chat about your chum Hess. More private in here than on the other telephones around the place. When I told the PM you and Hess were getting along rather well, he insisted on having a word'

George picked up the telephone handset. The Brigadier stood nearby, listening, arms folded.

First things first, Churchill said. Did the Major enjoy a drink or was he one of those drab, bible-thumping Scots Presbyterians who skulked around as if the world had ended yesterday. George said he had a fondness for gin. He enjoyed a cigarette, too.

'Excellent, excellent,' the Prime Minister said. 'I've yet to find an abstainer whose opinion on anything is sound. A fellow who doesn't enjoy a drink is a fellow with something to hide. That's my rule when it comes to sizing them up. Never lets me down. Now, time for getting right down to tin tacks...'

Churchill wanted to know how best to deal with Hess and George, apparently, was just the man to ask. The Brigadier had told him so. So, what were Maclean's thoughts on Hess? Was he barking mad. Not that it mattered all that much.

'Crackers or otherwise,' Churchill said, 'we've got him and we'll make good use of him. The Romans would have put him in a cage and trundled him through the streets... but even a Prime Minister can't authorise that these days. A pity, but there it is.'

'Well, sir,' George said, 'I'm no headshrinker. I can only go on what I see and hear. Personally, I think he's off with the pixies. But he's not off with the pixies all the time. He'll be fine, quite rational one minute, and then he'll get these flashes of rage... and half a minute later he's rambling on about horoscopes and the stars and some astrologer he has in the background in Berlin. Then he might go completely silent for two or three minutes. It's as if he's in a trance. When he comes out of it there's the feeling that he hasn't a clue what he has been saying. I think the quacks call it a split personality.'

Churchill blew smoke rings from his cigar.

He wanted to know what George made of the Hess demand to be taken to London without delay.

'I'm told,' Churchill said, 'Hess has been prattling on about talking with people in high places.' And what was the problem between Hess and Charteris and Villiers. The Brigadier had mentioned something along these lines.

George was guarded in his observations on Charteris and Villiers. They seemed to be no-nonsense types. Knew what they were doing. However, their suggestion that Whitehall might decide Hess was insane and should be sent back to Germany had unsettled Hess.

'Go on,' Churchill said. 'How would you deal with Hess? Don't hold back. Toes are sometimes there to be stood on.'

George cleared his throat. 'Well,' he said, 'there's a risk that if we push Hess too hard he'll just dig his heels in... call our bluff. And it is a bluff. Just because he might be a bit crackers doesn't mean he's a fool. Besides, I can't see us sending him back saying he's unhinged. Then we'd be the ones who were crackers.

'You're asking me what we should do, sir? We should do what he wants. Let him feel he has a bit of say, that he can call some shots. He says he wants to speak to people in what he calls higher places... well, get him down there. And when he arrives ask for a list of who he wants to talk to. No middlemen, just Hess and whoever. Although I suppose it really would be Hess and whoever plus the hidden camera and the hidden microphone.

'Top-shelf Nazis, like Hess, see themselves as having some sort of destiny to rule the roost. The Master Race. It's a born-to-rule-the-world mindset. I tell you now, sir, he won't be spilling whatever beans he has to spill to anybody up here in Scotland. We're the monkeys – myself included. He wants to speak to the organ grinders. He just uses people like me to pass the time.'

Churchill said, yes, he wasn't entirely unfamiliar with that born-to-rule mindset. Some might say it wasn't confined to the likes of Hitler and Hess. 'The uncharitable might have the temerity to venture that I'm actually a product, a rotund example, of that mindset. But, then again, someone has to take the lead.'

George smiled at the Prime Minister's self-deprecatory tone. For a man with a war to win, Churchill managed to display a dry sense of humour.

George said threats were unlikely to work on Hess. 'They might take the wind out of his sails for a minute or two,' he explained, 'but he collects himself in a couple of shakes and he's back to being a man of destiny. He'll have thought about the repatriation threat. He knows we won't do it. He knows he can just sit here, fold his arms, button his lip and wait for us to do what he wants.

'And, sir, the sooner we get him out of here, the better for all concerned. If the Jerries get wind of where he is they'll go after him. They might even be onto Hess as we speak. Personally I think he's a softer target here than hidden away down in London. I think the Brigadier might have reached the same conclusion, but that's one for you and the Brigadier... and the weather. You can barely see fifty yards outside.'

Churchill agreed. Arrangements for the prisoner's safe transfer from Scotland should be set in train. Would Major Maclean be kind enough to pass the telephone to the Brigadier? George complied.

The Brigadier listened, nodding. 'Right,' he said, returning the telephone to its cradle.

'Winnie seems quite taken by your views,' the Brigadier said. 'Excellent. He says it's a good idea to get Hess down south. Can't say, in the circumstances, that I disagree. He wants you and your colleagues to stay with Hess for the journey south. The less rattled Hess is the better. Can't see us making a move today. Not in this weather. Damned pea-souper. According to the Signals boys, the forecast says it's widespread and well set in. Be lucky if we could manage twenty miles an hour.'

There would be a briefing later in the day.

'Your two – Captain Fraser and Sergeant Inglis – and Villiers and Charteris. Some of our lads in uniform, too. I'll get Rutter on the job. He can pull in the Marines who stopped you on the way in here. They'd have a couple of heavy vehicles we can make use of, too. We'll either do the entire journey by road or we'll get ourselves to the nearest RAF base that isn't fogged over. And, Major, not a word to our fellow upstairs.'

George nodded. His lips, he said, were sealed. He'd await Rutter's instructions. In the meantime, he'd get back to his card game in the kitchen. He was thirty shillings up. He was on a winning streak. It was the only piece of luck he'd had in recent times. That and the prospect of offloading Hess.

Chapter sixteen: The fog of war

No plan of operations extends beyond the first encounter with the enemy—
Field Marshall Helmuth Von Moltke, Militarische Werke, 1892.

Duthie swore under his breath. The peat bog sucked at his boots. Every slurping step was an effort. The mist was dense, sodden like a kitchen sponge.

A few yards ahead of Duthie, Chrysalis was barely visible. The two had strayed from the track marked on the Ordnance Survey map and described in *The Scottish Tramper Field Guide.* They were lost in the fog of their own deadly mission.

'We'll rest... just for a few moments,' Chrysalis said.

A voice from the mist shouted: 'Stay still and identify yourself.' The accent was Geordie. Chrysalis and Duthie dropped to their knees. Duthie felt for the silenced Luger pistol in the inside pocket of his oilskin.

Two shapes emerged from the gloom. Their green berets and camouflage smocks marked them as Marines.

'Now aren't you a sight for weary eyes, and that's a fact,' Duthie said.

The taller of the two soldiers, a sergeant, was in no mind to exchange pleasantries. The weather was foul. He was cold and wet to the bone. Even a mug of NAAFI tea would be welcomed.

'You're a long way from the Emerald Isle, Paddy. What brings you here?' the sergeant said.

'We're bloody lost is what brings us here,' Duthie answered. 'Took a wrong turn on the way for a dram over at

Rowardennan. Been plodding around for hours, so we have. If you'd be kind enough...?'

The sergeant nodded towards the canvas bag slung over Duthie's shoulder. 'Open it.'

Duthie drew his silenced pistol from the inside pocket of his oilskins. He fired two shots. The Marines fell to the ground, blood splattering from their heads. Quickly, Duthie stepped forwards. Standing over the bodies, he shot each in the face again and returned the pistol to his inside pocket. Matter-of-factly, he said: 'I suppose this means we're not that far from where we're going?'

It also meant, Chrysalis knew, that when the patrolling Marines failed to return to Altskeith, the alarm would be raised. The mission to silence Hitler's Deputy would lose any element of surprise. And without surprise, there was no chance of success.

He looked at the bodies and the placement of the shots. Duthie's immediate instinctive reaction to the challenge from the sergeant said the IRA man was that of a natural close-in killer. There was no gap between thought and action. It would be, Chrysalis understood perfectly, unwise to upset Duthie. At least until he'd served his purpose.

'You know your business,' Chrysalis said.

Duthie, impassive, said: 'These two wouldn't be the first, not by a long way. And they won't be the last.' There was an iced coldness in his voice when he added: 'So, do we get on with this, or what?'

Chrysalis nodded. There was no time to lose. The clock was ticking.

'We need to move quickly, before the bodies are found. Help me with these,' he said, pointing to the Marine camouflage smocks. 'Put them on. Leave the oilskins here. We'll keep going, get as close as we can. After me, stay close.'

Chrysalis moved into the mist. Duthie followed. The ground was firming beneath their feet. Within ten minutes the two were back on the path that had petered out in the mist near Rowardennan, the path the two patrolling Royal Marines had taken from Altskeith.

Twenty minutes later, the yellow glow of headlights cut through the pea soup. Chrysalis crouched. He counted four lights. Two vehicles came to a halt. The whiteness of Altskeith was clearly visible, reflected in the vehicle lights. Duthie sniffed the exhaust fumes that floated in the mist. The sound of boots on gravel could be heard as the drivers climbed down.

'Right, let's have you,' a voice barked. 'After me, kitchen round the back. Tradesman's entrance. Tea and biscuits.'

Then another voice shouted: 'You, upstairs, sort those bloody blackout curtains. And who's the bright spark that left the headlights on? Move yourself… switch the lights off.'

Duthie and Chrysalis fixed their eyes on the merest thread of light that seeped from a curtained first floor window. There was a hurried, jerking movement as the curtains were drawn fully open by a Marine. For two or three seconds, before the curtains were closed, the thread of light became a blaze. Standing, hands on hips, in that blaze was the man they had come to kill.

Then the misty gloom, like a grey shroud, enveloped Altskeith. There was no light from the trucks and there was no light from that upstairs window.

'Was that our man?' Duthie whispered. 'Because if it was, you'll be on your own. There's no bloody way in the wide world we can get up there. Maybe you might want to give it a try, but not me and that's a fact and a half. In my book, suicide is still a sin, or didn't they tell you that in your German church?'

Chrysalis resisted the urge to tell Duthie he was not in a position to dictate what Chrysalis would or wouldn't do. Duthie was quite capable of turning his pistol on Chrysalis and vanishing into the mist. He was, as he had shown, a man untroubled by killing without hesitation.

'I did not come here to have us killed,' Chrysalis, his voice lowered, said. 'We will finish our work here and when it is done, we will make our way to safety. We will return to the cottage. I will receive our instructions, by wireless and, in a few days, we will be in Berlin.'

***

Beyond the greyness, less than 100 yards from the two intruders, in the sitting room at Altskeith Lodge, a Marine captain, a second lieutenant, a sergeant, Rutter, Villiers, Charteris, and George, Danny and Finola assembled to hear the Brigadier reveal that Hess would be taken to London by road sooner rather than later. The order to move quickly came from London.

'Road will take a fair bit longer,' the Brigadier said, 'but Whitehall says train or aeroplane could be too risky, especially closer to London. You never know where Jerry fliers will turn up down there. Prisoner and escorts will be on the move south as soon as the fog shows signs of clearing.'

Nodding to the Marine captain, he added: 'You can brief your men when we're finished here. Extra ammunition all round. The Whitehall instructions are very clear. Hess is to be delivered alive and, hopefully, not kicking and screaming from some injury sustained between here and Whitehall. It's beyond question that the enemy has a strong desire to see our prisoner dead. And we shouldn't imagine he's beyond their reach here on our patch. Whether or not they know his location is another matter. In the event of some sort of incident en route you are to defend the prisoner with your lives.'

George and Danny exchanged glances. They would have preferred the Brigadier to have said 'our' lives.

The Brigadier caught the exchanged glances and cut in quickly. The Whitehall order applied to all in the room. Naturally, he and Lt. Col. Rutter would be travelling south with the convoy.

In the meantime, there would be no further questioning of Hess until he was in London.

'We'll babysit the bugger, nothing more, from now on,' the Brigadier said.

Then, to George, he said: 'You're rather chummy with our Mister Hess, Major Maclean, what do you think? How will he feel about this? Rather pleased, I imagine. Off to see people in the highest places. Back there on the top shelf where he believes he belongs.'

George answered the Brigadier's indulgent, almost cavalier, tone with a deliberate flippancy that could allow the inference of insubordination. He believed Hess would be little short of delighted. The decision to spirit the prisoner to London at the earliest opportunity was singularly sensible. Obviously, the Brigadier had played a part in that commendable decision.

He added: 'Perhaps, Sir, you being the senior man here, you might want to break the news yourself. Hess has a preference for dealing with people in high places. I can ask him to pop down. I don't think he has a full dance card at the moment.'

There was no perceptible response from the Brigadier.

Danny winked in the direction of George.

Charteris opened his mouth to speak. He was halted by a raised eyebrow from the Brigadier and a nod to Rutter.

'Our organisational wizard,' the Brigadier said, 'will outline the nuts and bolts of the transfer of Hess. Details of the transfer have already been approved by Whitehall.'

'The journey by road from Altskeith to London will take between 13 and 15 hours,' Rutter advised.

'The vehicles you heard arriving a short time ago, those were our chaps from the roadblock where we got the once-over on our way here. They'll keep the place tight as a drum until we get going.

'When we leave, we'll travel in convoy via Aberfoyle to Stirling. Our convoy will consist of two heavy vehicles and three motor cars. Half a dozen Marines in each heavy vehicle and two marines in each car. From Stirling we'll motor, via Edinburgh, down the east coast. Major Maclean, the prisoner and two marines will travel in the motor car in the middle of our convoy.'

Danny was unclear about the implications of journeying to London.

'It's an overseas trip for me. I was wondering about vaccinations and maybe an allowance. When I was in France during the last stramash we got a few extra bob for every week we were over there'.

The Brigadier nodded and smiled away Danny's mischief.

'Any sensible questions? None? Fine. We're all clear on what has to be done. Good, carry on. I'll keep you posted. You should be ready to move at an hour's notice.'

The Brigadier rose from his leather armchair. He smiled towards Rutter. 'First class briefing,' he said. 'Expected nothing less, of course. Born to organise. Shipshape and Bristol Fashion as they say in the Senior Service. Now, what about a glass of sherry? Port? A dram? Come one, come all. Drinks on the house, Dunolly's house, to be exact.'

Charteris and Villiers nodded their acceptance. Danny said he felt obliged to sample Lord Dunolly's cellar. Finola expressed a similar feeling of obligation to her elders and betters.

The Marine captain, lieutenant and sergeant declined. They needed to brief their men and have them ready to move out.

'At the drop of a hat,' Rutter said.

The Brigadier nodded and turned to George. 'Sensible suggestion of yours,' he said. 'Me breaking the news to Hess. Butter him up a bit. Render him a bit more civil. Why don't you pop up and invite him to join us.'

***

There were two almost simultaneous explosions as George returned with Hess. The stick grenades lobbed by Chrysalis and Duthie had four-second fuses. The first stick grenade was thrown by Chrysalis. It landed between two heavy vehicles on the gravel near Altskeith's solid front doors. Debris from the two heavy vehicles was blasted into the signals room on the ground floor. The duty operator, peppered by shrapnel, was killed instantly. The blast collapsed his lungs and threw his body across the room. The radio equipment was destroyed.

The second stick grenade was thrown, by Duthie, towards the first floor room where Hess had been seen. Chrysalis had left his companion with no option but to join the attack.

Inside, on the first floor, the sound of shattered window glass was followed by a deafening crack and the orange swirl of flames. Less than a minute earlier, the grenade would have killed Hess and George Maclean. The decision to brief the prisoner in the ground floor sitting room saved their lives. They cheated death by the merest of margins.

The initial attack took less than twenty seconds. Moving silently towards the heavy vehicles and Altskeith Lodge, the assassins threw two more grenades and, just as silently, retreated into the greyness. They waited, weapons cocked. A dozen crouching Marines, fanned out through the front doors of the building, clearly visible in the flames of the blazing heavy vehicles.

The twelve were cut down in a spray of bullets from Chrysalis. Ten were dead in the instant. Two lay breathing their last.

Chrysalis and Duthie retreated further into the mist. This was not the time to press home the attack, the German said.

'They don't know how many we are. We'll keep it that way. Keep them guessing and keep them inside.'

'And we don't know if we got our man,' Duthie sniped.

On the first floor, two Marines were using exquisite eastern carpets to smother the flames that had come with the blast of the stick grenade. In the ground floor signals room, two more looked quickly at the lifeless body of the signals operator then, through the gap where there had been a window, at the bodies of their dead comrades.

For a few seconds that, to those present, seemed to last an eternity, there was quiet after the carnage of the explosions and the gunfire.

In the sitting room, Villiers was the first to speak.

'Everybody stay down,' he shouted. He needn't have repeated his entreaty. Nobody, at that moment, was moving. The Brigadier and Rutter were crouched under one end of a long, solid, teak table. Danny and Finola were curled under the other end. Villiers and Charteris lay flat by the big open fireplace. Hess and George sheltered behind a red leather sofa.

The Marine lieutenant and his sergeant burst into the room, weapons in hand.

Rutter moved from under the table. 'We need a situation report, Lieutenant,' he said. 'You and the sergeant, get moving. Casualties. Wounded. What's still in working order?'

Rutter seemed a different man from the one Danny had come to know. More decisive and analytic. As though the heat of battle had brought out a different side to him.

'Any injuries here?' Rutter asked, looking around the sitting room.

Charteris was seeping blood from a shallow head wound sustained when, throwing himself onto the floor, he'd crashed into the brickwork around the open fireplace. There were no other injuries. Hess, however, was ashen-faced, visibly shaken and unsettled by the attack.

Villiers glared at the prisoner. 'I'd say some of your pals from Berlin have just made their intentions very clear.'

Hess shot back: 'And I would say, Herr Villiers, that somebody in this room told them where to find me. Somebody here wishes me dead.'

Hess and Villiers stared at each other, unblinking.

Any further exchange between the two was stifled when the Marine lieutenant and the sergeant returned and reported thirteen dead, including their captain. The signals room and the prisoner's quarters were destroyed. Two of their comrades were unaccounted for. They had failed to return from a perimeter patrol. 'A fair bet that whoever just had a go at us also did for our two out on patrol. They must have come over the peat bog,' the lieutenant added.

'Anything else?' the Brigadier asked.

'Two heavy vehicles destroyed,' the lieutenant said, 'and, without the signals room, we're isolated. We're on our own.'

'I don't suppose,' the Brigadier asked, 'you have anything by way of good news?'

The lieutenant tilted his head and breathed in deeply. 'We have one heavy vehicle untouched behind the building and we have the ten men who were bunked down near the kitchen when this lot started,' he said. 'And we have the two who've been upstairs and the two taking a look at the signals room. Sixteen of us in all – that's counting myself and the sergeant here. We've got the doors and windows covered and I've just put three men on the roof. I suppose that might pass for good news.'

The Brigadier threw a question to the room: 'Options?'

Villiers said, 'We make a run for it, that's my idea of the best option. There wouldn't be more than two or three, maybe four, out there. No more than that. You use a small team for what they're up to. In and out and off they go. A bigger team – ten or twelve – wouldn't be easy to pull together quickly, if at all. And a bigger team wouldn't have hit and run. They'd have come straight in and found what they were looking for, no messing about.'

Hess, agitated, demanded to know how the attackers had been able to target his first-floor quarters. He repeated his assertion: 'In this room there is somebody who told my attackers where to find me. Someone here wishes me dead.' He appeared to be on the verge of hysteria.

The Brigadier nodded towards George. 'Let's hear what Major Maclean has to say about this,' he said. 'You appear to have placed some considerable trust in the good Major.'

'Herr Hess, I am sure our Brigadier will confirm to you that we have orders from the very highest places to guard you with our lives,' George said, speaking in German. Then he added: 'I doubt there is any person in this room who will depart from these orders.'

George was dissembling. But this wasn't the time for him to say he believed that German sympathisers or German agents, and most certainly German Military Intelligence, had probably been aware of where Hess was from the moment he set foot in Lochard House to his transfer to Altskeith.

It wasn't the time, either, to say he believed that someone on the inside – in Whitehall or in the Second City of Empire – was playing a deadly double game. George could do without a hysterical Hess.

The Brigadier motioned Villiers to continue his observations on what plan of action might be considered.

'So, we'll assume we're up against a small group. Whoever is out there,' Villiers said, 'doesn't know we've lost radio and telephone contact. For all they know, we've called in the cavalry. They won't know, either, if they've despatched Mister Hess here. So they'll make their move soon. They've come this far, they won't back away now. They'll want to see a body, the body of Mister Hess.

'They're on foot. They came across the peat bogs. That's their best way in and out. By vehicle along the road from Aberfoyle would have been far too risky.'

The Brigadier pressed Villiers: 'We probably know all that. I asked for your plan of action.'

Villiers was silent.

After a moment, Charteris took the lead: 'We make a run for it. Leave half a dozen of the lieutenant's boys to lay down covering fire while we go like the hounds of hell... into the heavy vehicle at the back… into the cars… four or five hundred yards and we're out of their effective range… along the loch road to Aberfoyle and the local police station. You're the senior man. Just give the order.'

The Brigadier turned to Danny: 'Sergeant, you saw your share of action in the last Big Show, Highland Light Infantry as I recall… stay or go… back foot or front foot?'

Danny was a front foot man. 'We should take it to whoever is out there. In France, the Germans called the HLI "Hell's Last Issue.' When we came at them, the Germans knew they were in for a right fight. So, we'll give them one. Plenty of covering fire from the Marines, and we run like the clappers to the vehicles. We'll be out of harm's way in a minute. If we stay here, whoever is out there is calling the shots. We're fish in a barrel.'

'No time to lose, sir,' Rutter said to the Brigadier. 'Your orders?'

Six soldiers would remain at Altskeith, the Brigadier said. They'd lay down covering fire while Hess, Major Maclean, Sergeant Inglis, the lieutenant and six Marines made a 25-yard dash from the rear of the building to the unscathed heavy vehicle. The soldiers would also provide covering fire while Charteris, Villiers, the Brigadier, Rutter, Finola and three Marines dashed for the cars that had brought them from Lochard House.

'One car in front, heavy vehicle next and two cars bringing up the rear,' the Brigadier ordered. 'Then we hammer it along to Aberfoyle, hunker down in the local police station and call in some extra pairs of boots from the Military Police at Stirling Castle. The chaps we leave behind here will have to fend for themselves until then. Any questions?'

There was silence.

'Right,' the Brigadier said. He turned to the lieutenant and his sergeant.

'Get your men organised. Ready to go in ten minutes.

Automatic weapons and spare magazines for everybody in here, with the exception of Herr Hess, of course. We might be needing more than service revolvers for this one.'

'I'll have two of my boys bring the weapons and I'll get the rest in position for our dash,' the lieutenant said.

Hess was grey-faced. His dark eyes were unblinking, vacant. Hitler's Deputy was afraid. The self-assurance had vanished. His mission to Britain was not going as planned.

George looked at Hess. He thought of the Nazi rallies he'd witnessed in his student summers in Berlin. The drums and flags, the swagger of the uniformed thugs, the adulation of the masses, arms raised in the Hitler salute. He'd picked them then for cowards and bullies. The grey-faced, fearful, Hess standing there in the Altskeith sitting room confirmed that long-held view. Hess was an empty man. A shell of a human being.

Two Marines appeared. They distributed automatic weapons and spare magazines.

'Some of you will have handled these before,' the shorter of the two soldiers said, 'but a freshen up never goes astray. Watch what he does.' He pointed to his comrade.

'Right,' the taller man said. 'Lovely bit of kit this is. A life-saver and a widow-maker all in one. Now, load this way. Safety on. Safety off. Point. Firm grip. Squeeze the trigger and Bob's your uncle. Simple. Can't go wrong. Aim for the central body mass and keep shooting until the target is down. Always finish them off.'

The lieutenant returned. 'Ready to make our move in five minutes, sir,' he told the Brigadier. 'The heavy vehicle group out the back with my men. Yourself and the others out the front.'

'Any sign of movement out there?' The Brigadier asked.

The lieutenant shook his head. 'We don't know what we're up against.'

Four minutes later he, and six of his Marines, were dead. They would not be the last to die protecting Adolf Hitler's Deputy that day.

Chapter seventeen: Do or die

To each, there comes a special moment in life when they are figuratively tapped on the shoulder and offered a chance to do a very special thing… what a tragedy if that moment finds them unprepared—
Attr. Winston Churchill.

A spray of bullets sliced through the lieutenant and his men the moment they started their dash from the kitchen to the heavy vehicle at the rear of the building. They dropped like condemned prisoners through a gallows trapdoor.

Hess, George and Danny instinctively fell to their knees and rolled away from the half-open kitchen door. Crab-like, they scampered towards the sitting room.

The gunfire that mowed down the soldiers and their young officer was followed by the blast of a grenade tossed by Chrysalis from the cover of a thicket of trees. The grenade landed on the canvas canopy that covered the rear of the vehicle. There was an eruption of orange. Shards of metal flew through the air. The vehicle was engulfed in flames. Its tyres and petrol tank exploded.

A brief burst of fire from Duthie, breaking cover, raked the front of the building. Too late, the defenders on the roof saw grenades tossed towards them. They had no chance. The explosions sent tremors through the solid stone building.

On the ground floor, stray bullets from Duthie's rapid fire ripped through curtains and shattered the sitting room windows. The bullets felled Charteris and Villiers. Charteris, his elbow exposed to the bone, lay in a state of shock. Danny, using his belt as a tourniquet, worked to staunch the flow of blood.

Finola crawled towards Villiers. He was dead. Near the door of the sitting room, two Marines crouched, their faces pock-marked from flying shards of glass. Their sergeant, unscathed, sat hunched, weapon cocked and at the ready, by the ripped curtains.

Hess was on his knees, shouting in German, waving his arms, beckoning to the others in the room. This particular member of the Master Race did not, there and then, have the demeanour of a leader of men.

The shouting stopped when Finola, darting over the motionless body of Villiers, delivered a stinging backhander to the face of the prisoner. The force of the blow sent Hess sprawling. The Brigadier and Rutter stared, taken aback by the swiftness of Finola's action. She returned the stare. 'Girl Guides first aid training,' she said. 'A good, hefty smack always does the trick with a shouter. The instructors at Spean Bridge said much the same.'

George raised a hand. Finola stopped talking. 'He was shouting that there's another way out,' George said. 'He says there's another way out. I was right all along. He has been here before.'

Looking at Rutter, George demanded: 'What's he talking about? You know this place. You're Dunolly's man. What's the other way out?'

The question to Rutter was answered by Hess. His hysteria despatched by the slap that had sent him sprawling, he reverted to English. He had visited Altskeith in 1937.

'Herr Rutter knows nothing of when I was here before. I came in secret. Your Herr Rutter is only a servant. A servant in uniform.'

There was no visible response from Rutter.

Hess continued: 'I was in London at our Embassy. It was easy to slip away. An Embassy car to a private airstrip near Gatwick and a private flight north. I came here to see Lord Dunolly. He seemed not unsympathetic to our Reich. He was not alone in his admiration for our New Germany.'

The pieces were falling into place.

Hess was cut short by the Brigadier. 'We can have it chapter and verse when we get out of here. Not right now. Whoever is outside will have another go. Where's this other way out?'

There was, Hess said, a door in the cellar below the kitchen. It lay behind a pyramid of casks of port and sherry and Muscat and malt whisky. These were the jewels in Lord Dunolly's private reserve.

'Behind the door is a passage that runs to the trees behind this house, a passage of perhaps forty or fifty metres. There is an electric lighting switch just inside the passage. Lord Dunolly took me there. He made a joke when he showed me. He said if the Communists in the coal miners ever rose up and came for him, he would escape through the passage. It was his secret. Nobody else knew. He showed me the key to the padlock on the door. He said his was the only key. It was the same key that he used on the padlock on the inside of the trapdoor at the end of the passage. When he opened the trapdoor we were in the trees.'

The Brigadier snapped: 'The sergeant and his two men will remain here. They're our rear-guard. And you, Sergeant Inglis, you too. Never hurts to have an old HLI man in the mix.'

Danny had seen a few rear-guard actions in his time in the trenches. Most were terrifying. None were easy and all were bloody. Involuntarily he sniffed. He could almost smell the blood and the sourness of cold sweat.

The Brigadier turned to Charteris. The wounded man was conscious but white with pain. 'We'll get you hunkered down behind one of the sofas,' the Brigadier said.

Charteris would be alone in the sitting room. Two Marines would position themselves in the hallway, covering the front door. Danny Inglis and the Marine sergeant would position themselves by the kitchen door.

'The rest of us will make our move through the passage from the cellar,' the Brigadier said. 'Maclean and Captain Fraser in front. Herr Hess next. Then you, Rutter. And I'll be the tail-end Charlie. When we get outside, we'll stay under cover. If we can get round the front to the motor cars, we will. If not... we stay hidden and hope to God our rear-guard polishes off whoever is out there.'

It took two bullets from George's service revolver to shatter the heavy brass padlock that secured the door to the passageway in the cellar. The noise in the confined space was near deafening. Slithers of brass became shrapnel and punctured four of the prized private reserve casks. The confined cellar space was instantly thick with the mingling sweet scents of fortified wines and the spiced aroma of malt whisky.

The door swung open easily. Inside the passageway, it was as dark as any of Lord Dunolly's coal mines. 'The switch,' Hess said. 'The switch is there on the wall. Somewhere on the wall.'

George stepped inside. His hands ran across the rough, damp brickwork. He could feel nothing. He reached for the wall on the other side of the tunnel. Nothing. Then, the smoothness of a Bakelite switch. A click later, and the darkness was gone. Half a dozen light bulbs cast a dim yellow glow along the length of the passage. The smell of mould reminded Hess of the boiled cabbage he'd been forced to eat as a sickly child. He gagged. He could taste the memory.

Closing the cellar door behind him, George led the group in Indian file along the length of the tunnel. A shot from his revolver smashed open the padlock on the trapdoor. He pushed upwards. There was no movement. The trapdoor had not been opened for years. Some roots had worked their way through the edges of its thick timbers.

Hess, then Finola, moved beside George. *One. Two. Three. Go. One. Two. Three. Go.* The trapdoor opened. Pine-scented air filled their nostrils as the group scrambled up and into the thicket of timber. The rear of Altskeith was no more than forty metres away through the lifting mist. There was, for perhaps a minute, neither sound nor movement around the building.

Then, from the front of the building, came the roar of a grenade and the crack of an automatic weapon. Smack. Smack. Smack. A crouching figure, firing from the hip, ran, towards the fractured, half-open heavy main door of Altskeith Lodge. Two Royal Marines, the door sheltering them from the blast, found their target. The running man, legs shattered, crumpled on the steps that led to the door, his weapon cast aside as he fell. He screamed. He was going nowhere.

One of the soldiers shouted at the wounded attacker: 'How many more are out there? How many? Tell me or I'll kill you here and now, sure as God.'

The man pleaded for help. The plea was ignored.

'How many,' the soldier demanded.

'One. There's only the one,' the man said. 'For Jesus' sake, help me.' The Ulster accent was unmistakeable.

'Where's your murdering mate... where,' the soldier shouted.

His questioning was halted – and answered – by the chatter from Danny's automatic weapon levelled at the figure running towards Altskeith's kitchen at the rear of the house. The figure ducked and rolled and returned fire. A bullet smacked into Danny's shoulder. He fell back against the frame of the kitchen door. He slid down, clutching at the wound, blood seeping between his fingers. Another bullet from the rolling man silenced the Marine sergeant by Danny's side. The bullet pierced the sergeant's heart.

From the cover of the thicket of trees around the trapdoor of the passageway that ran from Dunolly's cellar, George raced towards Danny. The attacker, now on his feet, levelled his weapon at George.

Instinctively, George ducked and felt the whistle of a bullet that missed his head by two inches, no more. The bullet was fired from behind. It struck the attacker high on his right arm. He dropped his weapon and clutched the wound.

George straightened, and sprang towards the wounded attacker. A second bullet was fired from behind. Again, the man was struck high on the right arm. Again, George ducked.

Finola raced past him, smoking service revolver in hand. She pounced on the still-standing attacker. The Spean Bridge training was put to brutal use. A hammer-blow punch thudded into the attacker's wounds. He doubled up. Finola's knee thudded into the man's face. He was sprawled on the ground when Finola stamped a boot on the man's right arm then pushed the cocked service revolver into the man's bloodied face.

'I'll blow your head off if you so much as blink,' she shouted, pushing the barrel of the revolver harder into his face, breaking the skin.

Some desperate, pleading words left his lips. He was speaking German. 'Sorry, I don't speak Jerry,' Finola said, again pushing her revolver against the man's face.

George, knelt by the wounded Danny, examined his shoulder wound and said: 'You'll live. Straight in. Straight out. You'll be lifting pint glasses in a week.'

Danny struggled with a forced smile. It failed to disguise his pain and his fear. Half-conscious he was remembering, again, the trenches of Northern France around Arras and Douai and the faces of the men who succumbed to seemingly minor wounds, men who simply died of shock.

George was reassuring. Danny would be fine. Promise. They'd be into a car and off down the loch to Aberfoyle quick smart. There was a doctor there. And, if needs be, Danny could be in the Infirmary at Stirling within an hour. But only if he needed X-rays. It might not come to that. It was a through-and-through wound, George said again. Straight-in-straight-out.

George looked at Finola. 'That knee-in-the-face trick of yours,' he said. 'You didn't learn that in the Girl Guides.'

'A simple thank you would be adequate,' Finola said. There was the trace of a smile on her lips.

A Marine appeared behind Danny in the kitchen doorway. It was, he said, all clear round the front.

He added: 'There was only the two of them according to the sod we did for on the front steps. The one back there, and you got the other one round here. The one at the front won't be long for this life. Bloody Fenian took a few in the legs. One of the lads is round the front keeping an eye on the bugger. Not that he'll be making a run for it.

'Your man Charteris, the London bloke, is back where you left him in the sitting room... still knocked about... but he's better than our lads on the roof and' – he looked at his dead comrades and their young lieutenant – 'these lads here.'

He lobbed a webbing haversack towards George. 'There's field dressings and morphine in this,' he said. 'It looks like you could use them on Sergeant Inglis there.'

George stood. 'You stay here and keep an eye on this toerag,' he said, nodding at the downed attacker. 'Captain Fraser can slap some of these dressings on Danny. I'll get round the front and look at this Irishman of yours... then we'll get going right away... The cars are still in one piece?'

The Marine said the three cars were untouched. A bloody miracle it was, too.

George made to move when Rutter, the Brigadier and Hess appeared from the thicket of pine trees. The Brigadier, revolver in hand, moved quickly, almost running, and stood over the wounded attacker. He cocked the weapon, and in that instant the attacker moaned 'Kingfisher... *Der gute Kamerade.*'

George recognised the words. They were from a German Army song... *Once I Had a Good Comrade.*

'God almighty,' George said. 'It's you... you're bloody Kingfisher. The inside man. You treacherous swine. And this bugger is Chrysalis.'

The Brigadier squeezed the trigger, and the German

was dead, shot between the eyes. Hess, five yards behind the Brigadier, recoiled at the noise and the swiftness of the killing. Rutter, alongside Hess, neither moved nor showed any reaction.

The Brigadier stepped away from the dead man's body, levelling his pistol at George and the Marine. He ordered them to kneel. 'Captain Fraser, too,' he added. 'Weapons on the ground. Now.'

The momentary refusal of the three to comply instantly ended when the Brigadier mortally wounded the Marine with a shot to the chest.

George and Finola did as they were told. They kneeled.

Hess, terrified, began to bargain. There were those in high places who would see the Brigadier well-rewarded for ensuring Hess arrived in London safely.

The Brigadier was dismissive. There were those in high places who had much to lose by the arrival of Herr Hess in London.

'Before the utterly unnecessary outbreak of hostilities between Britain and Germany, you could have served some purpose. Now you're just a liability. You're surplus to requirements, a liability. Worse, you're a coward and a traitor.'

Rutter stepped between Hitler's Deputy and the Brigadier.

'You think I won't shoot you, Rutter,' the Brigadier said. 'I've wanted to shoot you ever since you arrived at Lochard House. You and your damned phoney commission. Lieutenant-Colonel my rear end.

'You're not a soldier's bootlace. You're only wearing that uniform because Dunolly needed somebody to water the plants and keep an eye on the silverware for the duration. You're a smarmy filing clerk. That's what you are. You're the trouble with this country. You and millions of soft-handed, spineless sods like you. And Herr Hess here… back-stabbing Hitler, the only man who will stand up to the Bolsheviks and the Jews.'

Rutter stared at the Brigadier. 'Back-stabbing? You're the

only back-stabbing swine here.' His voice was firm and unafraid.

'I'm many things, Brigadier, but I'm no two-faced traitor. Go on,' he said. 'Shoot me. Whatever happens, you're finished. You'll never get away.'

The Brigadier shook his head.

'On the contrary. I'll be the only one left standing. You all perished in the attack. How very sad. I'll say how bravely you fought. I might even recommend a medal or two. How would that be...? Posthumously, of course. It will all be hushed up by Whitehall. They'll run the line that Herr Hess is alive and well and spilling the beans. But Berlin will know otherwise, I'll see to that. And when this soft, pathetic little country of ours hoists the white flag, I'll be the one who gets a medal.'

Hess crouched behind Rutter. George and Finola were silent. Both knew that the Brigadier, having despatched the Marine and Chrysalis, had four bullets left in his revolver. After Hess and Rutter were downed, the two remaining bullets would be reserved for them. Then, after reloading, the Brigadier would finish off Danny.

Rutter had made the same cold calculation. Comes the time, comes the man, a school teacher had once told him. He could take the first bullet. There was a chance, just a chance, that George and Finola could overpower the Brigadier before the second bullet found Hess.

Rutter lunged at his tormentor. Instantly, George sprang towards the Brigadier. There was a single shot. The Brigadier crumpled, blood pumping from a ragged exit wound in his thigh. The last thing he saw before he passed out was Danny, half-sitting, a pistol dropping from his hand.

'I never trusted the bugger. A bit too chin-chin,' Danny said. 'A Glasgow copper's sixth sense. Never fails.'

There was silence. George and Rutter helped the crouching, trembling Hess to his feet. Finola turned to Danny. 'This copper's sixth sense of yours,' she said. 'You left it a bit damned late to let us in on it.'

A Marine, the only surviving soldier, emerged from the half-open kitchen door, his automatic weapon at the ready. He had crawled, slowly, cautiously, from the shattered front door when the shooting began. He surveyed the carnage. The grenade-blasted heavy vehicle. His dead comrades. The bleeding, unconscious Brigadier.

'God Almighty,' he said. 'They got the Brigadier.'

George corrected him. 'No, we got the Brigadier,' he said.

The soldier shook his head. What did the Major mean? Who shot the Brigadier?... and why?

'Explanations later,' George said. 'We have to get away from here first. What about the other one round the front... the one you shot.'

The soldier drew a finger across his throat. The other attacker was dead. Stone cold. He had bled to death. What were the Major's orders?

George looked at Rutter. 'You're the senior officer here, now,' he said. 'Orders?' He half-expected the direction 'carry on, Major.' After all, until a few minutes earlier, Rutter had not shone as an obvious leader of men.

Instead, Rutter spoke without hesitation or a hint of adrenalin-fuelled bravado. His voice was barely raised: 'Into the vehicles out front. Herr Hess, Major Maclean and myself in one. Captain Fraser and Sergeant Inglis and Mister Charteris and our Marine in the second. So what do we call you, Private...'

'Private Forrest,' the soldier said. 'Private Sandy Forrest.'

'Right,' Rutter directed. 'Into the motor cars. Pack one of those field dressings in the Brigadier's wound, staunch any bleeding, fill him up with morphine and put him in the boot. Straight along the loch. Stop for nothing until we reach the police at Aberfoyle. Any questions?'

There were none.

***

The dancing image of flames first flickering and then leaping from the burning roof of Altskeith was framed in the rear-view mirrors of the departing cars. Half an hour later, the bloodied and shaken survivors of the attack found the safety of the Aberfoyle police station.

Another thirty minutes passed before two army ambulances, two doctors and ten Redcaps arrived from their Stirling Castle headquarters. Danny and Charteris were taken, under Military Police escort, to Stirling Royal Infirmary. The Brigadier, watched by two Redcaps and a doctor, Rutter ordered, should be taken to the sick bay at the Castle.

'Just keep him breathing and write down anything he says. Myself, Major Maclean, Captain Fraser, Private Forrest and our German friend here will follow on to Stirling Castle HQ in ten minutes.'

Rutter looked at the grey-faced Brigadier. 'You'll hang for this,' he said.

'Quite the little jumped-up General, aren't you,' the Brigadier said.

Ignoring the barb, Rutter turned to the Aberfoyle police sergeant.

'Perhaps you have a private room and a telephone I might use.'

Alone, Rutter picked up the handset. The local telephone exchange operator asked: 'What number can I get you?'

Rutter replied, 'Whitehall one-two-one-two, thank you. And I'd be obliged if you didn't listen in. It could get you shot.'

The operator said she had better things to do than listen in to private calls, thank you. Rutter said he was pleased to hear this.

The call to Whitehall lasted for twenty minutes. Within the hour, Rutter, George, Finola, Private Sandy Forrest and Hess were behind the walls of Stirling Castle. The Brigadier, his wound cleaned, packed and dressed, was under guard in the Castle's small sick bay.

By then, Lord Dunolly's highland retreat was fully ablaze. White smoke billowed across the mirror-flat waters of Loch Ard. The smoke mingled with the clearing mist.

Chapter eighteen: Sleeping dogs

The Military Cross is awarded for an act or acts of exemplary gallantry during active operations against the enemy on land to all members of our armed forces. The Distinguished Service Medal is, when awarded, recognition of bravery and resourcefulness under fire—
War Department – decorations protocol (23B), 1941.

When darkness gave way to light, George and Finola left the Castle. Both were wearing the ill-fitting tunics and shirts and trousers supplied by the Garrison Quartermaster when they arrived.

Danny was sitting up, half-awake, almost light-headed, when the two entered the two-bed room, marked 'Private,' at the Stirling Royal Infirmary. Charteris, a few feet away, was heavily sedated. Blood had stained the bandages that covered his splinted wounded arm. Some blood had seeped onto the white, crisply starched bed sheets.

Seven hours had passed since the four parted company at the Aberfoyle police station.

'You took your time,' Danny said. 'I don't know what it is they've been pumping into me but it works a treat. Anyhow, what kept you? Rutter's bloody paperwork, I suppose. Still, no more complaints from me. I don't know where he got it, but there's some steel in that backbone. He's either a brilliant actor or my Glasgow polis sixth sense has seen better days.'

Finola Fraser suggested it might be a bit of both. There was, she was sure, much more to Rutter than met the eye. Whether or not they ever found out exactly what didn't meet the eye... well, there was a war on. People had secrets. Sleeping dogs were often left to lie, the cloak and dagger business was like that; conducted in a hall of mirrors.

'What's the verdict on you and our Mister Charteris over there?' she asked.

'I was lucky,' Danny said. 'Bullet in and bullet out, just like George said. No broken bones. Nothing vital damaged. There's a bit of a throb right down the arm. I suggested a nice drop of highland malt would soften the pain, but they said a needle was the way to go... and they were dead right.' He shook his head and added: 'You wouldn't credit this... I got through the last war with hardly a scratch and I get shot on home turf. No long-term damage, according to the Quack. They'll keep me here for a few days, maybe a week. Arm in a sling for a month after that, they say. Let the muscles knit, that's the idea. Good job it isn't my darts arm.'

Charteris had been less fortunate.

'I heard the doctor say the elbow was shattered,' Danny said. 'Bits of bone here and there. He'll have to drink with his other arm now. He was in a bad way. White as a shroud with the pain. Didn't say a word, not a whimper, when the doctor was poking about. Refused morphine at first but the doctor injected it anyway. They're going to operate today. He's a tough bloke for a Sassenach. Maybe he had a Scots Granny.

'So, what's the story up at the Castle? Rutter, Hess, the Brigadier... our young Private Sandy Forrest?'

George shrugged. There wasn't, really, that much he could add to what Danny already knew. Private Sandy Forrest had gone back to Altskeith with the Redcaps to identify the bodies. The Brigadier was in no immediate danger. His wound was messy rather than mortal. Regardless, he wouldn't be walking anywhere for a while. And he wouldn't, ever, be walking anywhere without a stick.

'I have a notion that they'll cart him off somewhere very private down south and have a good wee talk with him. I can't see it being the friendliest of discussions. Not too many pleasantries. Nobody would want to be in his shoes when he gets handed over. Anyhow, he won't get any sympathy from me. He made his bed... he can lie in it.'

Rutter, George told Danny, had been on the telephone to Whitehall half a dozen times. Hess, still demanding to speak with people in the highest places, was in comfortable quarters with two Redcaps watching his every move.

'Rutter says a security detail is coming up from Whitehall right now,' George said. 'They'll be in charge of taking Hess down to London. They're flying up and then straight back down with a Spitfire escort. An hour and a bit each way... depends on the weather. They ditched the plan to go down by road. Too long. Maybe too risky after last night. Always the chance of somebody else having a crack at Hess. Anyhow, that's their problem. Right now, I think we might be surplus to requirements. They won't need us any more and I can't say that I'm sorry. I'll tell you one thing, though. Rutter seems very, very pally with some high-ups down south... the way he was talking to them on the telephone. He was in another room up at the Castle but he wasn't keeping his voice down. Finola's right, he's a dark horse. From what I can work out...'

George never finished the sentence. A nurse entered the room. There was, she said, a telephone call for a Major Maclean. 'Someone by the name of Rutter. This way, please.' The telephone was at the nurses' station, just up the corridor. Second on the left.

***

Finola was adjusting Danny's pillow when George returned.

'I could get used to this,' Danny said. 'Pillow fluffed up and me nicely tucked in.'

Finola shook her head. Danny could get used to a thick ear if he said another word.

George looked at Danny and smiled. Sergeant Inglis

would have to settle for one of the nurses doing the pillow fluffing and the tucking-in for the duration of his stay at the Stirling Royal Infirmary.

Then, looking at Finola, he said, 'It appears that we're not yet surplus to requirements. Rutter wants us back at the Castle. Pronto. And then we're going down to London as soon as the Whitehall detail collects Hess. Rutter as well. He's going down with us. The Brigadier will go south on a separate plane. The doctors said there were no problems with moving him elsewhere. Don't know where, though. Somewhere right out of sight, for sure, well away from any neighbours. Somewhere the Whitehall hardmen have him all to themselves and won't be disturbed. I doubt we'll see him again. Not our business any more. According to Rutter we're to meet some bigwigs down there. Haven't a clue who they might be but they want a face-to-face account of what happened out at Altskeith. Chapter and verse.'

Finola raised her eyebrows. 'Bigwigs… we've fairly come up in the world. Babysitters one day and rubbing shoulders with bigwigs the next. So, I suppose we're off right now?'

George nodded to Danny: 'If there's any glory going,' he said, 'we'll make sure you get a mention.'

Danny doubted there was any prospect of glory.

'How it works,' he said, 'is if everything goes wrong, the likes of us down the ladder get the blame. If anything goes right, it's the higher-ups who get the credit. Why do you think I'm still a bloody sergeant?'

***

It was a bumpy flight in the Royal Air Force Transport Command Dakota from Stirling. Patches of low cloud and strong headwinds made it slow-going.

The best part of two-and-a-half hours passed before the Dakota reached the safety of Bristow Hall airstrip outside

London. The Dakota was escorted by three Spitfire fighters from RAF Turnhouse on the outskirts of Edinburgh.

The fighter escort was a necessary precaution as the transport plane headed south and further south. The unarmed Dakota was an easy and tempting target for any Luftwaffe fighters and bombers probing air defences in south-east England.

Hess and George Maclean sat together. Four big men, Whitehall men in trench coats, sat behind and in front of them. Rutter and Finola sat together. All were offered tea from a thermos flask and corned beef sandwiches by an RAF flight sergeant. Hess, dismissive, waved away the offer of refreshments. The fear that had near paralysed him during the attack at Altskeith had gone. He was back to being Hitler's arrogant and churlish deputy.

'Suit yourself, pal,' the sergeant said. 'I'll have them.' His words were lost in the noise of the Dakota's engines.

Three big, unmarked black cars met the Dakota when it taxied to a halt well away from the hangars at the Bristow Hall airstrip. Hess protested when he and George were ushered towards separate vehicles by the big Whitehall men. Rutter, smiling and reassuring, intervened when an agitated Hess demanded to travel with George and then insisted on being told where he was being taken.

Raising his voice, Hess said: 'I am not some nobody to be passed from hand to hand as the fancy takes you. You will tell me now what my destination is and you will agree to my demand that Major Maclean remains with me. I have grown used to his pleasant company.'

'Herr Hess,' Rutter said. 'You are being taken to somewhere very safe and very comfortable. You are here in London as you have requested. We will have you settled in and then I am sure we can arrange for you to meet the people you wish to meet.

'Major Maclean and Captain Fraser and myself have some formalities to attend to. Our superiors wish to hear details of the events that have so far taken place. You, of all men, surely understand the need to follow the instructions of superiors. I am certain Major Maclean will rejoin you when our superiors have finished with us.'

Hess was reassured. 'Of course,' he said. 'We follow orders.'

He extended a hand towards Rutter. There was a firm handshake. Then, from Hess, an unexpected apology. 'Herr Rutter,' he said, 'I forget too quickly that it was your actions that saved my life. And I forget too quickly my harsh words towards you. I was mistaken. You are a man of courage. You deserve to wear the uniform of a soldier. My only sadness is that our uniforms make us enemies.'

Rutter thanked Hess for his words. 'Most generous,' Rutter said. 'Now, perhaps, we should all be on our way.'

He watched as Hess was driven towards and then beyond the Bristow Hall control tower. Rutter wiped his right hand on his thigh. He turned to George and Finola. 'Bugger had very sweaty palms,' he said. 'Glad to see the back of him. Nothing but trouble since the off. Right, into our motor car, and into town. Half an hour will do it nicely. The driver knows where to take us.'

George was silent as the vehicle purred towards a city centre ravaged by nightly German bombing. In some places, entire streets had been flattened. Here and there a single residential building stood, untouched among the smoking rubble and gutted rows of houses. Fractured water mains turned bomb craters into deep ponds. Women filled prams with what they could salvage from the ruins of their homes. Two or three times the vehicle accelerated past skull and crossbones signs that warned: 'Danger – unexploded bomb – stay clear.'

This was the front line.

Women, children, cats, dogs, old people, men home on leave, firemen, nurses, they were all fair game in this war. London, Clydebank, Liverpool, Newcastle, Belfast,

Manchester, Plymouth, Coventry – every city was on the Luftwaffe's target list.

Seated alongside the uniformed driver, Rutter turned to George and Finola.

'All a bit reminiscent of Clydebank,' he said. 'Damned German savages. They'll reap what they sow, though. By the time this show is over, there won't be a building left in Germany. They started this awful business and we'll finish it. If they want savagery, we can show them how it's done. We will flatten them and then we will come back and flatten them again.' The vehemence in Rutter's words was chilling.

George thought of his days in pre-war Berlin. The beautiful buildings and parks and wide streets and museums and galleries. He thought of the cultured, generous, lively Germans he'd encountered in those student days. He imagined Berlin in flames. The savage would become the savaged. That was always the way of things. He knew this to be true. He'd studied history at Edinburgh University. He said nothing.

He looked at Rutter. The self-satisfied, penny-pinching Officer-in-Charge, Administration, Records and Allowances, Military Intelligence Glasgow/Clyde Sector of 24 hours earlier was nowhere to be seen. Perhaps this was his twin. Or perhaps the wolf had cast off his sheep's clothing.

The vehicle halted by the steps of a heavily sandbagged building in Whitehall. Armed sentries, bayonets fixed, checked the military identity cards of the three. They were escorted to a ground floor reception desk where the identity cards were rechecked. The sergeant behind the desk scanned a clipboard and ticked off the names – Rutter, Maclean, Fraser. He pointed to a wooden bench.

'Please, take a seat over there,' he said. 'You are expected. I'll telephone to advise you are here. Somebody will be along shortly.'

Ten minutes later, the three were escorted to a well-appointed first floor office. When they entered, they were met by a red-faced, middle-aged officer. His shoulder insignia marked him as a senior member of the Intelligence Corps. He looked unusually affable for a man whose core business was mayhem and duplicity. Of course, appearances could be deceptive. George thought of Rutter.

The affable, red-faced man introduced himself to George and Finola.

'Brigadier Frank Towler,' he said. 'Delighted to have you here. I gather you've done some rather sterling service in trying circumstances.' He turned to Rutter and offered his hand. 'Elphinstone, dear fellow. Glad you could make it. Touch-and-go from what I gathered from your telephone calls in the early hours. Bullets zinging about, Highland mansions in flames. And, finally Brigadier Ewan Stuart put a foot wrong. Well worth the wait. We've had our suspicions as you very well know.'

George and Finola exchanged bewildered glances. Towler caught their confusion. 'Plenty of time for explanations later,' he said. 'The main thing for the moment is to get written and signed statements from the three of you. Winnie wants the details, chapter and verse. The statements shouldn't present any great challenge to either of you two – reporters, I understand, are used to this writing things down business. Elphinstone is a dab hand at reports, too. I've seen a few in recent months. A rather dry style, but he doesn't miss a thing. Strong on detail.' Without waiting for a reaction, he continued, 'Just get it all on paper. Everything that happened up at Dunolly's highland hideaway. Who did what. Who shot who. When you're done, I'll send the statements straight to Winnie. You'll be here today and tomorrow, perhaps a bit longer.' He couldn't say for sure, but Winnie might well want to have a chat.

George's jaw dropped. Finola's eyes widened. 'Winnie?' they said simultaneously.

'You'll like him, I'm sure,' Towler said. 'Can be a bit gruff. Sees right through any flannel. Very dry sense of humour. For now, though, we'll put you up at the Services Club just around from Piccadilly. Very comfortable. Stayed there myself quite a few times. Even with rationing, they still do a good dinner. I assume the kit you're wearing was supplied by the people at Stirling. A bit on the long and baggy side, particularly for Captain Fraser. Can't have you looking like that in these corridors of power. The people at the Services Club can fit you out with something a bit more suitable. They have a cloak room full of uncollected glad rags, civvies mostly. Guests who left in a hurry or didn't come back. Their loss, your gain, really. I'll get somebody round to fetch you tomorrow, mid-morning. Better to be on hand if you're called to glory. Sign for whatever it is you need at the Services Club.'

George, raising his eyebrows, looked at Rutter.

'Yes, before you ask,' Rutter said, 'I'm sure His Majesty's Government can stretch to a bottle of gin, just the one, though. And Muscat for Captain Fraser.'

Towler cleared his throat. 'Well, considering the state of play and the size of the catch, one bottle of gin and one bottle of Muscat seems rather restrained. I'm sure our largesse could extend beyond that. Writing statements can be thirsty work. But business before pleasure. You should make a start on the statements. Wouldn't do to keep Winnie waiting.'

Rutter agreed. No, indeed, Winnie didn't like being kept waiting.

His tone suggested he and Winnie had crossed paths before.

Chapter nineteen: Corridors of power

When the air raid siren sounded, the dining room at the Services Club was empty save for Rutter, George and Finola and a waiter who made it obvious he'd rather be elsewhere. In bed, probably.

The clock showed midnight. It had taken all of the afternoon and early evening for the three to complete their statements in longhand.

Rutter looked at the dining room ceiling. 'Our signals boffins pick up the Luftwaffe about halfway across the Channel,' he said. 'That gives us twenty minutes to finish dessert and get downstairs to the shelter. You could just about set your watch by the Germans. They like to get everybody out of bed. Bugger up civilian morale while they bugger up the docks. The East End will probably be in for another hammering.' He shook his head. 'Still, Towler was spot-on; the Club does a very decent dinner in the circumstances. Mustn't grumble. We're the lucky ones tonight.'

Just how lucky was obvious in the dawn after the all-clear sounded. Londoners emerged from their air raid shelters to see the docklands fires still smouldering and to hear the sound of ambulance bells as bodies and survivors were pulled from the rubble. Rutter was right when, over dessert, he'd said the East End was in for another hammering.

It was mid-morning when a vehicle collected and delivered the three to Towler's Whitehall office.

'We've gone through the statements,' he said. 'Very thorough. Wouldn't have expected any less. They went up the line last night. Took a telephone call first thing this morning. We're expected in fifteen minutes. They'll give us a bell.

'We'll be seeing Winnie and one other, I'm told, in the PM's private room down below in the basement. Not many people get down there, all very inner sanctum. What's said down there stays down there. Buried deep underground. I assume that's fully understood.'

Rutter, George and Finola nodded. They understood.

'Good,' Towler said. 'Now a quick rundown on matters before we head down below.'

Altskeith had been sealed off from any prying local eyes. The bodies of the dead marines had already been removed. Some had been burned beyond recognition. The body of Villiers had been recovered. The corpses of the two attackers had been photographed and fingerprinted. The pictures and the prints would be checked against Belfast Special Branch and Aliens Registration Bureau records.

Charteris and Sergeant Inglis were on the mend although Charteris might take longer to mend than Sergeant Inglis. The gunfire at Altskeith would be explained in the local newspaper as an army exercise in the hills behind the estate. The damage to the building would be explained as a kitchen fire that got out of hand. As for Hess, he was being held in a secure location near Oxford. Brigadier Ewan Stuart was being held by Military Intelligence – 'at the Farm' – near Brighton.

'Two of our very best people are talking with Stuart,' Towler said. 'I imagine he'll have quite a bit to say. Our people know their stuff. I can't imagine they'll need to resort to arm-twisting. We'll have a couple of big fellows sitting in on the interrogation. One either side. Usually that's enough to get people chatting. It seldom comes down to anything nasty. Hardly ever, in fact. Ewan Stuart knows the system. The easy way or the hard way. Either way we always get what we want. He knows that.'

It was rather sad, Towler said, that Stuart was in such a predicament. He was a twice-decorated soldier. He'd served his country. Why had he turned rogue...? For now, that was anybody's guess.

The telephone rang. Towler answered, listened for a few moments and then replaced the handset. 'That's us,' he said. 'Winnie and one other await.'

***

Churchill's private underground room was comfortably furnished. There was a double bed with a reading lamp attached to the headboard. There was a torch next to the alarm clock on the small bedside table. One wall was lined with crammed book shelves. Maps of Britain and Europe covered the other walls. A well-used drinks trolley stood in one corner. There were leather-upholstered chairs and a cherry-red leather sofa for visitors.

The Prime Minister, sitting behind his mahogany desk, was puffing on a Maduro cigar. He'd had a fondness for them since a visit to Havana almost 50 years earlier. The desk was bare except for three telephones.

'Do sit down,' Churchill said. 'A job very well done. Captain Fraser, I assume... and Major Maclean... we spoke on the telephone. Face to face is always better, I feel. And Lt. Col. Rutter... Brigadier Towler... We meet again. Make yourselves comfortable.'

He turned to the figure by his side. 'Lord Dunolly,' he said. 'I should introduce Captain Fraser and Major Maclean. They've been your guests up in Scotland in recent days.'

Dunolly smiled politely, as a hotel concierge might smile at a guest.

Churchill said Lord Dunolly had rendered splendid service to King and Country in recent times. Rutter, too. He'd been Whitehall's eyes and ears at Lochard House for the best part of two years. 'Always a good idea to have somebody watching the watchers. A couple of times Dunolly here concocted a story to get Rutter down to Whitehall. Anyhow, perhaps Lord Dunolly might care to fill in a few gaps.'

Dunolly was happy to oblige. More than happy, he said.

He'd first met Hess during a top-level trade visit to the Ruhr coalfields in 1937. Some weeks later, when Hess came to London as a high-ranking official of the Berlin government, he expressed, through channels, a desire for a very private meeting, away from London, with Dunolly. The two met at Altskeith.

Dunolly continued: 'I thought it might be a commercial matter. It wasn't. He had the idea that my sympathies might lie towards his brand of politics.'

Hess, at Altskeith in 1937, said the British industrial and landed elite had much to gain from a natural alliance with a rising Germany. The German Embassy in London identified several within that British industrial and landed elite who might be persuaded to influence the development of such an alliance.

Dunolly smiled. 'I certainly wasn't one of them. It's one thing to run a business and it's another matter to side with the Huns. I lost two younger brothers in the 1914–1918 Show,' he said. 'It's not in my nature to forgive and forget. Simple as that.

'I didn't offer Hess an opinion on where my sympathies might lie and he didn't offer any clues as to who, over here, had a soft spot for Hitler. We left it at that. I haven't seen or heard from him since. I suspect that's because I didn't jump up and down and give the Hitler salute. He must have decided he had other fish to fry. That's where Towler came into the story. Perhaps he can take it from here?'

Churchill nodded. Towler obliged. He explained that he had served with Lord Dunolly's brothers in France. He was an infantry regular. They were volunteers. Towler had been with the brothers on the day they were killed.

'When the war was done and dusted, I visited the family and told them they'd lost two fine and brave young officers. It was the very least I could do. That's how myself and Lord Dunolly, before he was Lord Dunolly, came to know each other.'

The two met, occasionally, over the years in London. Several times they fished at Altskeith.

It was no great secret in the corridors of power, Towler explained, that the Duke of Windsor, before his abdication after less than a year on the throne in 1936, had quite open and cordial contact with some high-ranking Nazis.

'The man was a fool and a damned disgrace,' Towler added. 'Half of his silver-spooned hangers-on were closet bloody Nazis. I decided we could do worse than keep a close eye on some of them.'

Towler reeled off a string of names that could have been lifted from the pages of *Burke's Peerage* and *Who's Who* –peers, politicians, newspaper proprietors, and senior members of the military establishment. All of those named had flirted, to a greater or lesser degree, with the pro-Hitler policies of the British Union of Fascists led by Sir Oswald Mosley.

'This was when Ewan Stuart came into the picture,' Towler said. 'He was my immediate junior in Military Intelligence then. Not a bad fellow at all. Seemed quite solid. Very solid, really. Decorated. Exemplary war service. I briefed him to keep an eye on a few people.

'Managed to ingratiate himself – he could be charming when he set his mind to it – with some of Windsor's soft-handed chums and the titled. Even attended a few German Embassy functions. Stuart gave me a verbal report every now and then. So-and-so was having his wicked way with such-

and-such. Lord Somebody's youngest was spending summer holidays with some up-and-coming goose-stepper in Bavaria. Nothing really worthwhile. The usual smutty stuff. Boys bedding boys and sundry beasts of the field, and girls bedding everything on two legs irrespective of gender or soundness of mind.'

So, the investigation was dropped. There was a war on the way. Military Intelligence could do better with its time and money than have Stuart wining and dining and glad-handing in Mayfair.

Churchill cut in. 'And it was a while later, quite a while, that you received a second telephone call from Lord Dunolly. That would have been around the time he placed some of his property in Scotland at our disposal. Around the time Stuart was promoted and sent up north to look after the Intelligence sector there.'

Dunolly explained: 'Stuart telephoned me. He was rather jovial, thanking me for my generous contribution to the defence of the Realm – Lochard House and Altskeith. He said he hoped it wouldn't come to a war with Germany. After all, our two countries had so much in common. Half our Royal Family was German. I had the distinct impression Stuart was on a fishing expedition and that's what I told Brigadier Towler. Never heard a peep out of Stuart since that telephone call from him. When I didn't take the bait I suppose he thought it wise to keep his distance.'

However, his suspicions aroused by Lord Dunolly's telephone call, Towler moved quickly. 'It seemed to me that the Germans might have turned Stuart. If that was the case, we needed proof. We needed a man on the inside up north,' Towler said. 'Somebody we could slot in without raising eyebrows. I spoke with Lord Dunolly and he insisted that Rutter was just the chap. He wasn't exactly a stranger to hush-hush work.'

Towler paused, smiling at the puzzled expressions on the faces of George and Finola. 'Oh, didn't I mention,' he said, a hint of mischief in his eyes. 'Rutter did some outstanding work in Royal Navy Intelligence at the Admiralty during the First War. So top secret that he wasn't even on the Army, Navy and Air Force list. Officially, he didn't exist. I only found out when Lord Dunolly said he'd released Rutter for some economic intelligence work in 1914 and early 1915, wasn't it, Rutter? Various jaunts around Europe in the guise of a businessman. He could have been shot as a spy, you know.'

Rutter smiled, shrugged and pursed his lips. He really couldn't say.

'Well, if he won't speak up,' Churchill said, 'I certainly can. I was running the Admiralty at the time. I know all about Rutter's sterling secret service. He reported to me and only to me.'

Churchill asked Towler to continue. 'In the circumstances, it was blessedly simple to organise Rutter's Commission and,' Towler said, 'as far as Ewan Stuart was concerned, our Mister Rutter was up there to look after the paperwork and keep the wheels turning. On the side, of course, he was keeping a very close eye on everything that crossed Stuart's desk – in and out.'

The close observation of Ewan Stuart, Rutter said, had yielded nothing.

'He never put a foot wrong,' Rutter said. 'I had reached that stage where although I found the Brigadier to be an insufferable and offensive sod, I was starting to have doubts about him being a Jerry collaborator. He could certainly put on a good show. It wasn't until Altskeith the other night that... well, we all know the rest of the story.'

Churchill puffed on his cigar. 'Not quite all of the story,' he said. 'We have to rely on Towler's fellows to find out how, exactly, Stuart was in touch with the Germans and who he was dealing with.'

Towler said the Prime Minister could rest assured that Stuart would – 'one way or another' – fully cooperate with His Majesty's Government.

'Any questions?' Churchill asked.

There were none. That being the case, there was one other matter, Churchill said. On the basis of events during the past several days and the accounts of those events provided by Rutter, Major Maclean and Captain Fraser, Decorations would be awarded.

This might take some months. Citations had to be written and recommendations had to be made. The top secret nature of events surrounding the Altskeith affair meant there would be no official announcement of awards. No official photographs. No formal Buckingham Palace afternoon tea. A discreet private meeting at the Palace, though, might be considered.

As Churchill rose to end the meeting, George said perhaps, on the matter of Decorations, there was just one question. More of a well-meant suggestion, really. Far be it from him to presume. However, Sergeant Danny Inglis, Charteris and the young Marine private Sandy Forrest had done their bit at Altskeith.

Churchill nodded. He was quite certain that all concerned would be fully recognised for their outstanding contribution. It would be properly seen to.

Right now, there was a war to win. Tempus fugit. Better get on with it.

For Rutter and Finola, getting on with it meant a train journey to Glasgow and for George Maclean it meant remaining in the south, Towler said, when he returned to his office with the three.

Rutter would take charge of the Glasgow/Clyde Sector of Military Intelligence. The appointment came with a promotion from Lt. Col. to Brigadier. Finola, promoted to Major, would return to The Glasgow Herald, eyes and ears wide open for the duration.

'Apparently that family illness has cleared up rather well,' Towler said. Turning to George, he added: 'Hess is being settled into his new digs at our place near Oxford and we'll put you up there for the initial interrogation. You won't take part, of course. We have two very good people who'll do the nitty-gritty; talk Hess through his personal history, his rise through the ranks, his visits over here before the war. People he met, what they said, what contact they might have had with Berlin. You'll simply be a necessary familiar face for the first few days. Then we'll whisk you back to Glasgow. Duty calls, that'll be the line.'

And Ewan Stuart? Finola asked. Was there anything to report?

The interrogation of the wayward Stuart, Towler said, was yet to commence at 'the Farm' near Brighton. Overnight there had been some minor complications with his leg wound. Some further loss of blood. An infection that, one hoped, was being nipped in the bud. A rather irregular heartbeat.

'He's getting the very best of medical attention. More's the pity, really,' Towler said. 'The heartbeat business, though, is a cause for concern according to the medicos. Could be because of the gunshot injury... or the pressure he's under. Maybe a heart problem although there's nothing in his medical records to suggest this. We'll have to be careful. We don't want him popping off to meet his Maker... at least not until we've finished with him.'

The meeting adjourned. Sleepers were booked on the evening train to Glasgow for Captain Fraser and the new Officer-in-Charge Glasgow/Clyde Sector, Military Intelligence.

A car was waiting to take Major Maclean to Oxford. He'd be there in an hour.

***

Security at the 14-room Georgian house on the outskirts of Oxford was tight but unobtrusive. There were no military uniforms in sight. The vehicle carrying George was waved towards the front steps by men who might have been gardeners or farm labourers. Identification papers were checked.

Inside, George was escorted to an impressive ground floor sitting room. He exchanged handshakes with two men who introduced themselves as Colonel Peter Pegg and Major Nick Faulkner, Military Intelligence. They had been charged with the completion of the Hess interrogation. Pegg spoke first.

'A pleasure to meet you, George,' he said. 'You appear to have made an impression on Herr Hess. You're about the only thing he has talked about since yesterday. Well, you and his boyhood and his war service and what a sterling fellow Adolf is. And we couldn't shut him up when he got going about horoscopes and the infamous Professor Krafft. We know all about him, too. Confidence trickster of the first order. A drunkard to his bootstraps.'

He and Nick – 'first names all round, I think' – had been briefed on the Clydebank bombings, the IRA connection, the late Reverend Martin Lang and the 'business' of Ewan Stuart. Events at Altskeith, too. By all accounts, it had been a close run thing, according to Towler.

George said he agreed with Towler. It had been a very close run thing.

Pegg said the initial interrogation of Hess was almost convivial. There were conversations, in German, on the prisoner's early years, his First World War service, his infatuation with Hitler and his rise through the ranks of the Nazi Party.

The mood of the conversations was relaxed, almost informal, Faulkner said. 'We've found that the best approach for now is to butter him up. A bit of flattery and off he goes.'

Hess seemed to approve of his surroundings and his inquisitors. Pegg and Faulkner were men of substance, apparently. Their German, in all its nuances, was perfect, Hess said. They understood Germany and its destiny. They were not unlike Major George Maclean. When Germany and Britain united and succeeded in crushing their common enemies, Hess insisted, men of the mettle of Majors Maclean and Faulkner and Colonel Pegg would find themselves in positions of great influence. When, by the way, might Major Maclean arrive. And when might Hitler's Deputy converse with 'people in high places.'

Hess had been advised, Pegg said, that it wouldn't actually be possible for Herr Hess to meet people in high places until he named such people in high places.

'He huffed and puffed a bit before he got the message that when he gave us the names, we'd contact the names and they'd, presumably, be over the moon to see him. That won't happen, obviously,' Faulkner said. 'He won't be talking to anybody – except us, of course. When he tells us what we want to know, we'll have him under lock and key and out of sight for the duration. You get the impression that he's off in a world of his own half the time.'

George nodded his understanding. 'So, what happens now?' he asked.

'Well, we may as well fetch him,' Pegg said.

Hess beamed like a child when he was led into the ground floor sitting room. 'Herr Major George,' he said. 'I have been telling your colleagues of our adventures and misadventures.'

Hess looked around the room. His expression indicated he was comfortable in his surroundings. He felt safe, out of harm's way. His treatment could not be faulted. Herr Pegg and Herr Faulkner were, like Major George, cultured and intelligent men. He was rather enjoying the company of British officers who understood Germany and the German people. They understood that the Bolsheviks and the Jews and the Slavs were the natural enemies of two great natural allies, the Germans and the British.

The buttering up, George was certain, was working well. The effusive Hess had been given what he fed on – an attentive audience. In the language of interrogators, Hess was a 'real talker.'

What he talked about that day astonished his inquisitors. They'd need to brief Winnie without delay.

Chapter twenty: King and country

Towler/Churchill eyes only: Continuing interview with prisoner today disclosed matters that should not be committed to paper. Immediate verbal briefing imperative. Pegg—

   Churchill Prime Ministerial Archives: Miscellaneous Papers. Undated handwritten note.

Pegg, Faulkner and George Maclean sat opposite Churchill and Towler in the first floor reception room at number 10 Downing Street.

Pegg was the one to drop the bombshell. 'Hess believes, Mister Prime Minister, that there are within the Establishment persons who are willing to assassinate you, take control of Government and put the Duke of Windsor back on the throne, at which point this country will declare an alliance with Germany and we'll all be off confronting the Bolsheviks.'

Churchill asked: 'And will they? Try to do me in, that is.'

Pegg was unsure. The whole mad scheme might not exist beyond the prisoner's imagination. Then again, anything was possible. Even hare-brained threats had to be taken seriously. Nothing could be ignored.

Churchill looked around the room, puffing smoke from his cigar. He asked for names.

Hess had revealed four names, Pegg said. Two wouldn't be assassinating anybody. 'He mentioned Brigadier Ernest Milton, Royal Signals, and Colonel Carleton Forrester-Hawkins, Artillery. Both died on the retreat to Dunkirk last year. They'd had a brief dalliance with the Mosley mob in '37... a silly political fling before they turned on Mosley when they cottoned on to the fact the man was a disgrace and a traitor. At the time of the turning, the two of them gave Scotland Yard

Special Branch a list of ne'er-do-wells and halfwits. The Yard locked up a few and frightened the life out of the rest.'

'And the other two names Hess gave you?'

There was, Faulkner said, Baronet Elwes. Churchill raised an eyebrow... Elwes, the steel magnate.

'He must be in his eighties. Chummy with our unlamented Duke of Windsor as I recall. Isn't Elwes the one who went quite crackers?'

The Prime Minister was correct. 'Been in the madhouse for a couple of years now,' Faulkner confirmed. 'Has this notion that he's George the Third. Seemingly mumbles all the time about the loss of the American colonies and the Boston Tea Party. I had a word with the Quack at the funny farm this morning. He gave us chapter and verse in very fancy medical lingo. Basically, when you cut through the Latin lexicon, Elwes is off living on another planet.'

What, Churchill asked, was the connection between Elwes and Hess?

Pegg said the two had met several times in 1938. Elwes had visited half a dozen steel plants in the Ruhr. But even then it was no great secret that Elwes had started to lose his marbles. 'This leaves us,' Pegg said, 'with Lord Pilton, the banking bigwig. Awash with money. Landholdings in Northumberland, Ayrshire and Devon. Very well connected, very influential behind the scenes. Sees himself as being above the rules that govern the daily lives of mere mortals. A bit of a string-puller.'

Churchill snapped: 'Right now, the only influence that counts is my influence and the influence of The King... and Pilton, believe me, has no influence on either myself or His Majesty. Pilton paid for his title after the last war. Parvenu of the worst type. Bloody new money upstart. The suggestion that somebody like Pilton might hold some sway with His Majesty or the Prime Minister of Great Britain and Northern Ireland is offensive.'

Towler, familiar with Churchill's capacity for explosive

anger when he felt slighted, intervened. He said Pegg, not in a million years, would suggest Pilton could receive special treatment from Downing Street or Buckingham Palace. Good, Churchill said. Very good. Carry on.

Pegg nodded to Faulkner. 'We've established that Pilton and Hess met at a German Embassy knees-up here in London in the middle of "38,' Faulkner said. 'Pilton's merchant bank had some rather large investments in the German aeroplane business at a time when the Jerries, on the quiet, were building up their Luftwaffe. Pilton must have been worried that if we ended up in a war, he'd lose millions. Hess certainly had enough influence in Berlin to ensure Pilton's millions remained safe. In fact, Hess is quite convinced that Pilton will be overjoyed to see him here. Now, here's the really interesting bit.'

Ewan Stuart and Pilton were guests at an earlier German Embassy function in March, 1938. But their connection went back more than two decades.

Both served in Flanders and both spent several months recovering from injuries in a convalescent home near Lewarde. Both had been on the Board of the Services Club since 1934. They met at least twice-yearly at Board meetings. A few quiet dinners and the odd luncheon were possible, too.

'We've been doing some more digging,' Pegg said. 'This Martin Lang, the Chrysalis character. Stuart was the debriefing intelligence officer when Lang arrived from Germany claiming he'd fled in fear of his life. He was the one who signed off on Lang's clearance to stay here.'

George raised a hand to speak. 'Carry on,' Towler said.

'We have two separate issues here,' George said. 'But there's possibly a common link in Pilton. The first issue is Hess and the supposed plan to assassinate the Prime Minister, put the Duke of Windsor back in the Palace and snuggle up with Hitler.

'Think about it. Hess imagines nothing has changed since 1938. He'll just fly over here, meet up with people he believes are pro-Hitler, convince them to kill the Prime Minister and replace the King with the Duke of Windsor... then we're all chums off to defeat the Red hordes. It's all in the Hess Horoscope. It has to be right. Professor Krafft said so.'

'And the second issue?' Towler asked.

'The second issue is Ewan Stuart. It's clear as daylight that he was the one who used Chrysalis to call in the Luftwaffe on the targets that hadn't been flattened on the first night of the Clydebank Blitz... he was the one who got Billy Dalgleish killed and Robbie Kirkness near killed... and he was the one, when Chrysalis and Duthie made a run from Clydebank, who somehow let the Germans know where to send Chrysalis and Duthie to kill Hess.'

And how, Churchill asked, might Stuart have contacted Chrysalis and the Germans?

'He could have contacted Chrysalis directly in Clydebank,' George suggested. 'Or he could have made the contact with Chrysalis and the Germans through Pilton.'

Towler said George had presented a tidy enough theory about Hess and his contacts in Britain in 1938. But Major Maclean was assuming Hess was telling the truth – that there had been no contact since '38.

Churchill said Hess had no reason to lie. Hess wouldn't have flown to Britain if he didn't expect to be welcomed with open arms. He fully expected to make immediate contact with his pre-war sympathisers.

'But I keep coming back to the view that Hess is mad as a hatter. Have the Quacks had a look at him yet?' Churchill asked.

Pegg said two army psychiatrists had, secretly, been observing and listening to the Hess interrogation. 'The medical jury is still out on whether or not the man is barking. One believes he's utterly crackers and the other believes he's crackers some of the time and perfectly rational five minutes later. Apparently he's something called Oedipal – I gather it means he wants to climb into bed with his mother. Some odd German thing, if you ask me.'

'The important point here,' Faulkner said, 'is that the doctors insist Hess completely believes what he's saying when he's saying it. He doesn't know when he's telling lies. You could chop his fingers off and he wouldn't change his story... whatever story he happens to be telling at the time.'

Churchill asked Towler for a plan of action. How would the interrogation of Hess and Ewan Stuart proceed and how would Pilton be confronted?

'The questioning of Hess will continue, of course,' Towler said. 'But on the basis of his scatty state it's unlikely, beyond propaganda value, that he'll deliver anything of real value from now on. He's a bit like a trophy one hangs on the wall.

'However, I've no doubt that Stuart will have a great deal that should be shared with us – but we can't really push him until we're sure he can survive the pushing... the heart business... his general state. With Pilton, we've already made arrangements to put a watch on him around the clock. Where he is, who he's talking to. Mail intercepts, financial affairs, his merchant bank clients. He won't blow his nose or empty his bladder without us knowing about it.

'We won't collar him right now. Apart from the Hess ramblings – and Pilton will dismiss them, no question of that – we won't have anything to confront him with until Stuart spills whatever beans he has to spill.'

Churchill nodded. 'Anything else?'

Towler turned to George.

'I'm sure the Major will be delighted to be on the overnight train to Glasgow. Really, there isn't any more he can do in London or Oxford. Pegg and Faulkner will attend to Hess. Job well done, Major Maclean. Thank you very much. Hess will be miffed, but Whitehall can live with that. We'll spin a tale about Major Maclean being called off for duties elsewhere.

'Sergeant Inglis, by the way, is recovering from his wound.

No lasting damage, fortunately.' It went without saying that Major Maclean shouldn't, ever, mention events at Altskeith. The same applied, obviously, to events in Oxford and Whitehall.

Churchill looked around the room. He rose. 'Thank you gentlemen,' he said. 'Let's all get on with our work.'

***

Four days later, Rutter advised George that Brigadier Ewan Stuart had suffered a heart attack and died during his interrogation. He had revealed no information of value, certainly nothing that would implicate Lord Pilton in treason.

'I'm informed that there was no rough stuff that might have contributed to the heart attack,' Rutter said. 'The nasty wound, the journey south, the stress of being exposed as a treacherous dog, they were what really did for him. As a consequence, our Brigadier Stuart has taken his secrets to the crematorium with him. Of course, we'll continue to keep an eye on Pilton, but unless he hoists the Nazi flag over his London club, we can't lay a finger on him. I have no doubt that in war or peace, Pilton is the sort of fellow who will continue to prosper.'

Rutter was right.

***

In 1946, Pilton was appointed to head the Postwar European Steel Industry Reconstruction Task Force. In 1956, the Government of West Germany awarded Pilton its Order of Industry medal for his oversight of the resurrection of the steel industry in the Ruhr Valley. In the late 1950's, Pilton was central to the establishment of what is now the European Union. When he died in London 1973, he was Europe's wealthiest man. He was not given a state funeral.

Chapter twenty-one: Beyond the grave

It has been 25 years since leading Nazi Rudolf Hess died in a Berlin prison, but a newly declassified report into how it happened has apparently failed to answer unexplained questions about whether he really did kill himself—

Daily Telegraph, London, 17 March, 2012.

Rudolf Hess, frail and stooped, was found dead on August 17, 1987. He was 93 years old. He was Spandau's only prisoner. The prison was under the control of Britain, France, the United States and the Soviet Union. Each of the Allied powers, for periods of one month, provided guards for Spandau.

Hess had been in Spandau for more than 40 years when his body was found in a garden shed in the prison yard. Other Nazi war criminals came and went during those decades. Some, like Albert Speer, Admiral Erich Raeder, Karl Donitz and Baldur von Schirach, served their sentences and were released. Others were hanged.

The Russian prosecutors at Nuremberg argued for Hess to be hanged, too. When the judges said Hess would receive a life sentence, the Russians said they would never, under any circumstances, agree to the release of Hess.

The Russians were as good as their word.

Several times during his sentence, Hess attempted suicide. The British, French and the Americans believed Hess was insane and should be transferred to a mental hospital. The Russians said Hess, insane or otherwise, would remain in Spandau.

During the weeks before his death, Hess told his British prison guards that he lied during his interrogations near

Oxford in 1941. It was time, he said, to tell the truth. He was an old man. His days were numbered.

Hess told his British guards he maintained contact with a titled member of the British Establishment beyond 1938. The contact was maintained through the Spanish diplomatic mission in London.

Hess said the clandestine contact was one of Britain's wealthiest men. He had pre-war interests in the German steel industry. The contact had encouraged, in Hess, the inference that there were those in Britain who wished to see Churchill dead and the Duke of Windsor restored to the throne.

The guards reported the Hess conversations to their senior officers. The senior officers reported these to Whitehall.

Fifteen days after that information reached London, Hess was found hanged. A thin electrical cord looped around a window latch choked the life from the man who had been Adolf Hitler's Deputy and acolyte.

The official medical report from Major John Macintyre, the British military doctor at Spandau, said that on the physical evidence available, Hess had taken his own life. It was observed, however, that given the frailty of Hess and his poor health:

'The looping of the electrical cord around a window latch could have presented difficulties for the prisoner. Arthritis in his hands and shoulders could have made it problematic for the prisoner to raise his arms high enough to secure the electrical cord around the window latch. Nevertheless, in cases where an individual is determined to take a fatal course of action it is not uncommon for physical limitations to be overcome in the pursuit of that course of action. It might be conjectured that a third party or parties unknown could have played a part in securing the electrical cord. In such an event it can be conjectured that the prisoner may have been an unwilling participant in his own demise. Despite his frailty, it is unlikely that the prisoner would have failed to offer some

resistance. There are no physical signs on the prisoner to suggest he suffered any physical trauma prior to his death by strangulation. Notwithstanding the above conjecture, what can be said with certainty is that the overwhelming physical evidence must lead to the conclusion that the prisoner took his own life. He had a history of attempted suicide. The empirical evidence shows that a high proportion of successful suicides are the determined work of individuals who have a history of failed attempts at suicide.

The medical report was buried in the Whitehall archives until it was released in 2012 after a successful British newspaper application under Freedom of Information laws.

There is continuing speculation that Hess was murdered by two British agents sent to silence Spandau's last prisoner whose revelations, if they were true, would shake the British Establishment and the public perception that Britain's leaders were united in their determination to defeat Hitler.

Historical Fact

Rudolf Hess, after his mystery flight to Scotland in 1941, was held in custody in Britain until the end of hostilities in 1945.

In 1946, Hess was sentenced to life imprisonment after a hearing at the Nuremberg War Crimes Tribunal. He was convicted of crimes against humanity. The charges stemmed from his role as Hitler's Deputy until 1941.

During the hearing, some observers suggested Hess was insane. His behaviour in the dock was erratic. Several times he laughed for no apparent reason. Often he stared at his judges and prosecutors for hours. Other times he rocked back and forth in the dock. He asserted he was being poisoned by Jewish guards. He claimed he was suffering from amnesia then claimed he was feigning amnesia.

He began his sentence in Spandau Prison, Berlin, in 1947.

Aged 93, he reportedly hanged himself in Spandau in 1987. During his imprisonment Hess attempted suicide several times.

In March, 2012, top secret documents released in London revealed allegations that Hess had been murdered by British agents.

The motive for the alleged murder in 1987: the British government feared Hess was about to reveal details of a conspiracy, by members of the British 'establishment' to overthrow Prime Minister Winston Churchill in 1941.